The
Denied Ones

Suzanna Abigail King

ISBN: 978-0-244-04594-4

PublishNation
www.publishnation.co.uk

Contents

To my Mum, Jean Dorothy Pettit (1945-2014)
Many thanks for sharing your life with me
and being a wonderful mother.
Although you are no longer by my side to hold my
hand, you are now my guardian angel, watching over
me for forever.
Until we meet again.

CHAPTER ONE

Innocence of a Child

'Let's go out and play' said Jean to her sister Mary. They were unaware how lucky they were to live on a small island where the sky was clear and the sea filled with tropical fish and giant turtles. Their own pet turtle was over sixty years old.

This island, called St Helena, is situated in the South Atlantic Ocean about 2000 miles from South Africa where their father's family came from. Both their father and mother were born on the island

The island is too small for an airport so the only means of transport is the ships of all shapes and sizes filled with many different cargoes and mail. The island people would run to the beach, children with smiles of delight on their faces. Maybe they are delivering presents and cards for their birthdays or letters for their parents.

St Helena is well known as the island where Napoleon was imprisoned and died. It has been governed by many countries including Portugal, Spain, Germany, South Africa and now the United Kingdom. During the Falklands War it was put on the world map because it is the island nearest to Ascension Island where there is an airport which was used in the Falklands War in the 1980s.

After the girls had played, they went looking for their other sisters and brother and on the way home picked orchids for their mother.

The two young sisters and their siblings arrived at the gate which led into their yard where the chickens ran free outside a beautiful, white farmhouse. Everything seemed too quiet and still. As they approached the house, one of the neighbours

1

came running out to greet them with tears in her eyes and sadness on her face, not knowing how to tell the children what had happened. Instead she hurried the children inside where their mother was sitting in her chair. She was five months pregnant. Their mother's face was white. In a painful voice she said 'Your father is dead'.

The two girls looked at each other, then at the other siblings and just fell to the floor asking how this could be. They were unaware their father had been suffering from tuberculosis. He had eventually died at the age of 42 years old, leaving behind five children and a wife to fend for themselves on this beautiful island. This family originally would have been eight children but two boys died, one only six months old the other even younger.

After receiving this heart breaking news, Jean and Mary (aged nine and three), who had always been the closest out of the siblings, led the others outside. The family was torn apart by the loss of their father. He had been a quiet, kind, loving, family man, slim build and very handsome. Before the children were born he worked as a porter in a local hospital. Later he worked as a shop manager with his wife making sweets and other foods to sell in the shop. The hospital work was likely to have been where he picked up the T.B. infection. Though he must have suffered a great deal of pain, he never once complained.

They all would meet again in heaven, but meanwhile the family had to continue in this world which had now turned into hell, filled with pain and sorrow and emptiness. Nothing would ever be the same again. How would they survive without their beloved father, no longer there to guide them in life and to give them away when the girls would one day get married.

Rest In Peace William Benjamin, 1901-1943.

As the grave was filled in, his wife, Lillian, stood with tears of pain and fear on her face. They walked into the house in silence. Their mother said 'Please, someone, say something, your father and son would have not wanted us to be like this. He would have wanted us to celebrate his life on earth, the good times that we had with him.' With that the whole family seemed to relax and started to talk about his life and all of the good times, then there was laughter as well as tears.

When it was time for bed, Lillian heard Jean and Mary crying and went to console them.

'Your father is in Heaven now, watching over us all. He will always live in our hearts and minds until we meet him again. Until that day, we must be strong and look after each other, that is what your father would have wanted.' With that, she kissed them and said 'Now go to sleep.'

As the days went by, the family changed from happy to sad. Not having Father around meant there was only one wage. Lillian now had to be the bread winner as well as mother and father in every way possible. This was a women who was only forty one years old, a widow with five children and pregnant with her sixth child. Her youngest was only three years old and eldest 16.

Everyone now had to pull their weight. The children that used to play so happily on the beach after school now had to work in the local shop to keep them fed and clothed as well as look after each other. The eldest, Edna, and John, the second eldest and only son, helped serve in the shop as soon as they returned from school. Jean had to play the new role of Mother while her own mother went out to work full time. Poor little Jean and her two older siblings had to cook and clean and take care of the younger ones, Mary and Joan. This was so hard for all the children but not as hard as was for their mother as she saw her young children change from child to adult in what would have felt like minutes yet it was weeks and months. Not once did she cry in front of her children, but at night when she thought they were all asleep, you could hear her tears of pain while she wept. She could only dream of a new life of hope and happiness for all of them.

A day came when the whole world fell apart for the family. Lillian decided to pack up and move to England. She made enquires and then it came time to tell her family what they had to do to start a new life and say good bye to the island, knowing that this would be the hardest thing to do. 'How on earth can I do this? Take them away from their home and all the things that they know. Take them to a country that is so big and different in every way. Who will understand us and the way that we are? The way we speak, for our native tongue is South African not English. Oh my God help me. Help us all.'

Lillian had all these thoughts whilst walking slowly towards her children who were already in their little sitting room. She saw them with their faces looking up at her and on their faces were looks of hurt, pain, wonder, and fright of what had happened, the look of 'No not our mother, no, is she going to die too?'

Seeing the looks on their faces when she came into the room she said quickly 'I am fine,' and saw their relief. There was a long silence and then their mother spoke, with a look of hurt in her eyes as she tried to hold back her tears. She explained it would be good for all of them to make a new life in England.

Lillian knew that she had to try and make them see that it would be the best thing for all of them and a new life is what their Father would have wanted.

Jean asked 'What is going to happen to our house?' Her mother replied 'The house will still be ours, it will not be sold. It will be looked after by one of our neighbours and if life does not turn out the way we hope and pray for, then we will return home. Please do not ask me any more questions' Lillian said very sharply.

'I know it will be hard but we all must now pull together and be there for each other, no matter what life will bring to us.'

With this, a huge sigh of relief came from Lillian as the children moved towards her and held their arms around her tight, without saying a word. Their arms were their way of showing her they were all together and united in their grief and life itself. Never to be alone again, whatever life would throw at them. They would somehow find that family strength to pull through and survive together, whether it be in England or in St Helena it did not matter, as long as they were together.

Lillian sat down and stared into space.

Jean said 'is anything that I can do, Mother?' Lillian turned and looked at Jean, 'No thank you, I am fine,' she replied. But she knew that she could not share any more pain with her family as she knew that they had gone through enough already, without having to cope with their mother's pain of losing her soul mate.

As the night slowly drew to a close and the sun began to rise, Lillian knew that this was not only a new day beginning but the first day of being both mother and father. She knew that she had to start a new role, and with this thought she quickly got out of bed and headed to the kitchen to start the family's breakfast. She became aware of the sound of her children already there getting the breakfast ready and making sure everything was done. There was nothing to do when she came into the kitchen, and with that sight of her family doing all of this for her and showing their love and support she looked at them and smiled and said to herself 'We will be fine' knowing that they all would pull together and be stronger than ever before. No matter what, their mother had decided they would all support her.

After breakfast Lillian was left on her own. She walked into town thinking ' I hope that I do not see anyone that I know' as all she wanted was to go to the Town Hall and find out all the information she could about leaving this beautiful Island.

Returning home she thought 'Well that was not too bad. I only saw two people that I know.' That was enough, anymore she knew she would have broken down. She did not want to do that for she knew that this was the day she had to change into being both mother and father. To do that needed great strength and no weakness, well not in front of her children. Only when on her own would she be able to show her feelings. She could show them to no one else for this was a sign of weakness which would not be tolerated under any circumstances.

The only worry was when they would leave their home. Should it be before or after her baby was born. She went to a neighbour, a good, close friend, and told her the plans she was making. She asked her for her guidance. She was now seven months pregnant. Her friend very quickly said 'I think that you should stay until the baby is born, then move if you are still sure that there is no other way of staying here where I know you want to be.'

Lillian replied 'Yes you are right about everything you have said, but it is not me I have to think about now, it is the children and this little baby too. I have no choice but to make a new start for all of us.'

'This is the only thing I can do for my family and you know that my husband would have wanted the best for his family.'

Her friend replied 'But if life got better?' Quickly came the reply 'And what if it does not, then we could lose everything. I cannot take that risk. At least if I do this we can come back, to what who knows, but at least we will have a home to come back to. From there we will deal with things as they are, and who knows what will happen, we will have to see.'

'But thank you for your ideas and thoughts. I now know what to do and that is to stay until the baby is born. Then we will leave, maybe after a few weeks, when I am well enough to travel. As you know, the journey to England is about six weeks by boat as we have no airport.'

'And nothing will change that decision which is now made once and for all.'

As she approached the front door she stopped and took a deep breath then walked into the kitchen. She said 'children please sit down and listen as I have something to say to you all and it is very important.'

She started to explain where she had been, the huge decision she had made and the detail of how much it would cost. There was nothing the children could do but to accept it.

With that thought they sat and listened. Their mother asked if there were any questions, how they all felt and what they thought, knowing that it would not make any difference to her decision. Their response was 'we are fine, Mother, and agree. What do we need to do between now and when we leave? We will do anything for you, Mother, to help. And when the baby is born, don't worry; we will look after the baby so that you can take a break. Please try and relax, we know it won't be easy, but we will try even harder for you. We know it will be harder from now on and we are all willing to do whatever it takes. We are all family and Father would have wanted it this way.'

Their mother could now see how mature they were, yet still so young. None of them had really reached adulthood yet they were behaving as though they had. Other neighbours' children were playing their games as children do, but Lillian's children had had to grow up very quickly. One neighbour was Jean's age and still playing games with their friends. Jean had to look after her sisters Mary and Edna, no games for her, just pre-motherhood and home work. She was still at school and would not be able to leave until she was 15 years old, eight years away. Unlike other children, she knew already that life for her as a child was over, now she was taking up the role of part-time mother. So too were her elder brother and sister for they would feel the pressure more than Jean, though at times she was on her own.

As days turned into weeks Lillian knew that this was the day when her long awaited child, the sixth one, would be born. With that thought, she hurried to her closest neighbour and told her the baby was coming. The neighbour took her to her home and started to prepare for the birth. There were no mid-wives, only family and neighbours to help. After a short time the sound of a new born baby could be heard so strong and powerful.

'It is a beautiful little girl you have and she is fine.'

With that her mother just cried with joy that everything was well. She could now start a new life with her new born little girl and her other children.

After a week, Lillian thought of a name for her new born little girl, calling her Grace. This was the same as Jean's middle name so on this day when the children came home from school and work, Lillian told them of the name that she had decided. The next day she went into town and registered her name, saw the vicar and made arrangements for their sister's christening. With that news the children were all excited.

Soon the day of the christening was here.

They all started to take their seats in the church. The vicar stood before them and before he addressed the congregation he looked at Lillian and bowed his head slowly. He looked at the others and started the service by saying 'What a happy occasion this is.'

He went on to say about the last time that they were all gathered together on that sad occasion and how their father and husband was there is spirit. This should be a happy occasion still, not to feel sadness, but joy for this little girl, and to pray for her and to guide her in her life and in her sadness when she learns of her father's life and illness and finally death.

After the service, they all went back to the family's house where there was food and drink laid on to celebrate the christening of little Grace. When she was born there were no celebrations of the birth like there was with her brothers and sisters so this time her mother made sure there was. It was not her fault what had happened and she knew that when Grace grew up she wanted her to know that they did celebrate her birth or at least later when she was christened. The day went very well and everyone came to see her, this was no-ones day but Grace's, it was a beautiful day just like Grace.

The next day was back to normal for all the family, some going to school and some going to the shop to work. Lillian was alone at home with Grace, and her thoughts were of what had gone on the day before. With those thoughts, she looked at her little Grace and said 'Your father would be so proud of you, as I am,' then she hugged her daughter, put her into her cot, covered her up so that she could sleep.

As Lillian walked slowly away, she watched her little girl's face and noticed how she looked like her father, with the shape of her eyebrows and nose and even her little forehead.

She smiled at the sounds of her family returning. Their talking and laughing made her feel happy. Then she thought this is not going to last. She would have loved time to just stand still. She knew that it would not be long before one of the children would ask 'When are we moving to England?' With that, she knew that she had to make a new decision; she felt that she did not want to move. She felt that at her age of forty-two, it would be too late for her to change her ways. She knew deep down inside that she would never fit in the way that she had in St Helena, for her country was like a small village compared to England.

She could not stop any of them if they decided to go to England. She would feel lost without even one of them. She knew that she would have to agree and then let them go with her blessing.

Time moved slowly on. It was Joan who first said she wanted to go to England to train as a nurse. She had seen that there was a place in England where she could go to study and she wanted to try and see if she could. She could earn more money there while she was training and there were work placements available. After Joan had said her piece, there was complete silence, everyone just looked blankly at each other. Joan was only sixteen years old and yet had seemed to sort out her own life, knew what she wanted to do with it and how she was going to get there.

Although sixteen may seem very young, on St Helena this was not young as the age for leaving school was fifteen years old. There was nothing legal that Lillian could do to stop her from leaving school, so she gave her permission and her blessing to move to England, although inside she hoped that she would change her mind. She also realised Joan was like her mother, strong willed and strong minded.

Joan had got a position in a hospital and found accommodation to live. She was very excited at her new life and very much looking forward to it. When she arrived in England it was not long before she was settled into her new life and enjoying it, yet missing her family. She wrote all the time, telling them how she was getting on, what she was doing, and what she had achieved. When her letters arrived in St Helena, the rest of the family all sat down and listened as their mother read them out. Lillian was so relieved that things were turning out well, that Joan was settled and happy, her job was good and her new life was turning out much better than she had hoped. With this, the others started to think that they too wanted to make a new life in England. They too started to do everything just like their sister, to raise the funds to go to England. To start again and see whether the grass is greener on the other side of the world. The only way they would have the answer to that was to go to England, see for themselves and hope for the best.

Less than a year after Joan arrived in England, John, Edna and Jean joined her. Jean was then 19 years old, Edna 27 and John 21. So Mary, Grace and Lillian were the only ones left on the beautiful island far away from England. Once again the rest of the family had to say their good byes and best wishes and wave them off just like before. This time it was clearer than ever to Lillian that now she would have to do the same to be with them, to move herself along with the remaining family and that thought was so very sad for her.

But she now knew that it had come to this. A change had to be made for all of them. With that she also made arrangements for her and her two daughters to move to England and join the other members of her family who she missed and longed to be with once again. This time she would make sure that none of them would be apart ever again. When they were all reunited they would become a complete family and not separate but live in their new country until death came and moved them to a new, loving and peaceful home.

The day when Lillian, Mary and Grace arrived in England was winter and there was snow on the ground, white and cold to the touch. None of the family had ever seen, never mind touched, snow. Though once they were all together the weather did not matter, they were now ready to start a new life, with new jobs and new homes to live in. They all started to work hard and soon settled into their new lives, except Lillian who found it so hard without her husband beside her.

Lillian somehow found comfort. She began, in her own way, to settle in England. She mixed with the people the rest of the family met and worked with, and the friends that they had met and indeed their partners too. Still Lillian found it so lonely, she still hungered for her home and it was not here in England where the weather is so very different and so too are the people. They are friendly and helpful and yet this was not what she was used to. She was used to her small town and her friends and her familiar surroundings and no strangers. Not many were like her, where she was the stranger and everyone wanted to meet her and to know all about her and her family. Some people that she had met had not even heard of St Helena. She, along with the rest of the family, thought that this was 'Unbelievable' as this was where Napoleon was imprisoned and spent the rest of his life. Yet not many people in England seemed to know this. Once explained by the family, and especially Lillian, the English friends were amazed and wanted to know more about this little country as it sounded so wonderful to them. They wanted to know about their life style before coming to England. The most important question on everyone's mind was 'Why are you here and why did you leave your home?' Everyone turned and looked at each other wondering who was going to answer the question. After a few seconds of silence, which seemed a lot longer, Lillian replied 'All will be revealed soon, but not now, it is the wrong time and place.' With that everyone started to make small talk about where the rest of the family was going to live and who they were going to work for.

The family was at last on their own. Lillian and the two youngest sisters were feeling very tired after such a day and after spending six weeks at sea. This was the only way of travelling anywhere from their Island. Mother and sisters were now ready for bed and rest, then tomorrow would be the start of a new life together in their new home in England.

Lillian began to think about her home town which she had left behind. Deep down inside she knew that she would never return to where she was born and had lived happily with her husband and her children. As she began to think of those days, she could feel the tears that were so long overdue begin to fall down her pale face. She eventually fell asleep as she hugged her pillow. Then it was morning and she awoke to the sounds of her children. Two of the girls, as she would like to call them, were now fully grown women. They were full of energy and life and could not wait to venture into the outside world and see what this day would bring. Yet Lillian, even though she was happy for her children, could not help but feel so alone in this strange world she has entered. At her age of 54 years old she knew that it would not be easy to adapt if she could at all.

Lillian got up, and began to walk down the road towards the local shops. She noticed a market shop and wondered what it was, as where she had come from a market was in the open air, not a shop. She entered and with amazement came across things like frozen packets of vegetables, there were so many to choose from, and frozen chicken and other meats, all in packets. This was something that neither she nor her family had ever seen before, everything they ate at home was all fresh. She was amazed at this. The only things that she was familiar with were packets of crisps and nuts. It was things like bread and cakes, they were all freshly made on the day and never wrapped and never had dates on them.

This was something she was very concerned about, so she asked an assistant at the shop if there was a butcher anywhere near. The assistant gave directions to the nearest one and off she set. To her relief she found what she saw she was familiar with, fresh meat. She asked how much things like meat, chicken and fish were and explained to the butcher that she had come to live here with her family. He replied with a smile on his face and served her with what she wanted and even gave her discount on the total goods that she bought. She even bought eggs as they too were fresh. With her shopping now done and a smile on her face of which she had not had for some time she turned towards home. On the way she saw a greengrocer where she bought the vegetables to go with the meat.

When the two girls came home from work, they saw their mother once again cooking them a meal. This time she was singing to herself as she felt happy at last. They both looked at each other. Their mother turned around and said 'Dinner won't be long. How was your day?' They said it was very busy and hard but it was a good day and it was good to be home.

Soon it was bedtime, for not just the two girls but also their mother as she had a very interesting day and found it very tiring day too. They retired, the girls fell asleep. Lillian lay awake thinking about the day, inside she felt good and happy because she felt that she was still useful. She thought of what her husband would have thought of the situation and what she had done on her own and with that she fell asleep. Before long another day had arrived with its new challenges to deal with.

As the days came and went, Lillian grew more and more confident with her new life and soon started to settle down and enjoy the time with her family. She was able to watch them grow and be happy with their new lives, their new friends. She learned how these people had come into her children's lives and made them smile and laugh again. This was so nice to see, as Lillian knew how hard it was for not just her but also her children to go through what they had gone through and come out the other end smiling when it could have been worse.

Work was good and all of the children seemed fine except Grace, who was eighteen years old when she arrived in England. She had been in touch with her boyfriend in St Helena, but only her other siblings knew about this. She became very down and withdrawn, not too much though, as otherwise Lillian would have caught on that something was not right with her daughter. Then the truth would come out that her youngest was pregnant. Not being married that was just not heard of where they came from. So Grace told her sisters and they all said 'What are you going to do? You are here in England and not back home.'

14

Grace replied that her boyfriend knew, as she had written to tell him. He had said that she must come back home and marry him as soon as possible. With that, the decision was made, she had to talk to her mother about returning home, and settling down with her soon to be husband. Grace did not know just how her mother would react to this. She hoped that her mother would give her blessing to return home and settle down. Indeed that's exactly what her mother did. Though it was hard for Lillian to let go of her, she knew that Grace would be safe and happy.

The day came when Grace was to leave and sail away home to where she was born, back on that big ship, where she would start a new life of her own. Without her family with her on the day of her wedding, there would be none of her family to see her get married and start a new life. This made her feel sad deep down inside as well as it made everyone else, but no one showed it. They all spent as much time as they could with Grace and made memories that they all would keep and look on when they went their separate ways.

They all knew that things would never be the same again. Who would be the next to move away and settle down, maybe not back home but somewhere else in England? This thought was so frightening yet so exciting at the same time for all of them, except Lillian. She would love things to go back to the way they were and back on her home ground, but this was just a dream. Sometimes, the way life goes, you never know what is going to happen next, you just have to make the best of the situation no matter how good or bad things may be.

The awful day eventually came when Grace, the youngest of the family, was the one to be the first to leave the comfort zone of the nest and venture out into the big world, on her own to start her new life. At least she was going back home where she knew everyone and would be safe. As they all walked towards where Grace's ship was waiting, the family all had tears in their eyes, said their goodbyes and hugged each other so tight as if no one wanted to let go. But they knew that they had to and Grace walked the steps onto the ship. She continued to wave and blow kisses to her family though her heart like theirs was now filled with sadness. She also had joy at the thought of returning home. As the ship slowly sailed away out to sea they all stood there until they could not see it anymore, watching it slowly disappearing out into the mist and eventually out of sight.

They slowly returned home without a word being spoken. The emptiness inside each of them was like the loss of a loved one, even though they knew that they had not lost her, she was going home, but home a long way away. Still it hurt all of them, and upon their return home they were still in a silent mood. Lillian said 'Well at least I know she will be safe and happy. For that we should be glad for her, and not sad. She is about to start her new life. Soon you will do the same, so no more long faces. It took a lot for your young sister to do this and on her own as well. I am very proud of her and I will be of you all one day when you go out into the world and start a new life of your own.'

As the days turned into weeks and then months, life for all of them settled down, they all seemed to start to enjoy their new life in England. Having started new beginnings and new memories of their own, it was not long before one by one they were coming home to Lillian and saying that they had met someone and telling her about them and where and when they met.

Fortunately for Lillian, none of her other children were in the family way before they were married. This, she thought to herself, she was very proud of, as the way that she was brought up on that small but very beautiful island of St Helena would be looked down upon if you were to have a child out of wedlock. She thought it would never happen to her family as they were brought up very strictly indeed. Some might say too strictly as now the day came when Jean came to her and said that she was having a child and unfortunately she was not married nor was she going to get married to the father of her child. He was a school teacher at that time, and she was working as a house keeper for a very rich and yet very kind family who were moving back to Warwickshire to live. She would have to go with them or leave her job and then where would she live with her child? The decision was made that Lillian would stand by her daughter even though she very strongly disapproved of the whole situation. She was disappointed with her daughter too, and this the daughter knew very well as Lillian was of a Victorian age and made her opinions loud and clear, no matter who was hurt by them. That was the way it was and that was how it would be as long as Lillian lived.

CHAPTER TWO

Boyfriends and Births

So Jean moved to Warwickshire with her employers. When it came to having her child, Lillian did not go to the hospital to see Jean and so the baby girl was born and mother and child were alone together. Upon leaving the hospital, Jean returned to her employer's home where she lived, not knowing whether she still had a job or whether her mother would be there to see her. Jean was frightened about what would become of her baby. She was at the tender age of twenty-three.

By that time of her life she had lost her father and moved to a big country with everything new. She was a virgin and knew nothing about contraception. She had been out with friends for a drink, although had never had been able to drink back home in St. Helena. Now she had had a drink and was happy, then how could this happen to her? After all it was the first time she had ever had sex. When she told the father of her child, he did not want to know and left so fast it must have felt like the rushing wind behind her, leaving her all alone to face everything. So young and filled with fear of what would happen to her next. Where could she go, would her mother and the rest of her family disown her because of what has happened to her?

The day came when Jean went to see her employers. They all sat down and everything was sorted out. If Jean wanted to keep her baby she could do so as long as she could arrange for someone to look after the baby while she was working. That would be fine.

Jean was thankful to be able to leave the meeting with her employer but then knew she had to face her mother. She was not looking forward to this as she knew what to expect. On the one hand was a hard and strong talking too, and on the other how could she let the family down. What would her other brother and sisters think, not to mention the rest of the family and friends back home in St. Helena.

Jean did not expect what her mother came out with.

'You cannot keep the baby. You're in no fit state to be a mother. You have no husband and no place of your own. How can you support the child? Do not think for one minute that you are leaving the child with me to look after. I am not looking after your child for you. You will have it adopted. You cannot keep it, so you had better find out how to go about adoption, and fast.' Her mother was very angry.

Jean went to her room to see her baby girl. She had decided to call her Lilly. She was so small and beautiful, and needed her mother. This haunted Jean that night and she could not sleep with the thought of giving her baby away. How could she manage to keep her? The next day, her day off, Jean went into town. Her sister Mary looked after the her baby while she went to find out if she could keep Lilly and if there was any help for mothers like her.

Unfortunately for Jean, all she learned was that she was an outcast, and made to feel ashamed at what she had done to her family. That was England in late 1950s, in fact the same as St Helena. If you were not married and became pregnant, you were made to pay the price. In any way that society could. It was to put unmarried mothers into special hospitals where everyone knew why you were there, to give your baby up for adoption. What any of these mothers wanted did not concern anyone. The decision was made by the family and the subject was closed and never spoken of again. It was as if the young woman had never had a child at all. Unfortunately this was not a situation that only happened in England, no it happened all over the world, even in a very small island such as St Helena, where it would have been worse in a way for Jean as they lived in a village.

As Jean was on her way home, the thoughts of what she was going to do and how she could keep her baby were now running through her head.

She started to walk up straight and tall. It was not long before she was home to face her family and prepare to fight for the life of herself and her child. This was 1958. This year, along with years before, the thought of an unmarried mother was not heard of. In fact, when it did happen the young mother-to-be was made to pay the price of putting her family to shame. It happened in all families, whether you were rich or poor. The result was the same, shame and an out-cast you were and sometimes the name 'black sheep of the family' was used so that others would know about this woman and what had happened to her and did you really want someone like that in your family. So it was like a warning to others 'stay away from this one, she is unclean, and, if you dare to go there, are you prepared for what you are about to enter? You will be talked about.'

Now all of these thoughts were in the mind of Jean. The only thing she could think of was how she wanted to keep her baby, how she missed her father. These thoughts made her feel so low and worthless. How she wished she had never been born as she had failed her family, and now they would feel ashamed of her. She was frightened that she may be dis-owned by the family that she was born into. How much she could lose because of what had happened to her. This thought was unbearable. Yet she knew that she had to make a stand and try her best to do what was right in the long term for her baby and herself.

She felt like a criminal. But no, she was a young woman age of twenty-three who came from a small country where she had her first boyfriend when she was only sixteen. The first time she had any sexual experience was when she was twenty-three, and she had fallen pregnant. Now she was alone with her daughter. She had had no sex education and now as a mother she was having to learn the hard way, having to make decisions she should not have to make on her own. Yet here she was making them, how life could be so cruel to her. She felt so hurt and alone, how could the father just walk away?

His words had been 'Get rid of it.'

'I am a teacher. I have a good job and a good life and do not want to lose either of them. Go away and leave me alone. I do not want to know about the child or you. Get rid of it and do not ruin your life with a child. You are too young to have a child, for God's sake.'

'Get rid of it' was all she could think about. The one thing she would not do was to kill her child. This she was proud of, even though at present she could not give her child what she had hoped, she was pleased that she never took the money to get rid of her baby daughter.

She had the pleasure of not only holding her but naming her. Now all she had to do was to try and find a way of keeping her.

Thankfully her employers were so kind and thought so much of Jean that they did not want to lose her under any circumstances. As she approached the front door, where she was living in the staff quarters, she knew that it was time to make a decision that would affect her life and her baby's forever.

She was prepared to fight for what she wanted as much as she could, knowing that this was not going to be easy. But Jean had both her parents' genes in her, the loving, kind, loyal, hardworking ones. Sometimes the 'do not give in', gene from her father and the other one, the one that was 'stronger to serve' and the 'act first then think afterwards' gene, that was her mother's.

Jean approached her own front door and walked into her large front room. She was met not just by her sister Mary who had been looking after Lilly, but also her mother who had a look of mixed emotions on her face. Their mother had gone through so much, not only losing her soul mate, but also having to leave her country where she was born and had hoped to bring up her children. Lillian had expected be laid to rest with her husband and look down on her children along with her husband, both of them thinking 'well we have done well with our family. They have done so well and all have waited and found the right person to marry just like we did.'

This was clearly not the case. Sad it may be, but the truth is often so far different to the dream. With that thought now going through Jean's mother's head, there was a look of hurt, disappointment, pain and shame. Jean could see this as she walked into the room. The look on her sister's face was the same as her mother's. It was of 'you are my sister and I love you no matter what happens.' This was the look that gave Jean the final strength to overcome what the situation was about to become. So Jean walked into the room with the information leaflets in her hands and over to her sister, took her baby from her and sat down. She waited for her world to fall apart, with what her mother would say. The two sisters were so close, they had that special bond that siblings had. At least she knew that her sister would be on her side. This was what Jean was hoping and praying for.

Later on that night Jean got up to feed her little daughter. As she looked down at her, watching her feed, she said 'I love you and do not want to ever let you go.' With those words Jean started to cry, her tears slowly falling down her face onto her little girl's forehead. Jean just held her baby so tight, as if she was holding onto her own life, and what life itself demanded from her. As Jean put her baby down to sleep she slowly kissed her head, then walked away, back to her own bed and sat down. She put her head in her hands and wept. It was hard for her to keep quiet, Jean just could not cry quietly for her pain would not allow it. Her pain was strong and powerful, it came out whether Jean wanted it or not. She just could not control it. And why should she, for Jean wanted everyone to feel her pain, the whole world in fact. She did not want be the only one feeling like this.

She carried on crying until her sister Mary came and put her arms around her, trying to comfort the pain. Mary felt so helpless for there was nothing that she could do to stop the pain that her sister was feeling. All that Mary could do for her sister was just to hold her as tight as she could until she calmed down and stopped crying. This she did, and stayed with her until morning came when Mary had to go to work leaving Jean alone with her baby. As Mary walked to work she kept thinking to herself 'I wonder what Jean will do now. How will she be able to keep her baby even if she wanted to? How will she be able to support her and her baby? Where will they live as she will have to leave her job?'

Jean's employers had been so supportive, and not asked her to leave. They had given her time to sort herself out and decide what she was going to do about the situation that she was now in. Jean was so lucky in having employers like them.

As Mary was about to start work, Jean was back at home with her baby and with her mother and her employers sitting around the kitchen table discussing what Jean should do about the baby and her future. What would be the best for both Jean and her baby? Eventually they decided between them that Jean would have to give up her baby for adoption. There was no other way of keeping her with Jean, who had to continue to work as the father was nowhere to be seen.

So it was agreed that Jean's baby would be put up for adoption. Jean's mother was so pleased with that as she did not want Jean to keep the baby without a father, or indeed marriage. Even though Jean at the time of the meeting had expressed her ideas of keeping her baby, her mother would not hear of it and told her that she would not help her as she did not have a husband or partner to support her in any way. No one would want to know her as a mother with a child on her own. What would everyone say? If it got back home in St Helena, what a disgrace it would be on the family's name.

So poor Jean had no chance of keeping her baby and had to let her go to a family that could support and bring her up and to give everything that Jean could not give her. This made Jean feel so hurtful and sad. It felt like a part of her was about to be torn away, like some-one cutting off a limb and leaving it to bleed slowly, feeling every drop of blood flowing from her body and being unable to stop it. Eventually to be left feeling numb and lifeless inside.

The day came when it was time to give up her daughter. It came far too quickly for Jean as she wanted more time with her, as much as she could, but this was not going be the case. The reason given was that all babies had to be adopted within weeks of the birth. This was the case for Jean. Her baby was going to leave her, her own flesh and blood, and start a new and better life. The child would not know anything about her real mother, only why she was adopted due to the fact that her real mother was not married and could not cope and that would be that.

The knock on the door came. Jean did not move an inch. She just sat there with her daughter in her arms, holding her so tight with tears now running fast down her face and onto her baby's forehead, yet not awakening her. Nor did the voice of her own mother saying 'I am so sorry, please forgive me, I love you. Please make sure she will be loved and looked after. Please tell her I tried to keep her but could not. Tell her not to hate me for what I have done. I did not mean any harm; I am so young and so very sorry.'

With that, the baby was taken away from Jean. At that moment the baby awoke and started to cry as if she knew that the person holding her was not her own mother but a stranger. As the lady who took Jean's baby walked out of the house, the sound of Jean's baby still could be heard. When the woman got into the car you could still hear the sound of the baby crying.

Then there was silence all around. Nothing but silence. It felt so final and deadly. With it came a sense of pain, emptiness and sorrow. Now a new life had to begin, this time without the sound of Jean's little girl in the background. How strange it was, Jean thought to herself. 'How long will this feeling go on,' and 'will my life get any better now that I am the black sheep of the family and don't I know it.'

One could say that Jean had learnt a valuable lesson in life. To make sure if she met another man that he was not just after one thing, and to make sure that he wore something in bed. To make sure he was a good man to her and would treat her right as she was a good, kind and caring woman, not used to this country. Still learning the ways of the world and all that it brings to her door step. How to deal with it no matter how much it may hurt her.

Time went on. Jean and her family got their life back in some sort of order. Things were getting back to normal. The only thing Jean was very scared of was men. Were they all the same in England? Or were some of them good men? How could she ever trust another man again after what she had been through? Should she still stay on her own as at that point in time would be the best thing for her and her family. She did not want to go through hell ever again and she did not want her family to go through that either. The pain was too much to bear for anyone. And so Jean had changed from a young woman not knowing anything to a woman now knowing to watch for the signs when she went out with her sisters or friends for a drink or to a party. She was ready to walk away when she did not feel safe or if a man came onto her life in the same way that her baby's father did that night. She was not going to be fooled again by any man.

What Jean and her family went through was the worst nightmare possible and it changed her and her family forever. Nothing could ever be the same again. This made Jean stronger in herself. It had been a hard lesson to learn in life but one she learnt all the same.

Jean carried on with her life the best way that she could, yet with the thought of how her little girl was getting on with her new mother and father. Hoping that life would bring her happiness and joy, that she would be happy whatever life brought her way. Jean hoped that one day Lilly would come looking for her real mother. They would be able to sit down and talk, Lilly would learn about her natural background and maybe understand that is was not what Jean had wanted, to give her away, but that Jean had no choice at that time. It was the best thing for her in order for her to have a good and stable life, something that Jean at that time could not give her. It would have been just Jean and Lilly, and God only knew what would have happened. At least this way Lilly had a better chance in life with her new family. Hopefully her daughter could come to terms with this situation and find it within herself to forgive Jean, and thank her for at least giving her a chance, one that she could never have had otherwise if she had stayed with her own mother.

Jean knew that her baby was adopted by a good family with two parents to care for her. They had a good home and money to support her. This all added up to one most important thing and that was to give this little baby girl a secure and stable life. That is what they could offer, and her own mother could not. With this thought running through her mind, Jean was filled with feelings of both pain and relief. But she knew she had done the right thing at the end of day. It was not what Jean wanted but what was best for her baby girl that was the most important thing in the world. Although it was so hard for such a young woman to do, even though there was her family there for her, she still felt so alone and hurt and lost inside.

The following days were filled by Jean working hard and trying her best to get her life back to some sort of normality. Lately, even though the days turned into weeks and then months, her life was changing all the time. But not the pain that still was felt inside Jean's heart. That feeling never seemed to go. She just had to accept it and try to carry on. Jean once told one of her friends who replied 'I just do not know how you can carry on. If that was me, I would probably break down and yet you are so very strong inside. Oh I wish I was you.' At the same time, Jean was thinking to herself 'I wish I was her' for her friend's life was very normal and fulfilling, compared to Jean's.

A year passed and Jean was back to her old self, or so it seemed. For only Jean knew how she was feeling deep down inside, still feeling the loss of her child. Unlike other mothers who have lost their child through illness and had buried them and while in their mourning could at least go their graves, but not for Jean. She had no grave to go to. She was still mourning the loss of her first born child which is always the closest to any mother. For it is when mother nature takes over the human and fills her with the over-whelming feeling of life, and this feeling some humans try to fight but mother nature always wins the battle and fills the human with this feeling, whether they want it or not. In this case, Jean knew that she was right and she must now get on with her life as her baby had started her new life, and so must Jean. Somehow she must try her best to cope with the pain of being a failure in life at such a young age, to feel like that too is a shame but that was Jean's life.

It was not long before a young man came into Jean's life. He was a kind and caring, single and very keen on Jean. He took care of her and showed her the affection that she had needed for a long time. This was what life should be like for two single people, having fun and sharing what life has to offer. Both were of the same age group and together they were happy. Jean felt good inside, the pain of being used was gone, for this man wanted her for herself and no other reason, just to love and protect her and make her feel safe. He wanted her love most of all because he saw in Jean not the ordinary girl from next door but a kind, caring and loyal person with commitment, who had come from a different country with different values in life, in need of a good loving man who would take care of her and their family in each and every way possible.

This is what Jean had found in this man. He was not shy and it was lovely to be loved and wanted. The last person who made her feel so safe was her father, and she thought she would never feel that again. But here she was feeling safe again, thanks to this man. Then came the question, how long would she feel like this. Would it be forever until she died or he died, or just for now? How long is a piece of string, one could say. But for now she was happy and safe. That was good enough for her and her family as they too noticed the difference in Jean.

Jean had decided not to tell her boyfriend or anyone else about the fact that she had a child. It would only give her family more pain and hurt. For this reason Jean thought she would keep the secret to herself and hoped that it would never came out and that she could take it to her grave.

As it was so for Jean's father and mother, William and Lillian. When Lillian's mother did marry, her father was an American GI soldier. She never knew why her mother never married her father. It was war time and, like so many of the war times, there were always the war babies left behind. Maybe that was the case for Jean's own grandmother, and maybe it was the real reason for her mother to feel so strongly about children born without their father being there, or at least knowing who they were as she never did or ever would. So one cannot help but feel the pain and disappointment that her mother must have felt as she wanted so much for her family to be normal and not have a black sheep in the family. She felt she was the black sheep and she wanted so much for her children not to become one. In her own country, being a black sheep is to be looked down on for bringing shame on your family, and everyone would know who you were.

Therefore you were made to wear it on your own shoulders for the rest of your life.

Now one of her own children had become the black sheep of the family, bringing shame. This, in Lillian's eyes, was unforgiveable. Since her husband had passed away, she tried so very hard to keep the family safe and out of harm's way, tried to keep them on the road that was straight and narrow and hoped that her family would have a happy ending without unhappiness or shame, sorrow or pain. They had all had their fair share of that.

As time went by, Jean became happy and soon fell in love with her new boyfriend. She felt safe at long last. This was a feeling she thought she would never feel after all the pain and hurt and disappointment that life have given her. Jean thought 'at long last maybe it is my turn to be happy and laugh both inside and out and feel good.' One thought kept popping up in her mind, that she knew one day she would have to tell her mother before she found out. That was her worst fear. This would be unbearable to her after what she knew her mother had been through. With this thought, she asked her sister Mary, who was the closest to her. The two of them looked at each other in silence not knowing what to say. Then with the night closing in they went home still in silence, as Mary could see her sister in pain and the worried look on her face.

The next day Jean thought 'I will leave it for now and see how things turn out.' For all she knew the boyfriend to whom she had become to very close, could get bored of her and move on. She kept her secret safe, not telling others that she knew could not be trusted. This went on for some time and the relationship developed further and feelings got stronger between them. He really cared for Jean and showed her how much, he was always protective of her, no other male came near her or made any moves. This she had never had in her life, only from her father and mother but no other person outside of her family. This was something that was hard for her to sometimes deal with, but at the same time she felt safe and happy with him. He always put her first and was also a family man as he too came from a big family.

This was what she had wanted for such a long time. She had wished this man was the first she had become involved with. That what had happened to her before had never happened. She knew that this boyfriend would not have done what the last one had. She knew that this boyfriend was not married and not just out for what he could get and lied to get it. No, this boyfriend was not that kind at all, he was kind and caring and very loving and loyal to her. This she needed so much in her life. As time went on they became happy with their lives, but she still had kept that painful secret of her being an unmarried mother who had to give up her little girl, as she feared that she would lose her boyfriend. She imagined he would think 'what sort of woman is she?' and even though she tried as she might, she could not change his feelings about her as he was a family man and had often said to her that one day he would love to settle down and have a family of his own. How could she tell him her secret, even though more than likely he would have still stood by her and not left her in the way that she was treated before. She was not going to take that risk and not only lose her man but put herself through all of that pain again. This was just too much for her to go through, as she might not pull through as well the second time. That was the hardest thing she had ever done. So she carried on being happy and being loved and protected by her loving boyfriend and hoped that it would last and that they would live happily forever.

This feeling was so good for Jean, being with someone who loved and wanted her. But it would not last. Jean found to her horror that she was pregnant. This was not what she wanted to go through again. Jean still knew that her mother would never, ever approve of her being pregnant again, even though this time with a good, single man, who would stand by her. She knew that her mother had been brought up in a different country and a different way of life. In fact her mother was a virgin when she married her father and vowed that she would never, ever get married again, as she married her father for life, 'until death do us part.' This was what happened and thinking about how she missed her father, Jean began to cry, the tears running down her face were tears of pain and grief for the loss of her father that she had loved so much. He was the one man in her life that would never hurt her, but protect her, and this she missed so much, as well as his gentle, loving side, and his cuddles and laughter. The picture of him standing there such a good looking man, slim, with good bone structure. This she missed so much, as she knew that since her father had died things had changed so much, and her mother had to take the role of both mother and father. This had aged her. Her mother was in her early forties when her father died, she had had to make the change to a stronger person, even more strict than ever before, for she had to protect her family in their new world that was very scary for her with only her past upbringing. The way that she had brought up her children back in her own country where she knew the rules and the way of life and the people on the Island she knew, this was not going to apply here in England. This made her more determined to be strong and show that she was somehow still in control of her family in order to keep them safe in this world and to do whatever she thought was the right decision for her family because at the end of the day all she lived for was her family. Jean knew this all too well and she knew that she would once again disappoint her mother and let her family down. This hurt Jean so much inside as she loved her family, and was so close to them all.

As the days went, Jean knew that she had to do something and quickly as she would soon begin to show. She turned to her closest sister, Mary, and Jean told her that she was again pregnant. How was she going to tell their mother? Mary asked if Jean had told her boyfriend and Jean said 'no not yet I have only told you.'

Mary said 'you must tell him, and talk about what you both want to do. Will he marry you?'

Jean replied 'yes he would.'

'Well that is good, you can be a family,' With that came silence from Jean, then Mary said 'you do want to marry him don't you?' Still no answer, then Jean replied 'I am not sure.'

'What do you mean?' asked Mary.

'Well he loves me and is very kind and loving, but he is very strong minded, full of confidence.' This was not what Jean was, she was the opposite, very gentle and loving just like her father, meek and mild. Her mother was the one who was the strong minded one in the family and together they did make a good team. But Jean was not sure whether she and her boyfriend would make a good team.

A week later, after talking to her sister, Jean decided to tell her boyfriend and see what he would say. After talking to him, her thoughts were right, he did indeed ask her to marry him. This was just wonderful she thought to herself. Then she thought how her mother would react to her news. This thought changed the look on Jean's face, going from happy to sad. Her boyfriend noticed this change and asked 'What is the matter? Why the sudden sadness on your face?'

Jean replied 'you do not know my mother.'

After hearing how she had lost her father and how her mother had changed, how she knew that she would not approve of them, and what has happened, her boyfriend turned to her and said 'it does not matter. I will protect you and be with you all the way. Please don't be sad, I will be strong for you I will never let you down.'

This made Jean feel a little better, knowing that at least she had someone who was there for her. Jean somehow found the strength to tell her mother the news. She knew this would be hard, as this was not the first time. How would she feel this time round as her mother was the head of their family and Jean was so young and green around the edges? All of them had to go through so much is such a short time. Now, again, Jean had let her mother and family down. But she knew she had to tell her mother, and no matter how her mother would react she knew that her mother loved all of her family.

Their mother's up-bringing was so very different to their own. It was in fact much stricter than theirs. At least they had the pleasure of knowing their father. It may have been only for a short part of their lives, at least they would know all about him and his family, unlike their mother. She never knew her father, as her mother had her out of wedlock. In those days, the child born out of wedlock was known as a bastard, and this is what their mother was. Never knowing anything about her own father or his family. Just knowing her step-father, step-brother and step-sister. Living with a drunk for a father, who put them all through hell.

So there was not much love in their mother's household. Just abuse. Either from shouting or by being hit by their father.

Their mother was the only one who gave love, as well as working to feed her family. Working hard to try and keep her family together, which was not an easy thing to do and would take such guts along with sweat, blood and a lot of tears. Indeed it did until Jean's mother was old enough to get married. Not to a man like her step-father, but to just the opposite, one who she would settle down with and have her own family. And keep her family safe and very much loved, like she never had in own life. She made sure that her own family would have what she did not have in her own life.

And at least this time Jean's mother could hold up her head with pride and not hold her head down with shame as she was a young, married mother and the children that she bore were the flesh and blood of herself and her husband. At long last, the shame of her own family had now gone and been replaced with a good name and no shame. From now on she was Mrs L.V. Benjamin and not the shameful Miss L.V. Jonson. No, that was now dead and buried and a new life had now begun. Marriage was 'Till death do us part' and indeed that was to be true. Knowing all this, you could see how Jean's mother would react and why, as her own past would be coming back to haunt her and bring back all the hurt and pain that she had to suffer all of her childhood.

Jean was so sad and hurt for doing this to the family. How she wished that it was all just a bad dream and anytime soon she would wake up and everything would be very different, it would be so happy and pain free, just filled with laughter and any tears that fell would be tears of happiness and not sorrow and pain. With this thought, Jean turned to her closest sister Mary and told her of her fears; for Jean knew one thing that was certain, and that was that her own sister would stand by her and hold her when she fell.

When Jean told her mother, she knew she was not prepared for what was to come next. That her own mother could not deal with the pain and shame of not just her daughter's present life and what has happened again, but of her own life and reliving the pain and shame of it all.

There was no way of having an abortion as this was not allowed or even thought of in those days.

Jean's mother did not go to the hospital when Jean was in labour, so Jean gave birth with her sister Mary holding her hand and being there for her. Her own mother was nowhere to seen.

Even when Jean came out of the hospital, her mother was not there. When she came home, her mother said how she had felt about the whole affair. Even though Jean had said her boyfriend, the father of her baby girl, would marry her, it did not make any difference. The deed was done and there was no going back, for the shame was there again. This was unforgiveable for her mother, this was just too much for her to bear the pain and disappointment. There is a point in a person's life when they have reached breaking point, in other words the brain and body cannot deal with any more pressure. So that person will deal with the worst situation that they find themselves in, any way it can, in order to survive. It is Mother Nature at her best, the game of life is called survival of the fittest, and if you fail you die.

So with that, Jean was told by her mother that she would have to do the same thing as before and have the child adopted.

When Jean heard this news, straight from her own mother's mouth, she felt her whole life just collapsing all around her. This time her pain was more than before. She had tried to convince her mother that things were different, but she still had no choice as her mother once again was in control of her life and a decision had been made. Jean's mother thought that Jean knew nothing about bringing up a family of her own without a husband and how things should been done in the right way for everyone including the child. So Jean's second daughter was put into a foster home where she would stay with a family of their own two boys, and now this little girl. She stayed there being loved and cared for like a normal family for six months. In that time Jean was tormented.

She knew that she had to get her back. At least this time she had the father of her child there by her side, and also her sister Mary who was there for her and would always be there for her.

With this, Jean gained strength and told her own mother that she wanted her little girl back for keeps. That she was so very sorry for everything that she had done, and that this time would be so different. She had learnt her lesson. Jean went off alone to get her second daughter back to live with her for good. As her second child was not adopted and only fostered out, Jean thought that there may be a chance for her to get her little girl back and try and make a go of it. Her employers, once they saw her child, agreed that they would not replace Jean from their services as head house keeper.

The boyfriend did love Jean so much, and without Jean's mother's approval they stayed together, not being married or living together or anything like that. The two remained together, the father only being able to sneak in to see his own daughter as it was forbidden for Jean to see anyone outside the family or work place, that was her mother's rule. So Jean had to be very careful when her boyfriend could see his own daughter and girlfriend. They did this when Jean had finished work, then they would have their time together in Jean's own quarters. They would spend their time together though it was very little, as it was their time where no one could crowd them and where they both could think and try and plan for their future.

At times, the situation for Jean was very hard. Her mother still would not give her the support that Jean needed, she would not help her, yet she would never leave her side. She just wanted to show her that she had to do this on her own, though it may seem so cold to Jean, it was her mother's way of trying to make her strong like she had had to do. Only with her mother, she had to bring up six children on her own, and not just one child. She knew that Jean was not as strong as she was, but her mother had to try and make Jean strong enough to deal with being a mother.

When Jean turned to her mother for any tenderness, Jean's mother would look at Jean and refuse this, it was not an easy thing to do as she loved her family but she had to teach Jean a lesson the hard way, but a lesson that would make her strong enough to survive in this world. In time, Mary became a second mother to her niece and together Jean and Mary managed to cope.

Now Jean was with the father of her second child, society still would not accept this woman as a good woman with a good man by her side. For women like Jean were classed as undesirables and loose women, and if that was not bad enough, Jean was not white and not English. She was in fact foreign, which was even worse, as you were looked down on even more. It was not unheard of for a person who was not white and who may have been light brown or dark brown to be called nigger or blacky or wog. This language was indeed used towards Jean and some of her family as they were light and mid brown. Their father had been black and yet their mother was white, this did not matter to some people and Jean's little girl was white. This did not make any difference to society at all.

For this was a cold and cruel world that they now lived in.

Jean and her boyfriend lived the best way they could with the situation that they were in, seeing each other when they could and trying so hard not to get found out, but still trying to keep the relationship going no matter hard it would be. There was no doubt it would, but they were both determined to stay together as a family and maybe one day things would change for them for the better.

As the months went on, nothing had changed with their circumstances, though it was hard, they still lived life the best way that they could with the secret they had, that no-one knew about Jean's boyfriend, the father of her baby girl, still being on the scene. Especially Jean's mother, as far she knew Jean was on her own. She was taking care of her baby girl and there was no man to play the role of a father figure, who may stay there for a short term and not for the long term, for her mother knew that the only ones who would stay would be her own family.

But little did Jean's mother know that things would change for her family and this time it would not be any of her other children. No, it would be Jean again who became pregnant, and the father was the same father of her second child. Now Jean was pregnant again with her third child. Jean and her family did not know anything about condoms or any other protection against pregnancy, as back home things like this were never discussed. So therefore it was left up to nature itself and, unfortunately for Jean, nature had given her another baby.

Jean was beside herself with fear and worry for what her mother and the rest of her family would think of her and what they would say. Would they understand that Jean never did this on purpose, and that the father of her baby was there for her. In fact he had never left her side, and was indeed not just the father of this baby but was now the father of two babies and wanted to settle down with Jean and become a family.

But this was not going to be the case. As soon as Jean told her family, things would in fact change and not the way that Jean and her boyfriend had hoped for. No, indeed there was hell to pay for this. Jean's family, excluding her mother, comforted her and told her that they would stand by her no matter what would happen. But for Jean's mother it was to be a different story completely.

Now her mother just said 'I cannot cope with this anymore and you are on your own. I wash my hands of it all.'

So when Jean's baby girl was born, her sister Mary was there besides her, and no one else. Just the two of them. Not even the father. He was waiting for her to come out of hospital with their baby girl, whom Jean had given the name of Emma. Her second baby girl she had called Jesse. Both girls looked so much alike, and both looked like Jean, with their olive skin so beautiful in every way. Jean knew that she would have to try somehow and keep this little girl, and try and keep her little family together, but how could this be done?

When Jean came home from the hospital with her baby girl Emma, she tried to show her mother her new baby girl. She told her the name she had chosen for her. But her mother would not even look at her granddaughter; she walked away without saying a word to Jean and acted like she was not there. This hurt Jean so much, as she wanted the help and love of her mother.

Jean still had her sister by her side, and she knew that she still had her boyfriend, the father of her two girls. But she had no mother to turn to, like daughters normally do when they have a family of their own, or so it would seem outside of her own family.

She knew that it was not her mother's fault the way that she was behaving towards her, it was the way that her mother had been brought up, and the way that her mother had brought up Jean and her family.

As the days went by, things became even harder for Jean. She had to keep working and try and look after her two little girls. To try and sort out her feelings of hurt and pain, to deal with the pressure of when, how, where she and her boyfriend would marry and live. There was no room where Jean worked, there were no married quarters, only a single room for Jean and now her two girls. This was putting pressure on her, not only from her mother but from her employers too. Her employers had expected just Jean on her own, not Jean plus two little girls. They had said that so long as she could manage and carry on with her work as head house keeper the situation would be fine.

As long as she kept things going the same way, Jean knew that her job would be safe. But this is not what happened. Her boyfriend became very protective over Jean and his two little girls. Every time that Jean managed to see her boyfriend in secret, and they went out for a couple of hours while her sister would babysit for Jean, if any one looked at Jean, her boyfriend would ask 'do you know them?' If it was another man just looking in Jean's direction, the boyfriend would almost get into a fight because some other man had looked at his girlfriend. Eventually it did get worse, so much so that Jean just could not cope with her boyfriend the way that he was behaving.

As time went on things became very hard for Jean. She felt like everything was getting to her and no matter how hard that she tried to cope with her life and the way it was, she became very withdrawn. Her health was now starting to be affected, she did not sleep as much as she should, and she worked longer hours to try and get more money for her family. Her relationship with her boyfriend became harder and harder to cope with. She knew that she had to do something. She could not cope any longer with the situation of working and looking after her little girls, and keeping a relationship going with a man that had changed to a point that he had started to frighten her with his over protective behaviour.

She arranged to meet him and tell him how she had been feeling, how she just could not go on with the situation the way it was. That she had to go on in life without him. How sorry she was that things had turned out the way that they had, not just for her but for both of them. She wished him well in his life. Even though he had tried to talk her out of this, Jean knew that she could not change her mind. It was now the end of the road for both of them as a couple, though sad that it was, that was the way it had to be.

CHAPTER THREE

Lady Zara

From then on, that was the way life was. When Jean came home, she told her family what she had decided, and there was no longer any man in it. She would bring up her two little girls on her own, with or without help from her family, meaning her mother. Though Jean did not say the word 'mother,' she meant it. By Jean going through all she had, she had become much stronger. It was as if Jean was now fighting for her family's survival, as she knew that the rest of her family were not in the same situation, they were all fine with their lives.

Jean's life was in a mess. It was up to Jean to change that around and on her own she was prepared to do just that. Jean grew stronger, both in her body and mind. Jean slowly put her life back together again, managing both work and looking after her two little girls whom she loved so much. Every time Jean looked at her two girls she thought back to her first born. Her eyes would fill with tears of pain, and the longing to hold her little girl again and tell her how much she missed her. That she never stopped loving her, even though she was with a new mother and father and new brother and sister. Knowing that she was well loved and cared for was not the same as holding your own flesh and blood.

But Jean knew there was nothing she could do. Where her little girl was now, she was well looked after and very loved and protected in a stable family where she would grow up in a normal family life. Jean knew that her little girl would not get that if she had stayed with her, she was better off with her new family, no matter how much it hurt Jean. It was for the best for both of them. Jean just had to deal with this again. The only thing that Jean hoped was that one day her little girl would not hate her, but to try and understand the reason why, and to somehow forgive her, and maybe thank her. At least she had given her a good start in life, which was more than Jean could have given her. With the tears of pain, sorrow and shame falling down her face and her hands holding her head, Jean heard a small cry from behind her. It was Emma.

Jean stood up and wiped her face, then picked up Emma and held her tight. Jesse walked up to Jean, looked up at her mother who reached out one arm and put it on to Jesse's shoulders and pulled her close, holding her tight, saying 'I love you both so much.'

Jean felt the love and the need of her two little girls, and somehow felt happier. Emma stopped crying and started to smile. Jesse tickled her foot and she began to laugh. Jean gently put Emma down and the two girls played happily together.

As the two girls grew up, it became more difficult for Jean. Lillian came to terms with the situation, and she helped as much as she could, and so did Mary.

Even though there were the three of them trying to work and keep the family together, things were once again turning for the worse for Jean. The girls were now running around as you would expect any child to do. These were not the surroundings for two young children as Jean's quarters were very small.

The windows were easy to reach as Jean found out one day when she came back after work. She found Mary had caught both Jesse and Emma trying to reach the window cill. That scared Mary, they were both now exploring their surroundings every way they could. Once they had found their feet they were off.

As they grew, the girls were found in opposite directions. Jesse managed to sneak out of the door of their quarters and into the main house. Both Jean and Mary looked everywhere for her whilst minding Emma, trying not to cause a panic. It was difficult with such a huge house and its gardens. Thankfully Jesse was found in the drawing room by Lady Zara, and returned back safely with no harm done. Jean felt so upset and worried for the safety of her children.

The girls got into more and more mischief. They got bored just being able to keep to their side of the big house, and only being able to go out with their own family. Not being able to mix with the other children that came to visit the big house and were allowed in the gardens to play. Jean's two girls were not allowed, they would have to go out to parks and walks with their own family. The rest of the time they had to spend at home, playing in their tiny quarters.

Jesse and Emma were now four and two. Things were getting even tougher on all of the family. There were arguments about the girls and how it was getting harder and harder to look after them, to feed and clothe them, and to try and keep them out of the big house and the gardens. It was not just Jean who had to work but also Lillian and Mary, both had to earn a living as well as try and look after the girls. This was now affecting them all, and proving to be very difficult. When not working, they took it turns to look after the girls who were becoming very demanding.

One day Jean had just finished work. She was greeted by her mother and sister. This time not a hello or even a smile. Nothing but silence and a look from her mother, the same look as Lillian would give her children when she wanted to talk to them in a serious manner, or if they had done something wrong. Jean thought to herself 'oh no, what have I done now?'

Her mother said 'sit down, we need to talk.' Jean knew that meant her mother had decided something. She would tell Jean what that was, and this decision would again be final. Jean slowly sat, followed by her mother and her sister. Lillian began to talk about the girls and then about the past, Jean's past in particular. And with that, reopening old wounds that had hurt Jean before and now they were back to hurt again.

Lillian said 'I have watched and thought about this situation very hard indeed and I have tried, along with your sister, to help you with the girls as much as I can. But now it is causing great concern in the big house and it has been brought to my attention that it is starting to affect your work. You are getting more and more tired, and everyone is concerned for both you and the girls.'

'I worry about how you are going to cope as they get older and need more attention. And then there is their schooling. Not to mention where is everyone going to live. As you know, there is no room here, and you would have go and rent somewhere and pay all the household bills, which you do not have to do whilst living here.'

'I am sorry Jean. You have tried your best, but it is not enough. You will have to separate the girls and let either one or both of them live with someone else, in a family that can provide for them and give them a better life than you can give in your circumstances.'

At these words, Jean's pain came from her heart and turned into tears that rolled down her face and began to turn into a flood. No matter how Jean tried to control them, she just could not. There was just too much pain and hurt for now. She felt that she again had failed her family, no matter how hard she had tried to keep them together. She had proved to have failed again.

Jean also knew that her mother was right in what she had said. Her mother went on talking, reminding Jean that she was too weak to do anything, that she just cannot make the right decision. She had tried once before, and this was now the outcome of her mistake in making the wrong decision in the first place. Jean's mother told her that this was enough. She would now make the right decisions towards the girls, and that Jean would have to just deal with it and get on with her life.

'Get back to work and do not to lose your job. And do not bother with men anymore.'

Jean felt so very low inside. So much hurt, she wished that she had never been born, though she had never shared her thoughts with her sister and just kept her feelings inside

Her girls were her life and they gave her hope and so much love, she felt alive with them. Jean was only strong in body and not so strong in her mind, for she was like her father. He had been the weak one in their family, and their mother was the strong one. Jean knew it too well, and also knew that her mother would now take control of her life for the time being.

For next couple of months, Jean carried on looking after her girls, working and trying to do the best that she could. Jean was trying to show her mother that she could cope with the situation and indeed she did for a while until she got sick with being so tired and run down. Then her mother said 'this situation has to stop. You cannot cope any more. I will now sort things out, and you will not go against my wishes again, then things will be normal for everyone concerned.'

Lillian did just as she said that she would. She arranged for Emma to be adopted into a new family.

That time soon came. Jean had taken the day off. She was there when a car pulled up and a nice looking couple stepped out and rang the doorbell. Jean was looking out of the window holding Emma for the last time, as she had done before with her first born little girl. She saw the couple arriving and thought that they looked a friendly couple and hoped that they would take good care of her little girl and love her as Jean loved her.

Lillian showed them in. She said to Jean 'it is time to say your good byes now. This lovely couple have come to take Emma home with them.' The door opened further and in walked Jesse and ran up to her mother who was crying and still holding Emma tight in her arms. Jesse walked up to her mother and Jean, still holding Emma, had put her other arm around Jesse and held them both tight. Then she had to say to Jesse that her sister was going to live with this lovely couple and that Jesse would be living with her. With that, Jesse, being only four years old, started to cry and say 'no mummy no', and would not let go of her mother and even tried to hold on to her little sister at the same time. But it was no use, as Emma was handed over to her new mother. Jean reached out to Jesse to try and comfort her, as both of her little girls were now crying and so too was Jean. She knew that this would be the last time that she and Jesse would ever see Emma again.

After little Emma had gone, Jean, Lillian, Mary and little Jesse were left in the room, now all crying and holding each other and trying very hard to comfort each other. This was another day from hell. How would they all come back from this and carry on with life? There is just Jesse left in Jean's world. For now Jean was grieving for the loss of two of her little girls. Even though there were no bodies in their graves and no stones to mark them, Jean was in mourning for her girls. Jean could not go to and talk to them and lay flowers for them.

As the day went on, things went back to as normal as they could be, given the situation. Jean became very protective over Jesse and would always give Jesse all the love that she could and made sure that Jesse was safe at all times. In the time that they had together, she would often tell Jesse that things would be better, that no one was going to take Jesse away from her, and that they would all live happily ever after.

Even though Jesse had all the love in world that her mother and family could give her she became withdrawn and sad, for she was now on her own with no little sister to play with and cuddle up to and no more little sounds that her sister had made when they were laughing out loud and no more playing with their dolls and talking in their own little way. Jesse was missing her sister so much and not old enough to understand why she had to leave.

Everyone noticed that Jesse had changed and become very quiet. She would sit cuddling her sister's teddy and not respond to anyone in her normal smiling self, just with a sad face. So the family had to do something about this as they did not want Jesse to suffer any more than she was. They all took it in turns to play and try and talk to Jesse about what had happened to her sister and why she had to go and live with a new family.

When the family in the big house heard what was going with Jesse they even said to Jean 'you can bring her to work with you.' So Jean took Jesse with her to work and when the lady of the house (Lady Zara) saw Jesse with a long sad face she said 'come with me and we will go into the garden.' Lady Zara showed Jesse the big maze at the bottom of the garden and the woods. They both returned into the large lounge which was filled with so much beautiful furniture and paintings, and deep piled carpets where your feet would disappear. Zara would pick up Jesse in her arms and gently place her on her lap and tell her about the woods where there were little fairies and how they would play.

Jean would come into the lounge to find Jesse sitting on her employer's lap, laughing, on her face was the smile that her mother remembered. Here it was again. Jean thought to herself that she had got her little girl back from that dark and lonely place. How good it was to not only see but to hear her laugh again, and with this Jean thanked Lady Zara. She replied 'you both have gone through so much. It is time for you to start again, a fresh new start, and learn how to smile again yourself, and fill this house with laughter and no more tears of pain. So when you come to work, you must bring Jesse with you at all times, as we look forward to you both not only my head house keeper but family also.

From that day Jean and her little Jesse were made more like family than employee. Jesse was very much made to feel like family as Zara would take Jesse shopping with her. When people would ask who Jesse was, Zara would say 'this is my little God-daughter' and would buy Jesse anything she needed. Jesse was allowed in the big house at any time. Zara had a family of her own, a son and a daughter, and when they were there, so was Jesse. Jesse was treated as the baby of the family and welcomed by all in the big house.

In summer there would be children who were friends of the son and daughter and Jesse would go into the garden and play as one big family, only Jesse not born into money, like the other children.

She was unfortunately born out of wedlock and from the other side of the track, the poor side. Yet Jesse and her mother were never made feel like that, and Jesse was now living on the rich side of life. Her past was slowly disappearing into a dream that she once had and never to dream it again. Jesse went on to have the world at her feet, learning about her new world and how they lived and behaved, how they talked as well as dressed. Jesse indeed was now turning into a little lady and dressing like one. Even though she was not old enough to attend school, she was being groomed for her new world and she became very well spoken and polite.

At Christmas, the whole house would change into Santa's home, filled with holly and a huge, real Christmas tree that stood from floor to ceiling in the lounge, covered with lights and tinsel. At the bottom of the tree there were piles of Christmas presents. When the family, and of course Jesse, were called into the lounge, everyone had to sit around the tree and was told that Father Christmas was coming in person to their house to deliver their Christmas presents.

When Jesse heard this, her heart began to race faster and faster as she waited with the rest of the household for Father

Christmas to come. A knock sounded at the lounge door and Lady Zara said 'come in.' The door slowly opened and in walked Father Christmas, on his shoulder was a red bag filled with presents. He gently walked into the room towards the Christmas tree and slowly sat down on a big chair.

Then he said in a low voice 'has everyone here been very good all year? As you know, I only give presents to the good and not the naughty.'

With that, everyone said 'Yes I have been good Father Christmas.' Then he looked into his bag and began to take out the presents. He called out the name on each present and gave it to the person, they in turn would say 'thank you' and then sit down and begin to open the present.

And then it was Jesse whose name who was called out. Jesse was the youngest and was so excited as she ran up to Father Christmas and fell into his lap. When Jesse looked up he just smiled and gave Jesse her present. Then Jesse turned around and, with all eyes on her to see if she would run back to her seat, she saw Lady Zara look at her. Jesse walked back very slowly, sat down and began to open her present. It was a walking, talking doll, bigger than Jesse, and not made of plastic but something that looked just like real flesh. It was so fragile Jesse was told to be very careful with her.

This was not the only present that Jesse would receive for Christmas, this was the one from Father Christmas. When he left the room, the family began to open the presents around the tree and there were more presents for Jesse. When everyone had opened all of their presents the room was filled with laughter and everyone there had on their faces a red glow from laughter, their hearts filled with joy and especially for Jesse for this was her best Christmas ever.

At the door to the lounge, waiting there, was Jesse's mother who had watched her little girl see Father Christmas and collect her present and then open the other presents around the tree.

But most of all to see her little girl smile and to hear her laugh aloud again and to see her playing with her new presents and see her showing them to everyone there. The sight of all this made Jean so very happy and the tears of joy fell down her face as she had seen her little girl happy, knowing how much she had gone through and how far she had come since then and how proud she was of her little girl.

Jean stood with a smile and a little tear drop started to fall on her face, this time for joy. Jean's heart was filled with joy and happiness and a warm glow could be seen on her face. This felt so good, Jean wished that this feeling would last forever and never go, and that her little girl would grow up always being happy.

Winter passed and the household was preparing for spring. The garden was showing signs of new life. Jean's little girl was nearing her fifth birthday and would be going to her first big school soon, leaving her little friends at her kinder garden school and moving to her new private school. Knowing that, Lady Zara, who had welcomed Jesse into her family, now started to teach her to read and to tie up her own shoe laces.

Zara would give Jesse a reward such as a brooch. Later, the presents would be things like a gold bracelet and then a diamond swan brooch. Each time a reward was given, Jesse was told 'keep them always, and every time you look at them, it will remind you that you earned them through your own efforts. In this life, if you want something, you must work for it.'

As time went by, the rewards started to mount up. Jesse's mother kept them in a box for Jesse so she could look back on them and tell her grandchildren how she came to have them.

When Jesse went to her new school she soon fitted in with the other children and showed signs of being a gifted child. She was able to do things without being shown a second time, and showed she loved to learn.

The teachers at Jesse's school commented on her ability to learn and how she enjoyed a challenge, that Jesse was a very bright and intelligent child and would go on to achieve anything that she wanted in life.

When Jean arrived home with this news she was so proud of Jesse and so were the rest of her family and Lady Zara and her family. They all knew too well what Jesse had gone through in her life as well as her mother and her family and this time there was good news. It seemed that at last life for Jean and her family had changed for the better.

But most of all that little Jesse had gone through her own pain of losing her sister. She had managed with love and understanding from her mother and her family and Lady Zara welcoming her into her family. Somehow making sure Jesse felt that she would never again be taken away from her mother and family like her little sister. The nightmares that used to wake Jesse up in the night had stopped at last, and life seemed to go on as it should.

Jesse's mother always met her after school. One day Jesse was not there. After some time Jean returned home thinking Jesse had gone home for the first time on her own, but she was not at home and no one had seen her. The whole household was about to go out and search for Jesse when the doorbell rang and there she was next to the mother of one of her school friends, saying that Jesse had tea at their home. Jesse had been well behaved and it was a joy for her own little girl to have a friend like Jesse.

Jesse's friend's mother walked to her car and drove off down the long driveway. The front door closed and all eyes were on little Jesse. Not faces of approval or happiness but of relief that nothing had happened. That she was home safe. Then Jesse was told to go the drawing room. She turned around and saw her mother and Lady Zara talking and then looking at her. Jean said 'go on Jesse, I will be there in a minute.' Jesse continued to the drawing room and shut the door behind her. There she waited. She stood up and went to the window and was looking out when the door opened and in walked her mother and Lady Zara. Jesse waited for them to speak.

First was Jesse's mother, saying how she had gone to meet Jesse at school and how worried she was when she did not find Jesse there where she was supposed to be. How it is not safe at her age to go off on her own, and the dangers of the outside world, that Jesse had always been protected from and never knew about. But now she was learning a hard lesson, life on the outside could be far different from her world that she was growing up in.

From now on, Jesse would no longer walk to school with her mother but would be driven there and back. Jesse was not to go to any of her school friends' houses again without permission and that would be the rules of the house. Lady Zara explained her friend was not of the same family circumstances as Jesse, and that her friend's family were not in the same society as Jesse now belonged to. She went on to say that her friend and maybe others in her classroom were not upper class, only middle class and were not suitable to be seen with.

CHAPTER FOUR

New Beginnings

How Jean wished her life had not turned out the way that it had. She wished so many times that life was different, but it was not so. At least this time it had changed for the better. She would do whatever she could to make Jesse's life happy and safe, give her love and be proud of her, never being ashamed of her and never sending her to Coventry, like her own mother had done to her. This was not going to be the way she would be with Jesse. She would always stand by her. Her mother would always be there. Jesse would know her mother would never walk away from her.

Jean was still in contact with her friends from when she lived in the Midlands, but had not seen any of them since they had moved, she had only spoken on the phone. It was sad to leave them behind, but Jean was so pleased to leave the past behind her and start again in a new area, meet new friends and have a new life. This time with no thought of bumping into someone she knew, she was not yet ready for that to happen.

Jean was just happy that here she had met new friends, and when she did go out she enjoyed herself and did not worry about who may walk in the room where she was. She looked forward to seeing them once a month. And knowing that Jesse would be looked after at home and would be safe with whom she had chosen to look after her.

One day, a friend from the Midlands called and asked if she would come back for a visit. It would be nice to see each other to catch up and see how Jesse was in her new school. Jean replied that she would as she would also like to visit her family.

She put the phone down, thinking it would be nice to see her friend and her mother, sister Mary and her husband, Bob, and their new baby when it was born in a few months time. Should she stay for the weekend or would she feel that she could only stay for the night? It would depend how she felt or coped with being there, with all the memories that would somehow come flooding back to her, whether she wanted them or not and who she might meet.

All of this she knew she would have to face one day, and this would be the time that she would have to be very strong, not just for herself but her little Jesse and her sister too, as well as her mother. For this time she had turned around and she was happier than ever. At last things were going well for both Jesse and her mother, and this would be the time to show and tell how things were and hopefully for Jean's mother to be proud of her.

With this thought, Jean knew that she would have to go back and this time she would hold her head up high, with her little Jesse beside her. She knew that she had the strength to do just that. She would more than ever not let her past come back and put her right back where she once was, weak and full of shame. No more, she had made mistakes before, but now she had learned from them and would not repeat them ever again and put herself or anyone else through the pain and hurt that she still felt deep down inside, but now she was coming to terms with everything in her past.

Jean received a phone call from her sister, Mary, asking how she was and when she would be coming to visit them. Jean told her she would try for next weekend. Maybe this time she would be able to put the past behind her for once and for all. Even though Jean and her family had carried on with their lives, she did not know whether those who knew her at the time of her pain and shame would still think she was the same old Jean, the black sheep of the family, who would lead a life of no hope and no future.

This was not the way things had turned out for Jean. She had learnt her lesson well and now had moved on, taking care of her little Jesse and making sure that life would be better. Jesse would not be affected as her mother was, and she would grow up strong and do well at school and make friends and live in a safe loving world. She would know what there was to know and not be so green as her mother was. For at least Jesse was born in England, not in a small country where things were very different.

And Jean knew she would never ever walk away from Jesse, if she needed her in anyway. Not like her own mother had done to her, even though it was the way of showing her that she must not let down herself and her family. This is not the way of the family, and it was also of the Victorian ways as that was the time that Jean's mother and father were born. Things were so very different then to now, and yet the morals were very much the same. That is one thing that she would make sure that Jesse had throughout her life, that she always had her morals and stood by them, always, and never let herself down in anyway by doing something that she did not want to and to try and protect herself in any way that she could in order to be safe.

Jean's family was brought up to respect others and their opinions, whether or not she agreed with them. They would still show their respect to them and hopefully they would show the same. They would always look after their appearances making sure they would look their best at all times, as the first impressions are the ones that people always remember.

This was one thing the family agreed about their upbringing that they were very glad they had. Some families know never, ever, to disrespect parents, or any older member of the family, and never answer back to them, even though you might think at the time their decision was not one that you may have hoped for. They did it for a reason and a good one at that. Still you would never curse at them at any time.

All of the family would teach their own families this lesson. And so did Jean teach Jesse, she was glad to have learned it and be able to pass on. Jean hoped that one day Jesse too would pass it on to her own family, for this lesson was not only a good way of life, but it also made sure that the family would always be close, and be there for each other, whatever the situation.

The day arrived when Jean had arranged with her employers to take the weekend off and go with Jesse to stay with her sister and her husband. On the way there Jesse was so excited about seeing her Auntie and the rest of the family. Her mother was thinking how much they had both gone through, and how much they had changed for the better. How happy they both were now. She hoped her mother would see the difference in both of them and feel proud and be able to put the past behind them for the last time and move on with their lives.

This was the one thing Jean hoped for, to be able to show her mother she had learnt the lesson of life and learnt it well. She had moved on with her own life and it was better than before. Jesse too had moved on with her life and was turning out to be a smart little lady with all of her own graces and had been taught to respect her elders. Her mother would see that and now be proud of her and forgive her for bringing shame on the family. They would be close again as the rest of the family was to their mother. Jean wanted to be there with them, all holding their heads up high and not down in shame.

When the train pulled into the station, Jean looked out of the window and there was her sister Mary standing on the platform waiting. Jean and Jesse got off and gave Mary a huge hug.

They all walked from the platform to the outside of the station and onto the main road leading to the town centre. Jean held Jesse's hand very tightly, so tight that Jesse said 'Mummy you are hurting my hand.' Jean looked down and said 'I am so sorry. Mummy did not mean to hold your hand so tight.' Jean then looked up at her sister with a look of fear in her eyes, and said 'this is hard for me. I thought that I would be stronger than I am.'

Mary replied 'you are stronger than you think. You will be fine. That was then and this is now. Look how far you have come. Nothing will happen. You are a different person now, you are strong.' She took Jean and Jesse's hands and said 'let's go and get you both home and have something to eat as you must be hungry by now.' Jesse replied 'yes, I am hungry Auntie.' They walked towards a car in the car park, where a young man stood waiting. As they approached, he opened the car boot, ready for Jean's suitcase.

Jean gave Mary's husband a hug and kissed him on the cheek. 'It seems such a long ago since we have all seen each other. I am so glad that you married my sister as she is so happy, the happiest I have seen her since we were children.'

'It has been a long time since I have been this happy' said Mary, holding Jesse's hand. 'Now you both are here with me and my bump, who would not be happy?' She smiled and said 'now let's get going.' They all got into the car and drove off towards Mary and Bob's home.

As they drove through the town centre, both Jesse and Jean looked out of the window at the shops with all their beautiful window displays. They were trying to make the passer-by stop and buy their products, whether it be clothing or items for the home or the latest records in the charts. All looked so tempting, as if they were saying 'come in and buy me you know you want to.'

The sun was shining bright in the clear blue sky. Everyone looked so happy with smiles of joy on their faces, enjoying the sun that was beaming down on them after a hard cold winter. The snow had been cold and deep, the only ones who enjoyed it were the children who played in it, building snowmen and playing snow balls with each other. Jean thought of Jesse who played in the snow with her bright new wellingtons that she had bought for her by Lady Zara, how she did enjoy the snow and now it was summer and Jesse, who was dressed in her summer dress like so many other children, loved the summer when she would go out into the garden and down to the dockland and see the boats.

With her mother, or Lady Zara, she would walk to the shop that would always be open in the summer to sell everything that you would need for your trip in your boat. Jean knew just how lucky that Jesse was, as not everyone had a dockland at the bottom of their garden where you could moor your own boat for the winter and then go to the shop where your boat was, and buy anything that you needed for your trip. Then Jean remembered the day when Jesse went missing as she was playing in the garden, how everyone in the house went looking for her. The gardener went into the small woodlands that were part of land which was owned by Lady Zara and her family, but later returned without Jesse. The rest of the household searched the house from top to bottom. Everyone looking in every cupboard and under every table and even behind the long draped curtains in every room, even the big music room. Jesse was nowhere to be found. Not even outside the front, or in the garages under the cars. Everywhere they could think of everyone looked and Jesse was nowhere to be found.

Jean remembered how she felt at that time. She had gone to phone the Police to report her missing. How relieved she was when the phone rang as she got there and the voice on the other end was the shop keeper on the long strip of dockland. He said Jesse was there and she wanted to buy some sweets, she was safe and could someone come and take her home.

How relieved she was, and the rest of the household, to hear she was safe and sound.

When Jean reached the shop, there was Jesse. 'Have you come to pay for my sweets Mummy? I am sorry, I forgot to bring my pocket money with me.' The look on Jesse's little face was so puppy looking and sad. Jean thought 'How can I tell Jesse off now?' And yet she knew that she would have to tell Jesse that what she had done was very wrong and she must never do it again.

It was not good for a child to go out on their own as there are some bad people about. Some might harm her if they took her away. Then she may never see her mother or family ever again. That was the last time Jesse wandered off on her own.

Then Jean remembered the walk back to the house holding Jesse's hand, looking at the boats and their owners. Some were sweeping the decks of their boats ready to take them out on a trip. The sun was beaming down, keeping them all warm. The sky that was so blue, not a cloud in sight. How, if you could draw the scene, it would be like a holiday abroad, like a postcard that you would send saying 'wish you were here', and how you were enjoying your holiday.

Jean thought how lucky both she and Jesse were to have the employers she had. They gave them so much. Not many people lived the way that they did. And employers who kept on a member of staff after what had happened. Many would have just let Jean go, as it could have spoiled their image. That was not what any one in that position wanted. Yet Jean's employers took that chance and turned the situation round to benefit both them. The outcome was that Jean was their head house-keeper and Jesse was now their god-daughter. Both were treated very well within the household.

On the drive to Mary's house, Jean's thoughts were of back at their home, where she felt safe, and not here where it all started. Where she did not know how she would feel when she saw her mother and other people from her past. How they would react towards her. If they would let the past be just that, the past. Now everyone had moved on, especially Jean and Jesse, who had gone through hell and back without being old enough to do anything about it.

Watching Jesse's sister go to someone that she did not know. Now having to live without her for the rest of her life, never knowing where or whether she is safe and loved. And, more important than that, wondering whether or not she would remember that she had an older sister called Jesse.

And this made Jean feel so sad inside. She started to feel the tears in her eyes, but she knew that she could not show them, especially to Jesse. She would become upset, and Jean did not want this to happen again. So Jean turned her face away from everyone in the car for the whole journey, and tried to distract herself by looking at the shop windows.

They soon reached their destination. Mary opened the door and said 'let's have a nice cup of coffee, and then we will have something to eat as you must be tired from travelling.'

Then Mary took them round their home and garden. Jean said 'you have done so well, and I am so happy for you. I am glad that your life has turned out good. You are with someone who loves you so much, and is a good man. He will look after you and your family and never hurt you.' Mary replied 'one day you too will find a good man like my husband, who will look after you both and be a good father to Jesse.'

Even though Mary and Bob's home was a two bedroom flat, it had everything in it that you could want. It also had a garden, though small in size, it was a garden all the same, and the rent was not too high. They could manage with all the other bills as well. The flat was nicely decorated throughout by Bob. Everywhere was gleaming with fresh white paint and soft shades of colour on the walls and it just looked like a flat out of a home style magazine.

And one could see that both Mary and Bob were very happy together. When their baby arrived, they knew it would be very much loved and wanted. It would be looked after the best way they could. Jean also knew her sister had got the perfect life, and she was very happy for her.

The next morning, after a good night's sleep, Jean awoke to Jesse singing and walking in and out of the bedroom, asking 'Mummy, are you going to get up now as it is a lovely day outside? Auntie asked me to wake you up as breakfast is nearly ready.'

After getting dressed, Jean found Jesse sitting down at the kitchen table. Mary was preparing breakfast for them all. She could hear Jesse and Mary talking.

'Oh Jesse, why so many questions this time in the morning? You must only ask one question at a time. Give the other person time to reply to your questions.' Then Mary replied 'it is fine really, Jesse is very excited as it is all new to her.'

They all sat down to breakfast, and planned out what they would do during the day. It would be a good opportunity for the two sisters and Jesse to spend time together.

They walked to the local park and Jesse played there happily on the swings and slide. The two sisters talked about how things had changed for them both. Then Mary asked 'after we have been to the shops, shall we go and visit mother as she will be finishing work soon? She knows that you are both here and would love to see you, it has been a long time since you have seen her.'

There was a sort silence before Jean replied, as she was thinking about the last time that she had seen her mother. That was back in the dark days of Jean's life, when everything had gone so wrong. There were some bad feelings between Jean and her mother. Things had moved on for the better for Jean and for Jesse. Indeed, Jean had changed, life had made her stronger than before. Jean had wondered if her mother would see the difference in Jean and Jesse, and see that Jean had learned the lesson of life. She was much stronger now and would never make the same mistakes again.

But most of all her mother would now be proud of her and welcome her in her arms again and not make her feel like she was still the black sheep of the family. Her mother would treat her accordingly, as Jean had gone through so much in her young life. She wanted so much to put all that was hurtful in the past, and carry on with her new life, and everyone could see how far that she had come and be proud of her.

After they had walked around the local shops they all got on a bus to see Jean's mother. This was not going to be easy for Jean, and her sister knew that too. When they arrived at the stop near where their mother worked, Mary held her sister's hand tight. She said nothing to Jean as they walked towards where their mother was working. Their mother slowly walked out of the restaurant where she was working in the kitchen towards to the two sisters and Jesse. The look on their mothers face was one of tiredness and happiness to see her two daughters and grand-daughter.

As their mother approached them, her face was now beaming with a smile and this was one thing that Jean had longed for. Jean was not sure if she would ever see this again on her mother's face, after all that had gone on before. Yet here she was, in front of her, with this beaming smile. Then she came close enough to hug her daughters. She first gave Mary a hug, and then she turned towards Jean and looked at her and gave her a big hug and said 'I am glad to see you. You look well.' Then turned towards Jesse and gave her a big hug and said she had missed her.

They all returned to Mary's flat and had lunch, then when Bob came home he would then take home their mother. In the kitchen, Jean and Mary prepared the meal while Jesse sat down and told her grandmother all about her new home, her new school and her friends.

As their mother was chatting to her grand-daughter around the kitchen table, the two sisters looked at one another and smiled. Mary said quietly, so their mother could not hear her, 'there, see, you have nothing to worry about. The past is the past. Don't worry anymore as there is no need too.' And with that they both carried on preparing their lunch. Then they all sat down together talking about how things had changed and how better things had turned out. Their mother was very proud of her family.

Bob arrived home from work. They all looked at each other, not believing how time had passed so quickly. Now it was time for their mother to return home. She turned towards Mary and Jean and said she had enjoyed her lunch with them and gave Mary a hug. She turned to Jean and said how happy she was to see how Jean and Jesse were.

The two sisters watched their mother disappear in the distance, then they sat in the lounge and Mary said 'I told you that it would be alright.' Jean replied 'I know you did and I am glad that things have turned out the way they did.'

When Bob returned, he suggested Jean and Mary go out the next evening and he would look after Jesse. It would be good for them to have some time together. Mary and Jean agreed.

Later, Jean gave Jesse a bath and put her to bed after giving her a big hug and kiss. She returned to the kitchen where her sister and her husband were still sitting.

Mary's husband asked 'where you will go tomorrow night?' Mary replied 'I shall have to think about that and maybe even sleep on it. It has been a while since we were alone together without mother or Jesse around, and it would be so nice for us to do this one thing before the baby arrives. After that, I may not feel like going out or even be able to afford it.' Jean replied 'yes of course we will go out, you are right as usual.'

The next morning, Jean woke from a deep sleep to the sound of Jesse talking to herself in the bedroom. Jean sat up in her bed and asked 'who are you talking to this time?' Jesse replied 'no one Mummy. Just saying to myself should I wear this dress today or this one?' She turned round holding the two dresses she had picked out. 'Mummy, which one do you think I should wear, the pink one or the blue one?' Jean got out of her bed and said 'which colour is your favourite?' Jesse replied 'blue', 'then the blue dress is one you should wear today.'

After getting dressed, they went to the kitchen where Mary was preparing breakfast. Jesse asked 'what are we going to do today? Will we go to the shops again and walk into town afterwards?' Her mother replied 'no, not today. This time we will walk to the park and then come home for lunch as it is very tiring for your Auntie Mary, as it was for me when I carried you in my tummy.'

After breakfast, they set off to the park as it was a lovely morning. The sun was shining bright in the cloudless blue sky. As they walked, Mary said 'I am really looking forward to tonight. It will be a nice break for you and for me, and we will not have to talk about babies or children and our families, just us for a change.'

Jean and Mary started to laugh. Jesse looked up and asked 'what is so funny? Tell me what you are both laughing about.' The two sisters looked at one another and Jean replied 'a grown up joke, nothing that you will find funny' and left it at that. The answer was good enough for Jesse and they all carried on walking towards the park.

Jesse asked if she could go on the swings. Jean replied 'yes, but be careful you do not hurt yourself.' Jesse ran towards the swings which were one of her favourite things to play on.

The two sisters talked and laughed together. Jesse played with her new friends she had made in the park. Jean asked her sister what time it was and was amazed to find it was midday.

They had been here for the best part of the morning, and it felt very good.

When they all arrived home, Jean made lunch for them all. Jesse asked if there was anything to do and was told to put the butter on the bread. Jean had put out the filling for the sandwiches which were ham and cheese and salads and all the pickles and sauces to go with them. Mary said 'Goodness, we will never eat all of this. What a spread you and Jesse have done. It looks lovely as well, thank you both for this.' Jean replied 'It has been a while since I made us lunch' and laughed as the last time that Jean had made lunch it was only a cheese sandwich. Mary replied 'Yes, I remember it well. That was a while back. But you have made up for it now by this today.'

Just as they cleared the table and Jean started to wipe the kitchen table, Bob returned from work looking hot and tired. Mary told him what they had been doing and Jesse said she had played with some new friends. Jean then told Jesse she was going out that evening with Mary and her uncle would look after her.

Jesse asked if her uncle would put her to bed and read her a story and Jean replied 'yes of course but you must be a good girl and go to bed when you are told,' Jesse replied she would. As the two sisters were preparing dinner, Bob looked after Jesse, both of them now sitting in the lounge on the sofa, side by side. Jesse held one of her favourite books that she had brought with her. She began to read to her uncle and then explained the pictures in the book and what they were. He said to Jesse what a clever little girl she was and Jesse replied her teacher said so too. Her uncle smiled and carried on listening to her read to him.

Mary said 'Jesse is so good at reading, she is very confident. You can imagine the pictures in the book yourself, as if she was reading to you, and yet we are not in the room with her. She seems to make you feel as if you are.' Jean replied 'yes I know what you mean, she has the way with words and how to tell a story. At least we know she will be a good communicator when she is older and not have trouble talking with other people. That is a good thing, it shows that she has self-confidence, which you need to get on with in life.' The sisters carried on with making dinner and talking about the night ahead and what they would wear and where they would go. Mary said 'I must ring and make arrangements for a taxi to collect us and take us home.' Mary made the arrangements and returned to the kitchen where Jean was just about to dish up the dinner.

While they were having their dinner, Jean looked over at Jesse and thought to herself how much she had grown up. Even though she was still very young in age she was not in her mind, it was a mind of an older child, not that of a seven year old. Jesse could take in anything that you had said to her and hold a good conversation with any adult. It was as if she had suddenly grown up into a girl several years ahead of her time. Even though she still liked to play with children of her own age, she would enjoy being with adults and talking to them or just listening to their conversations and taking everything in.

Jean wondered what it would have been like if she could have kept her other two little girls. Jesse would have grown up with an older sister and a younger sister. How they would have got on, each with their own personalities and all looking similar and only one of them having a different father, the other two the same father. How would they be as sisters Jean wondered to herself. Inside, her heart was filled with sadness and pain as the reminder of losing her two little girls and with Jesse losing her two sisters and having to grow up alone.

And all that Jesse and her family had gone through, all the pain that everyone had felt and all the tears that Jean had shed. How much she regretted losing her two girls and how much she loved them and would never forget them. While Jean was deep in thought, the others had noticed how quiet Jean appeared to be, the look on her face was a look of someone who was far away, somewhere else but not here in the same room as her family was, and this came not only to Mary and Bob's attention but also to Jesse.

Suddenly Jean heard Jesse's voice saying 'Mummy what do you think of that?' Again Jesse said to her mother the same question and again with no reply until Jesse then tapped on her mother's arm to get her attention, then Jean replied 'I am so sorry Jesse, I was miles away. What was the question?' And once again Jesse asked. Jean then gave her answer. Jesse then asked her mother 'are you alright, Mummy? Jean replied 'yes I am fine. I was just deep in thought that is all. Nothing to worry about' and the conversation went on to something else.

But it was not only Jesse who was concerned about Jean, it was also her sister, who at that time had said nothing to Jean at the table, but was concerned what it was that had caused her sister to withdraw into a world of her own. Mary had not seen that for a long time, in fact it was the time when everything in life for Jean had gone so wrong, and there was so much pain and sorrow that her sister had to go through. And today still, even though time had passed, she could see her sister was suffering inside in silence, feeling the loss of her two little girls. She knew that Jean would always feel this, but in time it would become easier to deal with, and on the odd occasions the full impact of it all would come racing back with all the strength and more than before, so that you would never forget. It looked like this was one of those times, so Mary decided to ask her sister if she was alright and if she needed to talk she knew that she could at any time. As Mary would always be there for Jean no matter what, she would always be there, and never leave Jean alone.

When everyone had finished their dinner, Jean stood up and said 'I will wash up' then her sister said 'then I shall dry up' and Jesse said 'what can I do then, Mummy?' Jean replied 'you can clear the table, please.' Jean collected the plates and walked towards the sink, her sister followed her and asked if she was alright. Jean replied 'yes I am fine, I was just thinking of how much Jesse had grown up, and how it would have been if she had her two sisters with her now. How they would have been, growing up all together.' Mary could see the hurt that was on her sister's face and then said 'well, if they were like you and our brother and the other sisters growing up then you would know about it. Think back to how you would throw a house brick at our brother, even though it was only a half brick, you threw it anyway.'

'Well he upset me so much and that was the nearest thing at hand I could find.'

'Remember you and our brother did not really get on together until now that is.'

'Yes, you are right, now I remember, but I do love him as you know, I love you all.'

'Well, think what our parents went through with all of us, and then mother left on her own to cope alone' Mary replied 'and think if the girls did not get on well, not all of them, then it would be like the old days of us growing up.' Then they both laughed as they then went on to talk about their memories of growing up together, and things that you did when you were a child, and what you got up to. When you arrived home, the trouble that you were in from your parents, who were always wiser than you and know better than you and sometimes did not see things the way that you did as a child.

Even though Jean could see that her family was happy and settled in their lives and everything was for once going in the right direction for everyone else, for Jean it was not, as it would never be complete without her two girls. The thought of that would always be there in the back of her mind, always thinking of them and wondering how they are and if they would grow up hating her for what she had done, and why she could not have kept them all together. And why did their mother keep Jesse, not knowing that Jesse too, for the first 6 months of her life, was also fostered and then returned to her mother, which was a real battle on its own and how much she wanted to try and get her two back and start living as a family again all together.

But the reality was that she could not get her two girls back as they were very settled and happy with their own lives. She would have to live with that for the rest of her life and she hoped that when Jesse learnt of the truth she would forgive her mother and try and understand the reasons why and know how much it still hurt and always would and how sorry her mother was and how much she wished things were different for all of them.

And how she hoped that all of her girls would grow up and when they knew the truth they would all be able to see that their mother had done the best that she could for all of them at that time and how much she regretted it and how much she missed them and how much it hurt, knowing they would never ever grow up together. As they should have done. And how ashamed she felt for letting her family down, all of them, and would have to live with that for the rest of her life.

As Jean was thinking these thoughts the tears began to fall down her face, and then she walked into the bedroom and sat down and cried, holding the pillow as she lay down on the bed, her heart broken. All the hurt and sadness and shame now fell down her face in the shape of her tears rolling down her now pale and drawn face. No matter how she tried to stop the tears, she just could not. It was as if the pain of the past had returned to remind her, so that she never forgot what she had done. And to make her feel the pain and shame of everything all over again. It was if nature was not going to let Jean ever get on with life and that her life was this, and no other, and that she would have deal with it and get on with it.

'How cruel life was' thought Jean, as she had tried to be a good person growing up and had never ever been in trouble of any kind and now life had rewarded her with pain for being good in her life. It just did not seem fair, Jean thought to herself, while she was sitting on her bed slowly wiping the tears from her face.

Then Jean stood up and walked towards the bathroom. She saw her sister coming towards her and as Mary approached she asked Jean 'are you alright?' Jean replied 'yes, I am fine now, thank you for asking.' Then Jean opened the bathroom door walked in and shut the door behind her.

As she looked into the mirror, she said to herself 'who would want me now, after what I have done? Everyone will think I am a wicked, uncaring woman. They would never think of the reasons why, and what it has done to me or my family. No, they will just turn away with a look of dismay on their faces as they walk past me in the street. Never stopping to ask why and how I am feeling deep down inside. For if they dare to they would then find the truth about how it feels to be a person like me in a country that is twice the size of the country where I was born, where the way of life here is so very different to the life style of where I was born and grew up.'

CHAPTER FIVE

Dominic

Jean changed into the clothes that she would wear to go out. As she walked into the living room, they turned around and looked at her. It was little Jesse who said 'Mummy, you look so lovely.' Jean walked towards Jesse and gave her a hug and her sister said 'You do look gorgeous' and her husband Bob agreed.

Mary and Jean went to the pub by taxi, the same one that would pick them up later.

As they drove into town it seemed different somehow. As Jean looked out of window she saw people walking, some on their own and some in couples holding hands. As she watched them she thought how it would be nice if one day she too could be walking along with someone holding her hands as someone else watched them. How lovely that would be and how lucky are they to be happy and how sad she felt inside.

When they arrived, Mary turned and looked at Jean with a big smile, her eyes full of sparkle as she was looking forward to going out with her sister, she knew it would be a very long time before she could do this again, for when her baby was born things would change and time out would be very rare indeed.

As the two sisters got out of the car and stood outside the pub, they knew there would be people they knew inside. It had been a long time since they were all together and they all were looking forward to having fun and a good laugh. As the two sisters walked towards the main doors of the public house, Jean walked slower than her sister, she began to fall behind Mary who had by this time nearly reached the doors. Mary turned around to see where Jean was, she was standing and looking up at the outside of the building in silence. Mary asked 'are you alright? What is wrong? Have you changed your mind? Do you want to go home?'

Jean replied 'no there is nothing wrong with me. I just wanted a moment to look and take in everything before I go in.' What she really meant was she needed a moment to take a deep breath before they went in together as her nerves were now getting to her and she did not want them to show and feel uncomfortable and maybe say the wrong things.

Jean walked in feeling very nervous inside and trying very hard not to show it. There came a voice from the bar. It was a friend that both of the sisters had not seen for a while, with a welcoming smile on her face, so pleased to see both of them again. The two sisters approached the bar and their friend came up to them and gave them a big hug and kiss on their cheeks, then bought them each a drink. They began to talk and laugh, everything just so natural as if they had always been together. The two sisters acted like they had never moved away, which was good for all of them as it could have gone so wrong. Sometimes, times apart change everything and there is nothing much to talk about as people also change.

While the two sisters were enjoying themselves, through the door in walked a slim, dark haired man, nice looking, and turned towards the bar. When he had ordered his drink, he turned and saw the two sisters sitting with their friends. One of the friends noticed him and said to the sisters 'look over there, he is looking at you.' Both sisters could see he was actually looking and smiling at Jean who in turn smiled back, before turning back to her sister and their friends, and thinking no more of it.

Later, the man was seated next to the table with the two sisters. One of the man's friends came and sat down, a voice from the table where the two sisters were sitting said 'hello, how are you?' to the man at next table. Then the two men started to talk and introduced themselves. They all started to get to know each other, what they did for a living, where they lived and how they knew each other. Before long, the two tables were engaging themselves in conversation, all of them enjoying each other's company. At the end of the evening, telephone numbers and addresses were exchanged with promises to keep in touch.

Jean and Mary arrived safely back home, full of joy and happiness, something that Jean had not felt for a long time. She told her sister how much she had enjoyed herself and thanked her for her stay, it had been just what Jean and Jesse need.

The next morning, Mary asked if Jean would keep in touch with the man she had been talking to her. Jean replied 'I am not sure, we will see what happens' and left it at that. Then Jesse and Bob came into the kitchen and they all had breakfast together.

'It is time to go now and catch the train home' said Jean. Jesse stood up and said 'I have packed my case, Mum.' As they all walked towards the car, Jean was holding Jesse's hand and she looked down at Jesse and thought how lucky at last they were together and how happy Jesse was as she was singing as she walked towards the car without a care in the world. Then Jean and Jesse were at the station waiting for the train.

They found their seats and looked out to waive to their loved ones as the train gathered speed. Jean and Jesse settled in for a long journey ahead back to their home and back to their normal lives, with their lovely memories.

When the train arrived, they found a taxi home. Once there, Jesse asked 'What is wrong Mummy?' Jean replied 'Why do you ask?' 'It is that we have just walked around everywhere, before we walked to our bedroom you put down the cases. Why did you not go to the bedroom first, and then look around? Jean looked down at Jesse, took her hand and said 'do not worry; it is just a thing I like to do that is all.'

One day a letter arrived from the man. He had kept to his word, and written to Jean, to her surprise, she thought what to do next. Whether she would reply or not, and if she did what would she say. She felt that her life back home was very boring, more uninteresting that his was, not thinking that he might like her and was trying to get to know her and maybe it was the same for her.

As Jean read the letter, she thought how nice it was that he had written to her and then began to think about the time when both Jesse and she were happy with Mary and her family. How she longed for the feeling of happiness, with someone to cuddle up to at the end of the evening and talk about their day whether it be good or not. A friend and lover, that is what they would be to Jean, and maybe a father figure to Jesse, that would be perfect to Jean, as that is all everyone wants, a family to take care of and watch grow and have all the memories to keep forever.

When Jean had finished her working day and put Jesse to bed, she went to the drawer were she had put the letter and sat down to read it again. A smile grew upon her face, thinking about that time and how much fun and laughter is was and how her life was now and wondered if anything would happen between this man who had made her laugh and made her relax, which she had not done for a long time and thought that she would never again, after too much hurt which was still there deep down inside.

It was more than a week before Jean replied to the letter as it took that long for her to think what to say, thinking that she did not want to bore him in any way, as he seemed have more freedom than Jean had. Just the same, Jean sat down and began to write back. Soon she had finished her letter and put it on the table in the hall ready for the post the next day. While she lay in her bed, Jean thought of her letter and hoped that he would reply.

Soon she received a reply asking to arrange a meeting. When Jean read this she was very surprised indeed that she had received any correspondence. What was she going to do was the next question. After sitting and thinking, she replied and found she had completed a full page. At the bottom she finished by letting him know that she would be very pleased to hear from him. Once she had done that, she sealed the letter and put it ready to be posted the next day.

After a few days a letter came back. When Jean saw it she was filled with joy and happiness that once again he had written to her. It said that it would be good to meet up the next time that Jean had time off, if this would be acceptable to her. As she read the letter, she had thought that yes this would be acceptable to her and how she would have to get in touch with her sister to arrange to stay in order to meet up with the man who now wanted to meet up again. And this would be nice as Jean would get together with her sister and family again.

So Jean phoned her sister and arranged another visit.

The day before Jean and Jesse were to travel up to see Mary, Jean felt very nervous about the visit. It was about seeing the man again; he had now gained a name - Dominic. How would it all go? Would it be the same as before, which was so very nice and relaxed or would it be unsettling for her or for both of them?

Jesse was so excited again, while her mother was more nervous than before and tried hard not to show it. Jean did not like Jesse to see how her mother really felt deep down. Jesse would then ask questions and Jean knew that she would have to explain and that would not be an easy thing to do to a child of that age. Jesse was now old enough to know things and understand to a degree.

At the station, Jesse was talking away to her Mother, but Jean was in a world of her own, staring out of the window with thoughts running through her mind. She did not hear a word that Jesse was saying to her.

Then Jesse said to 'Mummy, what do think? Should I or not?' Still there was no reply to her question, just silence. So Jesse took her mother's hand and squeezed it tight and then Jean turned to Jesse and said 'I am so sorry. I did not hear what you were saying.' Jesse asked why. Jean replied 'I was day dreaming,' an expression which Jean had used before. She would say something to Jesse and Jesse did not reply to the question, Jean would say that Jesse was day dreaming, so Jean used the same reason to Jesse so that she could understand and that there would be nothing for Jesse to be concerned about.

From the train they saw fields of green and others yellow depending on what crop they were growing, trees of many shapes and sizes and horses, cows and sheep, and then through towns and villages, some small and some large, some old and some new, all with their own style and beauty and with sun shining through, highlighting all their splendour in many colours and shapes, all looking so wonderful to the eye.

Soon they reached their stop and Jean started to feel very nervous about meeting up with Dominic again. She started to think that maybe she could make some excuses not to see him again and just to see her sister and family. Then she thought of what her sister might say about her idea and that she would be right and that as she had arranged and had travelled this far she should go on and see what happens and then she could decide from there on, but at least Jean would know one way or the other. Not wondering what might have been.

So Jean decided that she would go through with the arrangements and at least she would know and maybe learn from this experience.

Jean took Jesse through the station to meet Mary and Bob. All seemed very relaxed and soon they arrived at Mary's house. As they got out of the car the nervous tension returned to Jean.

Mary said 'tea will be ready in half an hour, so if you both want to go and freshen up you both have enough time to do so.' Jean was still thinking about the next day and the night when she would be meeting up with Dominic. It was time to meet up again, but not in company like before but on their own.

This thought to Jean was both exciting and scary, at the same time, causing Jean in her heart and mind to disagree whenever she thought of this and no matter how she tried she still had a fight on her hands between both her heart and her mind. The question is who would win in the end. Jean did not know.

She thought to herself 'there is no point in worrying any more, just enjoy life while you can.' She began thinking about her late father who had died at the age of 42 years old, which is no age to die, it is still so very young age to have to leave his family behind.

Suddenly Jean thought of what her mother used to say when things got tough, and that was 'be strong. Only the strong survive' along with 'do not cry in public, it is sign of weakness and that is when the others can and will destroy you if they can, knowing your weakness. So always be strong, do not show your weakness at any time. You must be strong always.' The sound of Jean's mother's voice came loud and clear to Jean. And with this thought she became stronger, remembering her own mother's voice and remembering how her mother was so strong all through what the whole family had gone through and what Jean and her mother had gone through.

Jean became stronger and was no longer worried about the night with Dominic but was looking forward to a future whatever that might be.

After the meal, the two sisters washed the dishes, both laughing and talking about everything and anything. When they had finished, they went into the lounge where Bob and Jesse were already seated comfortably in their armchairs watching TV.

The next day came and the sun was shining through the window of the bedroom where Jean and Jesse were still asleep. The birds were singing, circling around the skies above, and in and out of the trees without a care in the world. Unlike Jean, who had just started to wake up to the sunshine which was slowly moving towards the bottom of Jesse's bed. Jean pulled back the covers and slowly got up, trying not to wake Jesse from her sleep.

Jean began to think to herself about the evening ahead and about meeting Dominic again and what the evening would hold for both of them. How the evening would go for both of them, and what if Jean did not enjoy his company, and if that was the case what was Jean going to do. Then all she thought about was 'I want to go home.' She thought she must have a plan just in case this situation did happen. She would tell her sister that if things were not going to plan and she had changed her mind and wanted to come home that Bob would come and give her a lift home.

So with that thought Jean was comforted and was now feeling at ease with herself and began to look at what she might wear that night. Suddenly she felt like she was sixteen again, when she had her first love back home on the small island where it was safe and no harm would ever come to her. This thought made her feel warm inside even though the situation was not the same, it did not seem to matter. She was happy at last. It was a long time since Jean had ever felt like this, after all that had happened to her and her family, and Jean thought to herself it was about time she had some happiness in her life, just like everyone else around her.

This is what Jean had always wanted and had dreamed of for so long, it seemed like forever and a day. Jean thought this was not an impossible thing to ask for in life as all of her friends and family seem to achieve this and were all content with their lives so why not this time it could be Jean. How happy would her family and friends be if this could be achieved and so too would Jesse who is the most important person in Jean's life.

Suddenly Jesse walked into the bedroom and Jean's thoughts and dreams came back down to reality. Jean then thought of the day ahead, and not the evening. The day ahead would be with her family only and no outsiders, for this was more important to Jean than her happiness.

They all settled down to have their breakfast and talk about what they would do next.

As Jean and Jesse were in the bright shining bedroom Jesse was looking out of the window and saying 'Mummy look at the sky, it is so blue and there are no clouds in the sky' so Jean walked over to the window and together they stood looking at the clear blue sky.

Jean said 'we must get ready to go out now' and Jesse replied 'I am ready when you are Mummy.' They found Mary and Bob who had decided they would go out for a picnic as it was so nice outside.

Jean sat down and thought this is what life should be, peaceful and calm. Meanwhile Jesse had walked towards the playing area and began to swing. She started to sing to herself, her face lit up with joy and happiness. Jesse could see her Mother was happy as she could see her smile on her face and that filled Jesse with happiness.

It was not very often that she saw her Mother happy and at ease with life and now she was. And for that Jesse was happy, then some other children came and soon Jesse and the other children began to play together. Soon it was time for all of them to go home. As they were walking back, Jesse was talking about her new friends she had met, how much fun she had and she cannot wait until the next time when they would be coming up to stay when she could play with her new friends again.

Jean started to look forward to meeting up with Dominic again, and to see if she would have a nice evening with him and maybe they would arrange another meet.

After a while, Jean said 'well is time for you Jesse to get ready for your bath and then get changed into your night time clothes before you have your evening meal.' She walked into the bathroom where her mother was running her bath making sure that the water was not too hot for Jesse and putting in some bubble bath for Jesse liked her bubbles at bath times for she said that it smelt so nice. Jean would always make sure that there was bubble bath in her bath as it would make Jesse smile and laugh, this made Jean so happy both inside and outside, to see her Jesse happy with such a simple thing as bubble bath .

Then Jean was putting on her lipstick, taking her handbag and coat. 'Jean you look so lovely' said Mary, and Jesse said 'Mummy you look so lovely and you smell so lovely too.' Jean stood there and smiled with happiness as she felt so good about herself and this she had not done for so long.

And for once Jean thought to herself that maybe this time her life is changing for the better and the bad days of the past are now left far behind and that she would never ever live a life that was so painful and unkind ever again.

The doorbell rang, it was her taxi. Jean said good bye to her sister and gave Jesse and big kiss. She felt relaxed and happy to meet up again with Dominic and was looking forward to having a good time.

Jean reached the pub and saw Dominic at the bar looking smartly dressed with clean shaven face, standing all alone in a room full of people and yet looking so out of place on his own.

Jean walked in. As she approached Dominic, he greeted her with a smile and kiss on her cheek. He ordered drinks, they walked toward a table, sat down and began to talk.

Jean felt so relaxed with Dominic who seemed to be feeling the same way as his face was lit up with happiness. The two of them looked like a couple who had been together for some time. Even though there was no touching of hands or sitting very close. It seemed as if there was something between them and both seemed comfortable with each other's company. Both were laughing and joking. As always, the time passed so very quickly as it always seemed to do when you are having fun and the time had come for Jean to leave and return to her sister's home.

Dominic said time seemed go so quickly and asked if she would like to see him again and this time they would have a meal together. Jean agreed. As they left, he took Jean's hand and slowly moved to her, then he leant towards Jean and with the other hand he held Jean's face and kissed her on the lips, just a peck at first and then he kissed her on the lips again and then their lips were locked into a long kiss.

They both said their goodbyes, promising to phone each other.

On the drive back, Jean was thinking about the night and how she had enjoyed it so much and was looking forward to the next time that she would see the man who one day would become her boyfriend. She began to smile at the things that were funny at the time and how they both laughed together.

The front door opened and standing there was Mary, asking how her night had been. Jean replied it was just so lovely she felt so good and happy and this is what her sister had wanted to hear for such a long time. And both the sisters began to talk about the evening over a cup of tea.

In the morning Jean awoke to the voice of Jesse asking 'how was the evening?' and Jean replied 'the evening was a lovely one' and then Jean said to Jesse 'today we are going home,' Jesse replied 'do we have to, Mummy? Can we stay one more day?' 'No' was the reply from Jean 'I have to work and you have to go to school tomorrow.'

Jean had felt so good inside after seeing the young man again she felt that this happiness she felt she did not want it to end and return to her normal life again. But she knew that her dream weekend had to end until the next time.

After breakfast, they packed their cases and set off on their return journey.

Both Jean and Jesse just sat and looked out of the window of the train neither of them speaking to each other, just in their own worlds, thinking and dreaming. After a short while, Jean turned to Jesse and said 'are you alright, Jesse, you are so very quiet, more than usual?' Jesse turned towards her mother and said 'yes, I am all right. I was thinking about my new friends that I have left behind and that I cannot wait until the next time that I see them again.'

As Jesse then turned back towards the window Jean began to think about the weekend and how much she had enjoyed every minute of it, especially the evening out with the new man in her life and wondered if this would lead to anything more than a quick kiss and then goodbye.

Could this lead into her dream of being happy and in love? Would it last with no more hurt and disappointment like the last time? She knew it was so much to deal with, and how she had felt at that time in her life. How it had affected both her and her family. She would never want that to happen again.

It was not long before the journey reached the end and life returned to normal. The dreams of yesterday had come to an end. Jean and Jesse got up from their seats. As they walked outside they had a look on their faces as if to say playtime is over and now work time begins.

Jean saw a waiting taxi, so they took it home. On the journey, Jean was talking to Jesse about her day at school and what she would be doing the next day. Jesse replied she was looking forward to telling her friends about the weekend and the new friends she had met and asking what they had done. Jean replied with a smile on her face 'it will not be as good as your weekend was' and with that Jesse laughed and then turned her face towards the window.

Half an hour later the taxi driver slowed down and turned into the entrance of the drive way towards the big house then pulled outside the side door where only the workers were allowed to go as the main entrance was only used for the family of the big house and their guests.

The house where they lived, though small, was at that time empty as the rest of the staff were already at work. There was only Jean and Jesse at home so with that Jesse stayed in her room and Jean was in the kitchen tidying up and then made a meal for them both.

Jean sat down and began to think about the weekend and how much fun it was.

The phone in the hall began to ring. Jean went and picked it up. To her surprise it was Dominic. As soon as Jean said hello the man knew it was Jean on the other end and asked her 'how are you?' Jean replied 'I am very well, thanking you.'

He asked when he could see Jean again. She replied 'I am not sure as it depends on what days I am working.' He then said 'when can I call you again?' Jean replied 'next week would be good, then I will know when I am at work.' So with that they both said their goodbyes.

But instead of picking up her book, she sat there thinking of the conversation with Dominic, and with her thoughts there came a smile of happiness across her face and her eyes showed a sparkle, at last Jean felt happy inside and it showed on the outside.

Jean did not know that others around her had noticed the change and how much happier she seemed to be. Compared to how she had been for a long time, so very sad and hurt inside. It would seem that Jean would never ever get on with life itself she would always be stuck in the past and always feeling so hurt for everything that had happened to her and how it had affected both her and her family.

Now it would seem that at long last things were changing for the better. She knew it and was beginning to be comfortable with this feeling. There was no more feeling and looking sad and waking up in the morning trying to put a brave face on to hide the pain inside so that Jesse and everyone else could not see how she truly felt.

In fact even her own Mother noticed the changes within her daughter and for once had felt happy and hoped this would be the one to change her daughter's life for the better. Like her other family who had indeed been lucky in love and had all settled down, she hoped that Jean too would settle down and be happy, for that is all that she ever wanted for her family, to be happy and loved as she was herself.

The week went on as usual and then on Thursday Dominic phoned again. As they talked, Dominic said 'I could if you wish meet up with you at the weekend, if you are not busy.' Jean replied 'that would be good as I have Saturday off.' Then he said 'I will come up to you if that is alright and we can spend Saturday together.'

Jean replied 'that will be fine and I am looking forward to meeting up with you again' and they arranged the time. Jean sat down and with a big smile on her face was thinking about this weekend and what she was going to wear. She phoned her sister and told her the news. Mary was pleased to hear that her sister at last was feeling happy.

She heard a noise coming from outside it, was Jesse skipping towards the front door. Jean opened it to find Jesse standing there with a big smile on her face.

They sat down and Jean listened to Jesse explaining all about her day at school. Jesse told it with such explosion of joy and enthusiasm and energy, her face was lit up with all the feelings that she had felt at the time when each event happened. When Jesse had finished, she said to her mother how she was looking forward to tomorrow and that she would tell her all about it when she returned from school.

As Jean looked at Jesse, she would have liked to tell her all about her phone call and how it made her feel inside, how she was looking forward to the weekend. But Jean knew that she could not tell her, as she was so wrapped up in her own little world. She was so happy there too, and why not Jean thought as Jean was fully aware that sometimes not all children stay children for all of their childhood, so Jean wanted Jesse to be a child for all of Jesse's childhood days and then be an adult when the time came and not a moment before.

Jean remembered very clearly how hard that it was for her and her family when Jean was the same age as Jesse, and how Jean promised that Jesse would have the childhood that she deserved and no less.

At times Jesse was a big worry to both her mother and to the rest of the household. For Jesse had climbed out of windows to see what she could from the window ledge. In some cases the fire department had to be called as Jesse was unaware of any danger and had managed to climb out of her bedroom window and sit on the ledge, looking at the birds on the tree opposite her window as they were singing. Jesse had thought that the birds were singing to her and did not hear her mother or anyone else calling to her for she was sitting and enjoying the view from her window ledge.

Jesse was blissfully unaware what concern she had caused in the household. When the fireman arrived, the young man managed to climb out of the same window as Jesse and after a few minutes both Jesse and the fireman climbed back into the bedroom. Jesse was greeted by a huge hug from her mother and a look of relief of her mother's face saying please never ever do that again, do not climb out of windows, as it is very dangerous, you could fall and then you will be in hospital and or even dead.

Jesse's bedroom was on the third floor and outside her window were concrete paving slabs. The lawn was further away from the pavement so any falls could have easily killed her. So after that event there were bars fitted so that no one could get out or get in the window, making it safe for all. And when Jesse admitted that she also had climbed out of the lounge window they too had to have bars fitted.

And that was not all that Jesse had done. She also went on a walk about and managed to find her Godparents' son's music room which was filled with drum kits and several guitars both electric and acoustic, none of which were the cheap kind but the very best kind that money could buy including a Gibson and Les Paul. But Jesse did not know this and had great fun on the drums and the guitars. For about 2 hours she was there making her own music and having such fun, until she was found by the owner of the room who was shocked to see Jesse. But he smiled and took Jesse back to her mother who was so upset she could not apologise enough. The son said 'it is alright, Jesse had fun and there is no damage, only a few strings broken on the guitars, that is all.'

Since then Jesse never got into trouble again, and was now a good, well behaved, little girl. She had more interesting things at school to do now to occupy her mind, and everyone in the house was thinking 'thank God' as each day before you wondered 'where will you find Jesse' and 'what has she done this time' or 'what has she broken, and how much will it cost to replace it or repair it.' Though Jean's employers never ever made Jean pay for anything, as they looked upon Jesse as one of their own, and Jesse, like their own children, could do no wrong in their eyes as they were only children after all.

As the weekend was drawing near, Jean began to think about Dominic coming up to see her on Saturday. She looked in her wardrobe to sort through her clothes and find something to wear. This made her all hot and bothered. She sat down on her bed and thought 'am I going to wear one of the posh dresses? He has seen them before now and all that is left is just casual clothes' surely if she wore those he might go off her and think less of her.

Then Jean thought to herself 'no. If he is as he seems to be a nice man, then he would not think like that. He will think that she looks just as good in casual clothes as she does in posh clothes.' And if he does not think this, then he is not the sort of man that Jean would like to be with as he is not worth it.

So Jean picked something out to wear on Saturday and it looked very nice on her as she tried the outfit on and looked in the mirror turning around and around. 'Yes' Jean said to herself, 'that is the outfit I will be wearing on Saturday.'

Suddenly it was Friday again. Jean was awake before the alarm went off. She thought to herself what a wonderful morning this Friday is and tomorrow is Saturday, she was feeling so happy and excited inside and with a big smile upon her face.

She stood at the foot of Jesse's bed watching her sleep, thinking how lovely and peaceful Jesse looked, not a care in the world. Jesse breathed gently as she slept, her skin so soft to the touch and the colour a light olive, which turned to a light brown when the sun tanned it, and yet never going bright red and then brown, just turning brown, and never peeling like you would peel an orange or burning like the fires of hell and those who have burnt in the sun with their cries of pain while their skin blisters while it burns. No, Jesse had no worries about that ever happening to her so long as she had put on her sun cream she would always look tanned light brown and then have a dark brown tan and with her long dark curly hair flowing in the wind.

On Saturday, Dominic phoned to ask if she would still like to meet. Jean said that she would love to. She thought how nice it was talking to him again and how she was starting to feel about him and wondered if he could one day be a good father to Jesse and a good husband to her and they all could live a good life together, and there would be no more pain in her life only love and happiness and how nice that would be if that could happen.

Jean thought to herself 'if only I could bottle the time I would' but she thought that she had the memories of all the good times with Jesse as a child and was looking forward to many more times as Jesse was growing up.

The next day, Lady Zara took Jesse out for the day as she has done so many times in the past. She had always treated Jesse like a daughter even though she had a son and a daughter of her own, Jesse was always treated like the youngest of her family. Lady Zara took Jesse shopping and bought her clothes, anything that Jesse wanted Jesse got, all of which would be designer.

While Jesse was out, Jean had the day to herself and after doing her own house work she sat down to eat lunch. It was lonely for Jean, but it had been like this before and she thought how lucky both Jesse and she were to have an employer who would treat them like this. Not many children were born with a silver spoon in their mouths as Jesse was, even when Jesse went to school it was a private school and sometimes Lady Zara would drive Jesse to school in her Bentley car or have the driver take Jesse to school down the one mile drive. The house was like a mansion with a mile long drive to the main road and then to school. Lady Zara and her husband were very rich indeed.

At Christmas time, Jesse would be invited to open her presents from Father Christmas with the family, sitting there by the large real Christmas tree, surrounded by all the presents for the all of the family, being able to sit on Father Christmas's lap and telling him how good she had been for her Mother and telling him what she wanted for Christmas. While Jesse was telling him the things she wanted, Lady Zara had taken note of what was said, knowing that Jesse's presents would be sorted

Jesse showed her Mother what she had in the many bags. There were clothes and toys and jewellery. The look on Jesse's face with such a big smile and her eyes lit up like stars in the night sky. She was so very happy and clearly had had such lovely day. Jean was so pleased for Jesse as she knew that she could never ever afford such presents or the life style that Jesse was living.

Jean and Jesse sat down and went through all the things. Then Jesse helped Jean put away the new clothes. Jean watched Jesse play with her new toys, mainly her new doll which she started to dress. Jean stood there and watched as Jesse was so happy and then Jesse looked and said 'do you like my new doll Mummy?' and Jean said 'yes I do, and look at her new clothes. She is lovely. How lucky you are to have a new doll. I hope you thanked Lady Zara.' 'Oh yes' replied Jesse 'I did Mummy.'

Jesse was just about to sit at the table when Jean said to her 'Jesse, please leave your doll on the chair and not at the table. You know not to bring any toys to the dinner table.' so Jesse walked back to the chair where she had been sitting and put the doll down.

After Jean said good night to Jesse she walked back to the lounge. The phone rang, Jean answered, on the other end was her Dominic calling as he had done many times before to see what Jean and Jesse had done in the week.

Jean thought how it would nice if this man could be the one for her and maybe a father figure to Jesse and that they all could one day be a family living happily ever after just like the good old black and white films that you watch on TV on a Sunday afternoon, how if that dream could come true, how wonderful that would be, to live happily ever after for a change with no pain or hurt ever again just love and happiness.

On Saturday morning Jean awoke earlier than normal as she was so excited because today she would be meeting with her Dominic. It was a break for her from working as a house keeper which was very hard and demanding at times.

As Jean and Jesse sat down together to have their breakfast, Jesse asked her Mother 'What are we going to do today Mummy?' Jean replied 'you are going into town with Lady Zara.

Jesse ran up to Lady Zara and gave her a big hug and looked up at her with a big smile on her face. She was so pleased to see her, knowing that Lady Zara was going to take her out and spend time with just her and what fun that they would have together and how happy she would be.

Lady Zara hugged Jesse in return and said 'are you ready to go out with me? We are going into town as I have to get some things,' Jesse replied 'yes I am ready. Can we go now, Mummy?' as she looked up at Jean with a big smile. Jean replied 'yes you may go now' and with that Jesse took the hand of Lady Zara and started to walk towards the front door. Then, while walking, Jesse turned her head and said to her Mother 'good bye Mummy, see you soon' and blew her a kiss. Jean replied 'good bye Jesse, love you' and blew a kiss back.

Jean packed her case ready for the weekend, even though she would return on Sunday afternoon. Her train was from Sussex, as the house was in Roman Landing, Chichester, but you had to catch the train from Sussex to Leamington Spa which would arrive round about 4.30pm and then she would get a bus back home, and walk from the bus stop along the road and then the mile long drive to the house.

As Jean was packing, she thought to herself how it would have been if her other two girls were here with her and Jesse. Jesse would have her two sisters growing up with her and playing with her. Every time she would cry with pain that they were not there and wondered where they were and how they were and hoped that they were loved as Jean loved them and never forgotten them and how it hurt not to have them both there with her and their sister Jesse.

CHAPTER SIX

Leamington Spa

Jean sat on her bed crying, thinking about them all. Then she thought 'I must be brave and get ready to see Dominic.' She dried her eyes and walked down the long drive to the bus stop.

The train arrived on time and she sat down ready for the journey to Leamington Spa. She began to smile and thought of how much she felt about him and wondered if he felt the same about her.

All Jean could think was about Dominic and her feelings for him, she had not felt like this before, everything was so right between them, how happy he had made her feel. The next thing was a voice saying 'we are now approaching Leamington Spa station.' Jean stood up and reached for her case and then walked towards the door of the train ready to get out where she knew that Dominic would be waiting on the platform for her. She saw Dominic as the train slowly approached the platform. He walked towards her, Jean then put her arms around him and said 'it is so nice to see you again,' Dominic replied 'it good to see you, Jean.'

Together they walked to the car. He opened the door, Jean got in and sat down waiting for Dominic as he put her case in the boot. He drove off to where Jean and he would be staying.

When they arrived, he opened the door and they both walked into the flat. Dominic said to Jean 'would you like a coffee?' Jean replied 'oh yes that would be nice, it was a long journey.' Jean was feeling both tired and happy at the same time. After Dominic had put Jean's case in the bedroom he walked into the kitchen and put the kettle on.

Dominic said 'if you would like to have a bath I will run it for you,' Jean replied 'that would be lovely.' While he was in the bathroom Jean thought to herself how nice this was, for she had found a man that treated her right with love and affection, making coffee and now running a bath for her, how she felt about this was just what she had always wanted in her life.

After Jean had her bath and got dressed, Dominic said they would go out for a meal at the local pub where there was entertainment, as well as good homemade meals.

Dominic and Jean arrived around 7.30pm, he opened the door and they walked to the bar, where Dominic asked Jean what she would like, Jean replied 'I will have a lemonade please,' so Dominic ordered their drinks and they looked around for a place to sit.

They both decided what they wanted to eat and Dominic ordered the food for both of them. He sat down beside Jean, looked into her eyes and said how lovely she looked and how lucky he was to be with her.

Then he leaned over to Jean and gave her a kiss on her lips, Jean smiled and replied how lucky she was finding him as she was looking for someone like him for such a long time and thought she would never find someone like him and was glad she had.

During their meal the conversation led to how they both felt about each other and Dominic was the first one to tell Jean that he was in love with her, Jean's face was lit up with such a big smile and she replied 'I love you too.'

All through the meal Dominic and Jean just looked at each other and smiled with happiness on both of their faces and the conversation led to what they wanted to do in the future. Dominic said that he would love Jean and Jesse to move to Leamington Spa to live with him and start a new life as a family and maybe one day to get married. Jean agreed that would be a very nice thing to do, but she asked 'what would I do as a job?' Dominic replied 'I know that you will find it difficult to find a job like the one that you have right now, but maybe you could find a job with another family but this time instead of living with the family you could live at home with me and Jesse.'

'There are plenty of schools Jesse could go to and with me working we will be fine. I will keep my eyes open for any jobs here and send the information to you in the post for you to look at and maybe apply to them if they are good ones.' Jean said 'yes that would be good, maybe next year all being well as it was September and Jesse was only seven and next year she will be eight years old, giving her the last Christmas with her and Lady Zara's family.'

Also it gave more time to see if the feelings between her and Dominic grew more and more, it gave both of them more time to get things started for their new lives together as a family.

After their meal, they walked towards the dance floor and started to dance.

After a few songs Jean said to Dominic 'I have to sit down, my feet are hurting me.' They watched the band play, Jean started to sing to the songs to which she knew the words, Dominic just watched Jean enjoying herself, he too started to join in singing, he held Jean's hand while they sang, both of them looking into each other eyes, Jean's eyes lit up the room with so much love shining through while she looked at Dominic.

At the end of the evening, Dominic took Jean's hands and led her to the dance floor for the last dance, they danced very slowly, holding each other close and looking into each other's eyes until the band had stopped playing and the dance floor was clearing. There was still dancing, Dominic and Jean not noticing anything or anyone around them for they only had eyes for each other, nothing else mattered in the whole world at that time.

Next morning Jean had to return home. She felt sad that she was leaving and longed for next time she would return to the one she loved, Dominic.

The train pulled into the station and Jean got out, walked along the platform to walk to the bus stop before walking the mile long drive to home where Jesse would be waiting for her to return.

As Jean opened the front door she got as far as the lounge when she heard Jesse's voice singing away so happy and she thought to herself how wonderful life is right now as she has a beautiful little girl and man that she loved. Jean walked towards the sounds of Jesse singing away in her bedroom, As she opened the door Jesse ran towards her and wrapped her arms around her, saying 'Mummy you are home' with a big smile on her face.

Jesse told her mother everything that she had done on Saturday and Sunday, then she came back to the flat where they both lived which was the staff quarters about 4.30pm, Jean arrived back home at 4.45pm 'looks like you had a great time with Lady Zara and her family.'

Jean was so happy and her heart was at peace at last, just filled with love for Dominic and the thought of life with him and as a family with Jesse, one big happy family at long last. Dominic was accepting of the fact that Jean had a child, it did not put Dominic off at all, he had family who had children and friends too, he was so good with Jesse playing games with her when they were all together.

Jesse asked her mother 'what did you do, Mummy?' Jean replied 'Dominic and I went to see a band and had a meal,' Jesse asked 'what did they play, Mummy? Jean replied 'they played rock' n' roll music from the sixties. It was very good.' 'and what did you eat?' asked Jesse, Jean with a smile on her face replied 'we both had steak and chips with garden peas.'

Jesse asked 'is that what we are having then now, Mummy? It sounds nice, I am hungry.' 'No Jesse, we are not having steak tonight as it is very expensive to buy, I cannot afford that.'

When Jesse had gone to bed, Jean sat down to watch TV, but she could not concentrate as she was thinking of the time that she had spent with Dominic, and the conversations they both had about their future together as a family.

She began to write a letter to Dominic, asking him to send any local papers with jobs, so she could see if there were any positions suitable for her, they must be jobs that Jean could go home every day and not live in positions.

It would be so different for both of them and especially for Jesse as she was made to feel part of Lady Zara's family and treated like one. Jean knew that it would be hard too for her and Jesse to leave, whether it be just to live on their own without Dominic in their lives. It would be so different and still a very hard thing to do, knowing that Lady Zara and her family would do their very best to try and convince Jean to stay with them.

On Friday there was a large brown envelope from Dominic which contained a letter and a local paper. Jean was so excited to receive it. There were jobs, but none that Jean could apply for. In the letter it said that Dominic would phone on Saturday.

After Jean had put Jesse to bed on Saturday, she had a bath and put on her bed clothes. Only five minutes to go before Dominic would phone her. Jean was feeling so happy and the five minutes seemed like forever, then the phone rang. Jean stood up from her chair so quickly and walked to the phone and answered it saying 'hello' followed by the telephone number. It was Dominic.

They talked for an hour. Unfortunately there were no positions that were suitable for her. Dominic said that he would continue to send the papers to her every week, hopefully one day there would be a job suitable for Jean. They ended the conversation with 'I love you and good bye till next weekend' when Dominic would call again.

Jean thought of all of the things that both she and Jesse had gone through over the last seven years. Next year Jesse would be eight years old and it could be the year that they both had a chance to start again in a new life, the three of them, Dominic, Jean and Jesse, as a family at last. The one thing that Jean always wanted and had wished for was true happiness and love.

Christmas was approaching. The last Christmas that both Jean and Jesse would have with Jean working as a house keeper and Jesse being treated like family by Lady Zara and her family. She thought to herself what would the next Christmas be like. She knew that it would be nothing like the Christmas's that she had with Lady Zara's family, no, it would be nothing like it at all, it would be very small and quiet, no Father Christmas to see in their home bringing presents and letting the children like Jesse sit on his knee.

But it would be the three of them as a family of their own. Jean would do the best that she could to make it a good time for Jesse, though there would not be as many presents as Jesse would have got before, but it would be what Jean and Dominic could afford. There would be plenty of love to be shared, that is itself worth more than any presents that you could buy, for love is a priceless gift.

Jean saved hard to make the last Christmas for Jesse the best one for her and throughout the year Jean took note of what Jesse would like.

Jean also knew that this would be the last busy Christmas she would have to work with all the parties and dinners that Lady Zara's family had during the Christmas period and how hard it was too, busy making sure that everything was running smoothly in the big house and that the family and their guests had a great time.

Making sure that the big Christmas tree was ordered and would arrive on time and the decorations were good and arranged around the house and along with the snow of which Jean had never seen before until she came to live in the England. At Christmas there was always snow and cold wind, not much rain, which Jean hated in the winter time, it was far too cold for her, she always felt down in the winter time and not happy and often thought of home where it would be summer time and Christmas would be spent on the beach in the sunshine as it would be summer time in St Helena. In July it would be winter time with only rain to deal with.

It was the beginning of December and the big house looked so beautiful. Decorations hanging everywhere and the huge, real Christmas tree smelling so wonderful and looking so pretty with the lights and decorations. It felt like Christmas already. It was like this every year, feeling like Christmas day every day. Everyone in the house was so happy whether it be the family or staff, everyone was in the Christmas spirit.

Jean knew that this would be the last Christmas that both Jesse and herself would be a part of it. For next year they would be in their new home living as a family, Dominic, Jean and Jesse, having their own Christmas. Church in the morning would never change, as Jean and her family were Christians, their faith was Church of England and always went to church on a Sunday and at Christmas and had done so for many years.

Jesse was so excited. Every day she would get up singing and at night time she would go to bed singing as she was so happy, counting down the days till Christmas Day came. There was no stopping her. Jean was happy that Jesse was happy and they both showed it by singing the songs that could be heard throughout the big house, sometimes you could even hear Lady Zara and her husband singing, the house was filled with happiness.

After Christmas and the New Year, it was the first week of January. All the Christmas things including the huge Christmas tree had gone and the house returned to normal again. The good times were over and everyone including Jean wondered what the New Year had to bring.

She had received many local papers from Dominic, none of which had any suitable jobs, but she was still hopeful and prayed that there would be one day and hopefully she would be successful. Then both of them could move to Leamington Spa and start a new life as a family as Jean loved Dominic very much and he loved Jean the same.

Jean had thought to herself that she would not move until Jesse had her eighth birthday as she knew it would be unfair to move before then as Jesse's birthday would include a party with lots of presents, and knowing that the next year, on Jesse's ninth birthday, it would not be the same as her eighth.

No, it would be a small affair, just the three of them and only a small amount of presents for that would be all that Dominic and Jean could afford, but the best present of all would be that they would be a family at last, something that Jean had longed for, a Christmas and Jesse's birthday to be spent as a family from now on and no more having to work on both these events, just having fun instead. This thought made Jean feel so good and happy. She was looking forward to that life and wishing it could come sooner.

The months went by so very quickly it was now approaching the summer time. Soon it would be Jesse's eighth birthday, the last one in the big house. One day in the post came the local papers from Dominic, this time there was a suitable job to apply for, though it was not a House Keeper position, it was in the kitchen as a head cook in a local café in Leamington Spa town on the Parade. Jean had experience in the kitchen as she had worked in the big house making sure all the food for every occasion was prepared and cooked right, also the table was set out correctly, in fact everything to do with the kitchen Jean had done for the family for many years. So this job would suit Jean and she knew that she would get a good reference from Lady Zara and her family after many years of working for them.

Jean thought that she would apply. She wrote a letter telling them of what she was doing and how she wanted to move to Leamington Spa. She put the letter on the sideboard ready to post. Jean was thinking about the position and hoped and prayed that she would be lucky to get the job.

Jesse was a very bright girl who loved school with her friends. It was a private school and Jesse did well there at everything that she did and always had good school reports.

It was now summer and only three months before Jesse's birthday which was on 17th July when she would be eight years old. Jean thought to herself how quickly time flies by.

Over the next few weeks Jean heard nothing, then a month before Jesse's birthday a letter came. It said they were very interested in meeting her and asked her if she could come for an interview. Jean was so happy and arranged to go the following week. She knew that she would have to give a month's notice to Lady Zara if she got the position and that would be hard for her as she loved working for her and her family a great deal. It would be very sad, but if Jean had to make a fresh start in life she had to do this. A few days later a letter arrived confirming the date and time of the interview. Jean was so excited, she thought this could be the start of a new life for both Jesse and herself as a family with Dominic.

The day arrived, she walked into the café and asked for the manager. She was so nervous, her hands were clammy and she could feel her heart beating hard and fast inside her chest. At one point Jean thought to herself 'I hope no one can see my chest beating.'

'Good morning, you are Miss Jean Benjamin?' Jean followed the lady to her office. After the interview Jean came out with a big smile on her face as she was told that she was given the position if she wanted it. Jean had accepted the position and gave Lady Zara as her reference.

The date for Jean to start would be in two months' time; this was good for Jean as she would have a month to settle down in Leamington Spa before starting her new job. Jean had already sorted out a school for Jesse, everything was dealt with.

Jean arrived home tired from the journey but feeling very excited at the thought of a new life with Dominic and Jesse, all one big happy family. At long last, just what Jean had always wanted. It looked like it would not be long, once Jean had given in her notice they would leave in August, after Jesse's birthday in July, the last birthday at Lady Zara's family home. From then onwards it would be in their new home, just the three of them.

Jean thought to herself that as much as she wanted to tell Jesse the good news, she could not as Jean wanted to tell Lady Zara first, and knowing Jesse she just might tell Lady Zara, and that is not what Jean wanted to happen, it must be done the right way.

The next morning Jean asked to see Lady Zara. Jean knew this would be a very hard thing to give her notice in as she had worked for Lady Zara and her family for eight years, and was treated very well, and so was Jesse. Knowing that this year would be the last birthday that Jesse would have with Lady Zara's family, it was hard and very sad, but in order for her to start a new life she had to do this.

After the meeting, Jean came back feeling so sad, she had tears in her eye, knowing that Lady Zara felt the same way. Lady Zara did not want her to move away, and had said so in the meeting. But Jean had explained the reasons why and Lady Zara accepted her notice with regret. She told Jean that she would be sadly missed by both her and her family, especially Jesse as she had grown up there from birth.

All that day, Jean just felt so sad and while she was working she thought of all the things that had gone on in the big house and all of the good times shared every birthday, every Christmas and the schools that Jesse had gone to and how well she has done at school and the reports that showed Jesse to be a very bright child and happy to learn, also she had lots of friends that she played with at school. She was a happy child.

When Jesse came home from school, Jean knew that she had to tell her they would be leaving to start a new life in Leamington Spa. They would leave in August after Jesse's birthday. Jean knew that Jesse would not be happy with this news. Jean sat down with Jesse and said 'we are going to move to Leamington Spa and live there with Dominic. Mummy has a new job in a café/restaurant, where I will be head cook. We will all live in a new flat, and you will go to a new school and make some new friends. But we will not move until after your eighth birthday, you will have that here. We will move in August when you are on holiday from school and you will start your new school in September. It will be so much fun, you will meet lots of new friends.'

Jesse's face was no longer smiling. She had a blank look, not knowing what to make of the news. Jesse said 'what about my friends at school here?' Jean told her that she would make some more friends and that everything would be all right. There would be new parks to play in and a new town to shop in. With that Jean hugged Jesse and kissed her on her forehead and said 'now I must get the tea ready for us as it is getting late.'

After putting Jesse to bed, the phone rang in the hallway. It was Dominic. Jean told Dominic what she had done and how it all went, she also said how hard it was for both Jesse and herself, what a day it had been 'I never want to go through that ever again, it is too painful for everyone.'

Dominic assured Jean that everything from now on would be fine and soon they all would be together as a family in a new life in Leamington Spa. Dominic ended the phone call by saying 'we should not be sad, but looking forward to starting a new life soon. I love you, Jean.'

There were now only two weeks left until it would be Jesse's eighth birthday, the last birthday spent at the big house. Jean knew that she had to make it a special birthday for Jesse, so that she could remember it and look back on it over the years, and remember it as the best one ever. How lucky she was to have had such an up bringing as she has had.

Knowing that she would never have that again, things would be so different for both Jean and Jesse, from riches to rags, living like working class people would live and Jesse not going to a private school any more but to a state school, which would be so different for Jesse, but Jesse would adapt to the change and settle down.

In time, Jesse will live the life of a child living in a working class life, but she will have memories of once having a privileged life only lived by the rich, with all its luxuries that they can afford, as Jesse was born into this life and had enjoyed the life style very much. But now it will have to change and for Jean who had always wanted a family life for both Jesse and herself, with a man who loves her and would accept Jesse and who will grow to love her and one day adopt her taking on his name and therefore being a complete family unit.

It was the week of Jesse's birthday. Lady Zara had said she would arrange a birthday party for Jesse and her friends. The look on Lady Zara's face was one of sadness as she too would miss Jesse being part of her family. But that was how life was going to be.

Jesse woke early with excitement. It was her big day. She quickly got dressed. It was a Saturday and the sun was shining so bright in the blue sky above, Jesse ran to her mother saying 'it's my birthday' and kept saying it over and over again. While Jesse was running around the kitchen as she was so happy, Jean said to her 'happy birthday my darling little girl.'

Jesse knew that she was having a birthday party, it would start at 1pm, but she did not know that it would be the best ever party that she would ever have as it was her last at the big house, with the big hall and big rooms, the size of the house itself was the size of a mansion, so many rooms and halls and so many bedrooms and not forgetting the large music room filled with drums, guitars.

After Jesse had finished her breakfast, Jean told her to get herself ready as they were going into the village for some things. The real reason was to get Jesse out of the house so that everyone could get the house ready and the food done for the birthday party without Jesse seeing anything to spoil her big day.

Jean and Jesse were in the village, shopping, and then they had a coffee for Jean and a milkshake for Jesse in one of the local tea shops. The sun was shining through the window of the tea shop as it was July and getting warmer. Jean and Jesse left and walked around the village looking through shop windows. The time came when they both had to return to the big house. It was now 11.45am and the party would be starting at 1pm so now not much time left to get Jesse home and ready for her birthday party with her new dress which Lady Zara had bought for her. It was a designer dress with ribbons and frills and the colour was pink along with a pink ribbon for her long curly hair.

As they arrived back, there was only half an hour to go. Jesse was so excited she was roughly taking off her day clothes and Jean said 'please, slow down, you will rip your clothes,' with that Jesse said 'I am sorry, Mummy.' She then slowly began to put on her new birthday dress. Jean stood there looking at Jesse and said to her 'you look so lovely with your new dress and with your pink ribbon in your hair, happy birthday my darling.' Jean then gave Jesse a big hug and said 'we must go now it is time for your party to begin,' and together, hand in hand, they walked from their flat to the big house where Lady Zara and her family were waiting in the big hall, where there were ribbons on the stairs and balloons of all colours.

The party was held in the dining room as it was such a big room which would seat 100 people with ease. It was decorated with ribbons and balloons, there was a long table with plates of food and cups of soft drinks for Jesse and her friends and another table filled with presents for Jesse, all shapes and sizes, from her family and friends.

In the dining room there was a man dressed as a clown who provided the entertainment for the children, followed by lots of games to play and music to dance to. Jesse, her friends and Lady Zara's family were all having fun. The party ended at 6.00pm and then Jesse went with her mother back to their flat. Jesse was now very tired after all the fun that she had at her party.

When Jesse was in bed, Jean was in the lounge sitting in the chair, and her thoughts were of what a lovely day it had been for Jesse's birthday. She then thought of how nice it would have been for Jesse to have her sisters there, all playing together. How happy it would have been if Jean could have all three of her girls together and not apart, and that they had all grown up together and gone to the same school together as a family instead of Jesse growing up on her own never knowing about her sisters, only knowing about one of them and not her older sister. This thought brought tears to Jean's eyes as she always wondered what the other two girls were doing and how they were and if they knew that they were adopted. Jean hoped and prayed that they both were happy and loved and one day they could forgive her as she wanted so much to keep them, but it was not up to her and not her decision as if it was she would have kept all three girls and never ever given them up.

Jean was now crying with pain of not having all three girls together as a family. She just cried and cried. She prayed that God would not hate her for what she had done but forgive her as she had no choice in the decision and how much from the day they were taken from her she was filled with pain, shame and anger of what she had done. Every birthday and Christmas she was filled with pain as she loved them very much and always would, she had never forgotten them and hoped that one day they would all be together again.

The next day after church Jean went to the dining room to make sure everything was back to normal and that it was set out for any guests that Lady Zara would have. The table was set out and dressed for lunch and the room had no trace of any party ever been held the day before, it was looking lovely with the flowers and silverware on the table.

Meanwhile Jesse was in her bedroom playing with her walky talky giant doll. It was very expensive to buy, this was one of the birthday presents that Lady Zara had bought. The doll was taller than Jesse and could walk with her and talk to her. Jesse loved this doll. Even though she had lots and lots of other toys and games, Lucy was her favourite toy, she was so very happy playing in her room with Lucy and never noticed that her mother was not around.

Jesse had a toy room that was already full of toys and games and bikes, everything a little girl wanted. Jesse was such a lucky little girl. Jean came back to the flat and could hear Jesse's voice talking, she opened the door to find Jesse playing with her new giant doll. Jesse looked so happy, wearing a big smile on her face. Jean said 'Jesse, are you having fun playing with your doll? Have got a name for her yet?' Jesse replied 'yes, I am calling her Lucy' and went back to playing with her doll.

As Jean was making lunch, she was thinking of all the other birthdays that Jesse would have and they would never be like her eighth birthday. No, it would be much simpler and less presents that Jesse would have, but there would always be one present that is priceless and this is the love that she has for Jesse and knowing that Jesse would come to terms with her new life and will be happy with whatever she was and be happy with that, as Jesse was always taught that she must appreciate everything that she has been given.

And Jesse did just that, and always said 'thank you' and 'please.' She was a very well behaved little girl, even though she had a life style of the rich. She always appreciated everything that was given to her in her eight years of living at the big house with Lady Zara's family.

After lunch, Jean took Jesse to the park to play as the day was so nice and warm. The sun was shining in the deep blue sky and the people at the park with their children were wearing big smiles of happiness on their faces. Jesse went up to a girl and they started to play together and Jean sat down on a bench nearby. She could hear Jesse talking to this little girl telling her all about her birthday party and about her presents and Lucy her giant doll and what she can do, the girls were happy, talking and laughing together.

Jean thought to herself as she watched Jesse play that when they moved Jesse would soon make new friends and she would play with them like she is now. But it would be in Leamington Spa as they have a very big park with swans swimming in the man-made lake with a water fountain. Also they had a large bird cage filled with all sorts of birds along with a large café where you could buy ice cream and soft drinks for the children and coffee and tea. Also there were seats outside so that the families could watch the children play on the swings, roundabouts and big slide.

The weeks went by very quickly, and now it was August, not long before Jean and Jesse would have to pack their belongings and leave to start a new life for both of them in Leamington Spa with Dominic as a family. They both would start on a new adventure together, and who knows what the future will bring for all of them, but Jean was ready to make the change and hoped it would be for the better and would do her best in life for Jesse, but she still wished that it would be with all three girls and not just Jesse on her own.

CHAPTER SEVEN

Damaged Goods

It was Friday 3rd of August when Jean and Jesse left to live in Leamington Spa. The day before Lady Zara had a small leaving lunch for them, it was a very sad occasion because Jean had worked in total 10 years for Lady Zara's family and was treated like family. Jesse had become the third child of Lady Zara's family.

It was a sad lunch. Lady Zara had given Jean extra money to say thank you for all the years of service she had given, and for Jesse a leaving present of a gold and diamond broach, something that Jesse would look at and remember the life and times she had growing up with Zara's family, that she would never forget them.

Lady Zara had arranged a lift to the station to catch the train. Jean and Jesse gave Lady Zara a big hug and said their goodbyes. As the car pulled away down the drive both Jean and Jesse were waving goodbye, until they could not see Lady Zara and her family anymore.

Soon they arrived at the station. Jean and Jesse only had one suitcase each, they got on the train and sat in the first class, thanks to Lady Zara. Jean said to Jesse 'we are on our way, look out of the window and see the countryside.' Jesse had the window seat and replied 'I can see cows in the field, Mummy, and some horses.'

They arrived at Leamington Spa at 5.00pm. Dominic was waiting for them. When Dominic and Jean were face to face Dominic put his arms around her and said 'welcome darling' and then said hello to Jesse and smiled at her.

Dominic took their suitcases and they walked to the car park. Dominic then drove Jean and Jesse to their new home, which was a rented small two bedroom flat which was all they needed.

They walked into the flat, Jean took Jesse's hand and took her to what would be her new bedroom, it was very small with a single bed and a single wardrobe and a small window. Jesse said 'I like it Mummy, it is pink.'

After Jean had put away their suitcases she said they would all go out for a meal, so they all got ready and then went to the local pub where Jean had gone with Dominic before as it was a family pub and served homemade meals.

They returned to the flat, Jean said to Jesse it was time for her bath and then bedtime as it had been a long day and there would be lots to do tomorrow.

Within six months Jesse had settled in her new school and Jean in her new job as a head cook in the restaurant part of the café which was a very big place and opened all day and closed at night at 10.00pm. Jean loved her job very much and the people there were so nice, they all worked along together without any problems.

Dominic had asked Jean to marry him and this would be at the Registry Office in Warwick as they could not afford a Church wedding, although this was what Jean had always wanted, to be dressed in white and walking down the aisle with her family watching her, but not her father there to give her away, that was always going to be a hard thing to bear as she loved her father and mother very much.

The time had come for the wedding. Jean and Jesse were excited as they both had new dresses to wear and Dominic had a new suit. All the preparations were done, including the flowers and reception, with food and a DJ for the big day.

Jean, Jesse and Dominic were all excited as from today they would all be one family, though Jesse's surname would be different to her mother's name, Jesse would still be Benjamin, the only way that Jesse would have the same name as her mother would be if Dominic adopted her, then all three of them would have the same surname, something that Jean had always wanted.

After the wedding some of the guests came back to the flat. It had started to rain and the children playing outside came into the dry. Dominic saw Jesse coming towards the kitchen door. He pushed her back out into the rain and said 'stay out there you little bitch. Out there were you belong, you little rat' and then he closed the door and locked it so that Jesse could not get in. She had to stand there in the rain, with no coat to cover her from the rain that was getting heavier.

After half an hour Jean saw that the other children were playing inside and said 'where is Jesse?' She walked towards Jesse's bedroom, but Jesse was nowhere to be seen. Jean was panicking, where could Jesse have been? She walked into the kitchen and looked out of the window where she could see Jesse crying her eyes out in the rain and yet all the other children were inside nice and dry. Jean opened the kitchen door and Jesse ran in, then Dominic saw what was happening and came into the kitchen and said 'look at you Jesse go and get some dry clothes on otherwise you will catch a death'. Jean took Jesse into her bedroom and asked her why she was still outside. Jesse told Jean that it was Dominic who locked her outside, Jean did not believe that Dominic would do this on purpose, it must have been an accident as he seemed so nice to Jesse.

A few months went by and Jean was settled in her job and Jesse settled in her school. Jean would always collect her from school and bring her home. Dominic took every opportunity he got to be mean to Jesse when Jean was not around. He would put her down, calling her names and saying to Jesse 'don't say anything to your mother or I will hurt you and her. Do I make myself clear Jesse?' And Jesse would always say yes.

Then came a time when the manager of the restaurant asked Jean if she could work some of the night time shifts to do the meals. It would only be for a few hours, she would only have to work until 9.00pm and she would have the day time off instead. Jean said that would be fine as she knew that Dominic would be home and he could look after Jesse for a few hours, until Jean returned home.

One day she told Dominic that she would have to work the following evening but only until 9.00pm and she would be home by 9.30pm. She would be at home in the day time to pick up Jesse and make the tea and put Jesse to bed before she would go to work, Dominic said that would be fine, he could relax until Jean came home.

So the next day Jean picked Jesse up from school and they came home, then she made the tea ready for when Dominic came home from work as he worked in a factory and would be home by 5pm. After they all had their tea and Jesse had her bath, Jean put her to bed and said good night. She then walked into the lounge and said to Dominic 'I must be off now to work, I will see you later, I love you Dominic,' and Dominic replied 'see you later darling and I love you too,' and gave her a kiss on her lips, then she left for work.

Later in the evening when Dominic had drunk a few cans of beer he went to the toilet which was next to Jesse's bedroom. Dominic then opened Jesse's bedroom door and walked in. Jesse was fast asleep, not a care in the world, holding her teddy bear in her arms as she slept. Dominic lent over her with his trousers on the floor and he then pulled the blanket off Jesse and he raped her. He put his hands over her mouth as she screamed out in pain. After he finished, he slapped her across her little face which was now covered with tears and said to her 'if you ever tell your mother about this is I will kill you, and hurt your mother. You are my little bitch now,' then he walked out to the lounge and slammed the door shut.

Jesse was still in her bedroom. She was that frightened she had wet the bed and she stayed there until her mother came home. Then she came out of her bedroom and walked into the lounge where she could hear her mother talking to Dominic. She walked into the lounge in her wet night dress and stood there crying. Jean turned around to see her little girl standing there crying in her wet night dress and got up out of her chair and ran up to Jesse and gave her a big hug and said 'is everything alright, Jesse? What happened? Why did you wet your night dress? As Jean was asking Jesse, Dominic glared at Jesse and nodded, holding his finger over his lips. Jean said 'was it a bad dream Jesse?' and Jesse nodded 'yes Mummy, I am sorry, I have wet the bed' and carried on crying in her mother's arms. Jean replied 'it is ok. Let's go and change your night dress and bed.'

After putting Jesse to bed, Jean walked back into the lounge where Dominic was sitting in his chair. Jean said 'that is very strange as Jesse has never wet the bed, in fact the last time she was three years old and that was because she was over excited when she went to bed. I do not know why she has done it now.' Dominic replied 'Probably she is finding it hard settling down and not saying anything, as she doesn't want to upset you. It is a big change for her to deal with at such a young age.' Jean agreed and said that she would talk to Jesse the next day about it and try and calm her down and make her feel safe again. Dominic had a worried look on his face as he knew the reason why Jesse was crying and why she had wet the bed, not that he cared, though he did not want to be found out.

The next day Jean picked up Jesse from school and on the way home Jean said 'let's go and have some ice cream.' Jesse said 'oh yes, Mummy can we please.' They both walked into town, found a coffee shop and Jean ordered ice cream for Jesse and coffee for herself. After their coffee and ice cream arrived, Jean asked Jesse 'did you have a bad dream last night? What was the dream about, can you remember it?' Jesse replied 'it was about the bogeyman. He came into my room and frightened me.'

Jean asked 'where did you hear about the bogeyman?' Jesse replied 'Dominic told me if anyone is naughty the bogeyman will come into my room at night.' Jean said to her 'there is no bogeyman, it is just a story that is all. No one will harm you or me, you are safe. I will not let anyone or anything harm you while I am around, you are safe, so do not worry Jesse.

With this Jesse was fine and talked about what she did at school that day. They left and walked back home to Dominic's flat. Jean and Jesse got back home at 4.15pm, Jean said 'go and put your school bag away and help me with getting the table ready for tea, as Dominic will be home soon.' The colour went from Jesse's face as she heard the name Dominic and she remembered what he had said to her last night in her bedroom, that if she said anything to her mother she will be hurt and so too would her mother and carried on laying the table ready for tea.

Dominic arrived home and walked into the lounge. Jean said 'hello, how was your day darling?' Dominic replied 'it was ok. How was your day love?' Jean said that is was very busy in the restaurant, Dominic then asked Jean if she was working tonight, Jean replied no not until maybe next week. 'I am not sure, but I will have to work on Saturday this week, only for the lunch time and will be back at 3.00pm and I will start at 11.30am.'

'Could you look after Jesse for me on Saturday if you are not doing anything?' Dominic replied 'yes will be fine as I am not doing anything on Saturday and I could take Jesse to the park to feed the ducks.' Jean replied that Jesse would love that and thanked Dominic for helping look after Jesse. Dominic said that Jesse was his little girl now.

In the next few months things in Jean and Jesse's life had changed as Dominic showed another side to himself. It was not a nice side, in fact it was an evil side. He began to argue with Jean and then started to hit her and Jesse would receive the same treatment. He carried on raping her every opportunity he got when Jean was working, he would abuse Jesse either by hitting her or raping her.

Until one day when Jesse was in her bedroom and Dominic and her mother were in the lounge. Jesse could hear her mother screaming out loud so with that Jesse ran from her bedroom into the lounge where she found Dominic hitting her mother and then saw her mother run out of the room into the kitchen and Dominic followed shouting 'I have not finished with you yet. Come back here.'

Jesse ran into the kitchen and found that Dominic had picked up a carving knife and was about to put it against Jean's throat when Jesse ran between the knife and her mother. Dominic put the knife to Jesse's face and said 'get out of the way, otherwise you will get it instead of you mother.' Jean shouted at Dominic to stop and put the knife down and said that she was sorry for upsetting Dominic, she did not mean to do that. Dominic put down the knife and Jesse hugged her mother and began to cry, saying 'Mummy, I am scared.' Jean grabbed Jesse and they both ran out of the flat, they went to the house of one of Jean's friends, only down the road from the flat.

Once they got there Jean banged on the front door, shouting 'let me in.' The door opened, Jean pushed past her friend with Jesse who was still crying her eyes out with fright. Her friend, Jules, said 'what has happened? Come through to the kitchen and sit down and tell me all about it.' So Jean took Jesse into the kitchen, where by this time Jesse had stopped crying but was still clinging to her mother.

Jean explained what had happened that morning. Jules told Jean that the other day she had heard that Dominic was seen in the local pub holding hands with one of the staff and they had left the pub together. They were seen in the car park kissing. Jules said that maybe it could have been someone else and not Dominic as he seemed so happy with Jean and Jesse, then Jesse interrupted and said no. She had seen the woman as she had come to the flat one day and Dominic told Jesse to watch T.V and that Dominic and the woman were in her mother's bedroom, then they both came out. Dominic said 'don't tell mummy or the bogeyman will come and get you.'

Both Jean and Jules looked at each other and then at Jesse as they knew that she would not make this up, so it was true. Jules said to Jean 'what are you going to do? You can stay here, we have plenty of room and when you need someone to look after Jesse while you are at work that will not be a problem. You do not have to worry about living with him ever again. We will look for another place for you both to live and start again.' Jean said 'thank you. If you are sure that we can stay with you until we get another place to live.' And Jean stood up and gave Jules a big hug.

Jean and Jules talked about going back to the flat to collect their clothes. Jules' husband said 'no way are you going back there alone. I will go with you and Jesse will stay here with Jules. If he starts again on you then God will need to help him as I will give him what for as no man should raise their hands to any woman.'

With that Jules' husband, Jeff, and Jean walked back to the flat. Once there Jean opened the front door and both walked into the hallway to find Dominic had gone out. It was Saturday so he would have gone to the pub. Jean ran to the bedroom and packed Jesse's and her suitcases, along with Jesse's toys. It did not take long.

Jean left a note for Dominic telling him that the marriage was over and she and Jesse would never come back. She also said that she would look to get a divorce and she would get a solicitor to deal with this and that she wanted nothing more to do with Dominic ever again after what he had done and for the safety of Jesse it would be for the best for all of them.

They returned and found Jesse happily playing dressing up with Jules shoes. They both were laughing as Jesse was trying to walk in Jules high heels and Jesse kept falling over, the higher the shoes got the more Jesse fell and both of them were laughing out loud with happiness and joy and no more tears were on Jesse's face, just a smile.

This made Jean happy so she did not go into the lounge, she walked up the stairs with Jeff behind her into the spare bedroom. Jeff put down the suitcase and left Jean to sort out the clothes, he went down stairs to the kitchen to put the kettle on to make a cup of coffee for Jean, Jules and himself.

Jean came down stairs and said 'I am back now and we do not have to see Dominic ever again.' Jesse stood up and ran to her mother and said 'good Mummy, he hurt me and he hurt you.' Jean hugged her in her arms and replied 'it is ok now, your clothes and toys are in our bedroom upstairs.' Jesse said 'can I go and see our bedroom now Mummy?' Jean replied 'yes, come with me,' and they both walked up the stairs into the bedroom, where there were two beds. Jesse said 'can I have this one as it is by the window?' Jean agreed.

Jesse took out her teddy bear and put it on her pillow, then she took out a doll to take downstairs to show Jules. They found Jeff and Jules in the kitchen where Jules asked Jesse if she would like some milk and a chocolate biscuit. Both Jean and Jesse sat down at the kitchen table.

They stayed at Jeff and Jules' house for a few months and Jean carried on working. Jesse was looked after by Jules when Jean had to work a night time shift. Jean had made an appointment to see a solicitor in order to get a divorce. Afterwards she felt so low and hurt even though she tried to hide it from everyone and carried on like normal. Jesse could see how upset she was as many a time Jesse could hear her mother crying in her in the bedroom. When Jesse came in to see her mother she saw her eyes red and tears falling from her face so Jesse too started to cry and said 'Mummy don't cry. I am here, I will protect you. No one will hurt you.' Jean gave Jesse a big hug and said 'I am fine now,' so they held each other tight and then Jean said 'come on let's to go to the kitchen and make some coffee. What would you like to drink Jesse?'

Jules came in and could see how upset they were. She asked Jean how she had got on, knowing she had gone to the solicitor. Jean replied 'everything is now sorted. I will hear from the solicitor soon.' Jean had only been married to Dominic for a year and every day for the last six months there was always something wrong. Dominic and Jean would at times end up arguing or there would be silence between them, but in the year of their marriage it was Jesse who had suffered the most with the treatment of abuse both by being raped and by mind abuse, being called names like 'you little bastard' and 'damaged goods' none of which Jesse knew what they were as she was only eight years old, and had never heard these words before.

Jean said to Jules 'I am so glad that we are out of that situation as it could have got worse and could have put Jesse and I in hospital, I am so glad that you have helped us. Thank you again for all of your help that both of you have given us, I am so grateful. You both are really good friends, and I will return the favour in the future if there is anything that you need I will be glad to help you.'

Jesse was listening to every word that Jules and her mother said. She did not tell her mother what Dominic had done to her, as she was too frightened to say anything as she still could hear his voice saying 'I will hurt you and I will kill you and your mother if you say anything.' So Jesse kept that secret to herself and said to her mother 'I will protect you.' As her mother had said to her when they left that day.

Jean came across an advert for a bedsit with separate bedroom and shared bathroom. She told Jules and Jeff and they said 'you should go and see it. If you can afford it you should take it.' When Jean came back from seeing it, she told Jeff and Jules that she had agreed to take it as it was around the corner from Jesse's new school. They would be safe and no more harm would come to them again.

While Jean and Jesse were staying at Jeff and Jules house, things had changed, as Jesse would have nightmares and sometimes she was frightened that she would wet the bed again like she had done that one night that she and her mother were living with Dominic. Sometimes she would wake up screaming as she had nightmares, Jean would comfort her by saying 'I am here, you are safe now. The bogeyman has gone now. You will never see him again.' And with that Jesse would go back to sleep.

Jean thought to herself at times when Jesse was like this that no matter how she wanted her other two daughters to be with her and Jesse, on this occasion she was glad that they were not here as they too would have suffered like Jesse. Jean thought at least the two girls are safe and well and happy in their new lives with their new parents to protect and love them.

Jean had told Jeff and Jules about the night when Jesse was dreaming and what had happened. How she had wet the bed and what she said, calling out for mummy and saying 'I will protect you Mummy, stop hurting me.' All of them sat in silence and then Jeff said 'how could any man harm a woman and a child. He is an evil man. I have never hit or would hit Jules.' Then Jeff walked out of the kitchen, as he was upset with the situation.

Jules was upset that her friend was treated like this and so to was Jesse, but neither Jean nor Jules knew anything of the abuse that Jesse had done to her. Jesse kept that secret to herself as she did want her mother to get upset and she was worried that Dominic would find them and come and hurt them like he promised. Jesse knew that she had to protect her mother, not hurt her, by telling her she would hurt her mother's feelings, and Dominic would find out and come and get them and hurt them.

So Jesse kept her secret. As the months went on it was coming towards Jesse's ninth birthday. A month before Jean and Jesse had moved into their bedsit and started a new life on their own. Jesse had started to sleep better and the dreams were becoming less and less, the relationship between Jean and Jesse was stronger than ever as Jesse clung to Jean when they were out. If any man was in the same room as Jean and Jesse, she would sit on her mother's lap and watch every move anyone made, she did not want anyone to hurt her mother so it was her way of protecting her.

Jean arranged a little birthday party for family and friends. It was a good day for Jesse, she was once again happy with everyone paying her attention and making sure that Jesse had a good birthday. There was no mention of Dominic or anything to do with how things with the divorce were going. It was a happy day filled with smiles and laughter and lots of hugs for Jesse.

The next day Jean met with her mother who had also moved to Leamington Spa and had a room with a lovely family. Lillian said she was glad that Jean was out of the marriage as she did not like Dominic 'you should never have married a man like that, he was not a Christian. And you did not get married in a church like me and your father did back home in St Helena.' Lillian went on to say how disappointed she was with Jean, with having children out of wedlock and then getting married and not in church, what would her father have say if he was alive.

Jean started to cry with shame and told her mother that she was so sorry for this and that she would make sure that from now on things would be different for both her and Jesse. She knew that all of her siblings had married their loved ones and had children with them and they were all working and very happy together as a family. Jean was the only one who had brought shame to the family by having children and not marrying their fathers; she was the black sheep of the family and knew that her father too would have been very disappointed with her and her decisions which she had made so far in life.

Lillian told her to stop crying in public, it is a sign of weakness, 'if you want cry, then do it in private, like I have done many times in my life.' Jean stopped, dried her eyes and thought of what her mother had told her. Jean had rarely seen her mother cry but had seen her come out of her bedroom back home in St Helena wiping her eyes, now she knew why, it was a sign of strength and not weakness.

She had to be strong for them all in their lives and to show them how to be strong in their own lives.

Jean knew her mother was right, she had to be strong for both her and Jesse and carry on with life, to do the best for her and Jesse that she could. To make sure that in the future she would never get into a relationship like the last one and take more time and not to rush without checking out the man and about his past. She did not do that with Dominic, she only went by what he had told her, which turned out to be lies as he had cheated before on his last girlfriend, which Jean found out while she was going through her divorce .

Jean thought to herself she had good friends around her now and they would look out for both her and Jesse, they would not let anything happen to her or Jesse again, this time will be a start of a good life and no more pain and hurt from any man again.

Jean kept in touch with Lady Zara's family and wrote every week telling her everything that had happened. Lady Zara was well aware of the situation and had written asking her to come back to work and live with her family.

Jean thought of going back to work for her again, but thought she wanted to stay in Leamington Spa as she had her mother and her sister nearby and her friends there. She knew they would be safe and they were now starting a new life. Jesse was settled in her new school, well away from Dominic.

Jean received a letter from her solicitor asking her to attend a court hearing for her divorce in Leamington Spa Courts. The letter brought back all of the times of the marriage that were bad and how both she and Jesse had suffered in the year that she was married. Soon it would be at an end, and Jean would be free from him for ever.

On the day that Jean attended the hearing at the Court in Leamington Spa she came out with mixed emotions of feeling both sad and hurt and glad that it was now over for good. That Jean no longer was anything to do with Dominic or his family, from now on it was just the two of them, living on their own. Jean felt happy it was all over and returned home to where her friends Jeff and Jules were looking after Jesse.

Jean told Jules of what had happened in the courtroom, how Dominic had held up two fingers at Jean and how she felt seeing him again after all that she and Jesse had gone through. She felt so sad and hurt, yet she felt glad that it was now all over and both Jesse and herself could begin a new life together and that they would now be safe and no longer in any danger.

Jean told Jules that Lady Zara had said if she wanted to return to live and work there she was more than welcome. Jules asked 'are you going to go back then?' Jean replied 'I have thought about it many times, but I want to stay here in Leamington Spa, as my mother is here. Jesse is very close to her nanny. As you know, Jesse stays at my mother's at the weekends and sometimes looks after her in the evening, as you sometimes do as well. So I will stay here and both Jesse and I will start again for she is now settled down in her school and has made new friends here.'

The following week, when Jean collected Jesse from school she noticed Jesse was not her usual self. She was sad and silent, not saying much about her day at school like she would do normally. When they arrived home, Jean asked if she was alright, Jesse replied 'those girls called me names in the playground and hit me,' Jean said 'what did they say?' Jesse replied 'they called me a nigger and blacky and woggy, then they hit me on my face.' Jean hugged Jesse and said that she would see the headmaster the next day and sort things out as this is wrong and to make sure that it never ever happens to Jesse again.

The following day Jean went early to the school and told the headmaster everything, including that this was not the first time this had happened. It had now got to hitting Jesse across the face and how upset Jesse was by all this. She asked that this matter be dealt with and that it would not happen again. The headmaster was very concerned and told Jean how sorry that this has happened to Jesse and that he would see the children concerned and tell their parents, and warn them that this will not be tolerated at this school.

Jean told Jesse that she had seen the headmaster and told him and that he would see the other children and their parents, from now it would never happen again.

When they reached home, Jesse asked why would they call her names and what they meant. Jean had to explain that both Jean and Jesse's colour of skin was darker than the other girls as they were white skinned and both Jean and Jesse were of olive skin. They looked like they were Spanish and not English and that it was wrong to call names. She should be proud of who she was and never ashamed of her colour. Jesse then asked 'is that why they go red and burn and peel in the summer and I do not? I just go brown.' Jean laughed and replied 'yes Jesse, you will never go red or burn if you always use sun cream when you are out in the sunshine.'

After that things calmed down at school for Jesse. There was no more calling names from the other children, they had stopped and left Jesse alone for she was only nine years old. To have to go through this had upset her very much but did not show it to her mother. She had learnt to live with the fact that white people looked at her differently, but when it came to the summer time Jesse would say 'at least I do not go red and burn like you do, I just go golden brown and I look nice, you look like a tomato' and would laugh at them.

At Jesse's school there were girls that were black and there were girls who were from India and they too asked if Jesse was Spanish. Jesse replied that she was English and her mother came from St Helena, a little island that is British and ruled by the Queen.

After that the girls made friends with Jesse and she was happy and they all played together. There was no more problems with bullying, they all got on with each other, which pleased both Jesse and her mother.

As the months went by Jean and Jesse were happy together living in there bedsit. Jean and Jesse would go out visiting friends. One family of friends they would go and see was a single man called Gordon who knew all about what Jean and Jesse had been through. They visited Gordon who lived with his father at his father's house. He had no children, was a hard worker and a family man who helped look after his father. Gordon was born in the house where they both lived, along with Gordon's grandmother who was his father's mother. She had brought Gordon up after Gordon's parents got divorced, but Gordon left with his sister and went to live with his mother at first, then his mother returned Gordon to his father and kept his sister with her, they never saw each other again.

So Gordon was brought up a single child as his father never married again. Gordon's father's mother helped to bring up Gordon who in turn became Gordon's mother as well as his grandmother. Both Gordon's father and grandmother loved Gordon very much and gave him all the love that they could. Gordon never went without, he always had clothes and shoes and food on the table and a bed to sleep in, he was well looked after, and there never was any mention of his mother or his sister in their house again, it was just the three of them.

Gordon, like his father, went into the army. His father was a soldier and would ride a horse and had travelled the world. And so did Gordon. When she returned Gordon, his mother said 'you can have Gordon as he looks like you and I hate you. I will have our daughter and you will never see her again.' He grew up knowing that he had a sister, but never seeing her again, which did upset Gordon and his father and his grandmother, but they made sure that Gordon would have everything that he needed to make Gordon's life a good loving one.

Gordon lived in a three bedroomed terraced house in Leamington Spa which was bought by his father. It was a town house dated before World War Two, old fashioned in style with its old fashioned furniture inside with a coal fire in the lounge and in the bedrooms and a Belfast white sink in the kitchen and an electric cooker.

Gordon was a nice, kind man, not like Dominic who was loud and a party man, where Gordon was a quiet man. Gordon liked Jean very much and Jean liked him as they knew the same friends and Jean knew all about him, there were no hidden secretes to come out. Gordon was what he seemed to be, a nice, kind man.

Jean felt comfortable in Gordon's company. She never felt unsafe as she knew that Gordon knew all about what had happened to both Jesse and herself with Dominic. He had told her he knew Dominic, he was a nice man to women but would change once he was in a relationship, he would then turn and be mean. Then they would leave him because of the way that he had treated them. Gordon had never treated any woman like that nor would he.

Both Jean and Gordon had got on very well together and Gordon got on very well with Jesse. He even gave her a teddy bear that was once his, given to him by his late grandmother when he was her age. Jesse in time warmed to Gordon as he showed nothing but kindness to her and her mother, whom she loved so much.

Gordon would take Jean out for a meal once a week and sometimes take out both Jean and Jesse on a Saturday for lunch. They always had a good time. Jean thought if this could be a start of a new life filled with happiness with Gordon in her and Jesse's life, though Jean never talked about Gordon being her boyfriend and neither did Gordon approach the subject. They both just carried on enjoying each other's company.

Coming up to Christmas Gordon told Jean how he was feeling towards her and he would like her to be his girlfriend. Jean said she was feeling the same and she would love to be more than just a friend. From then on, Gordon and Jean were in a relationship and everyone around them were happy as they were so good together, this for once was the right thing to do for both of them.

Gordon had always been in the background when Jean visited Jeff and Jules' friends Dotty and Joe. Joe worked with Gordon in the factory in Leamington Spa, Gordon was a shy man and would talk to Jean when she came around to Joe and Dotty's house so they had been in the same circle for some time and everyone got on very well. There was happiness and lots of laughter.

Around Easter, Jean had been going out with Gordon for some time and their feelings for each other were now serious. Gordon moved in with Jean and Jesse and all was well, they all worked together as a team.

Gordon treated Jesse like she was his daughter with love and attention and never once hitting her or shouting at her as Dominic had done. Even though Gordon had been brought up by his grandmother and never knew his mother or his sister, he could see how a mother should be with her child. It was hard to see sometimes but it was nice to see too.

Gordon had never had a mother and child. As the father figure he was happy at last finding someone to love and care for, he was now a family man and he loved it. Gordon said to Jean 'we must start to look for a bigger place to live with a bedroom for Jesse and a bedroom for us.' The bedsit was only one bedroom so Gordon would slept on the sofa at night as he had to get up very early for work, and he would not disturb Jean and Jesse, he could get up and get ready for work, while they were sleeping.

They lived there for two years nine months. Then Gordon was told there was a two bedroom flat for rent in Leamington Spa, near to where Jesse would go to her new school as she would have to change from an infant school to a High School. The school was a five minute walk from the flat. Gordon arranged for them to see the flat and they both loved it. It was a big flat, with two bedrooms, a separate kitchen and their own bathroom. Everything that they had to share so far.

Gordon paid the rent for the flat and they soon moved in to start a new life. It was perfect for all of them. Jesse loved her new bedroom with new furniture and a new bed that she would not have to share with her mother. She was so happy.

Jesse moved to a new all-girls school not far from the flat. She was now eleven years old and was very happy in school, had made friends and stopped being afraid, as she felt that Gordon was so kind to her and treated her like his own daughter.

One day her mother has said 'how would you like to have a brother or sister,' and explained she was pregnant. Jesse hugged her mother and asked 'when will you have the baby, Mummy?' Jean replied in November, it was now April.

It would be Gordon's first child and he was very happy with the news that he will be a father. He told Jean that he would like her to give up working and now be a mother and housewife and that he would work and look after them all. She did not have to work again as he wanted to provide for them all as a family and one day they could get married.

Lillian was not so happy of this news and said that they should have got married first and then had children as she had done. Jean told her that they could not afford to get married yet as they have just moved and they had to buy everything for the flat. They would get married after she had the baby in the New Year, once they have saved up some more money.

Lillian was not happy at all and told Jean that she was the black sheep of the family and how disappointed she was of her to let the family down by doing this. She did not like Gordon much, but had accepted him because of her.

Lillian did not like Gordon because she was worried that he might turn out like Dominic and hurt both Jean and Jesse. Jean told her mother that Gordon was not like Dominic, that he was a wonderful, kind man who looked after both her and Jesse, and even told her to give up work and be a mother and a housewife, and that he would provide everything that they needed.

Lillian said that was good and hoped it would continue because Jean needed this in her life.

Jean walked into her bedroom, sat down and cried as she too had missed her father as he was such a kind and gentle man who had loved his family and his wife very much and now he was gone. Jean could see the pain in her mother's eyes, yet she never cried in front of her as this was a sign of weakness and she had to be strong to carry on in life.

Jean walked back into the lounge and said to her mother 'this time when I marry it will be for life. I know it will be, as Gordon is a good man. He gives so much to me and Jesse and is very supportive in everything that I and Jesse do.'

'He never complains about anything, just gets on with things. And he too has a family that is not complete.' Jean's mother said 'what do you mean by that?' So Jean went on to explain about Gordon's upbringing and all about his parents and how it had affected him as a child. That his father had passed away and the house where he was born was now rented out to a family. Gordon could not move back there to live as he wanted to start a new life and not live in the past as it hurt him.

Jean's mother then said 'I know how horrible that is to go through, not knowing your mother as you grow up. What an evil woman she is, women like that should not have had children as when you have children and you are married to the father you should stay married until you die like I did when I married your father, and not move away taking one of your children with you and leaving the other one behind.'

Lillian soon changed her mind and treated Gordon as a family member, not just her daughter's boyfriend. She was never happy before when Jean was married to Dominic. She, like Jean, never knew what had happened to Jesse while Jean was married to Dominic, for that was Jesse's secret, never telling anyone in order to protect her family.

In November and a week away from when Jean was due to have her baby, everyone in the family was so excited. Everything for the new baby had been bought and now it was just a waiting game. Then on the 30th November Jean went into labour and Jesse was looked after by her grandmother while Jean and Gordon were at the hospital. A little girl arrived, she had a little dimple on her chin just like her father, and she had blue eyes like her father and she had white skin too, not olive skin like her sister Jesse.

When Jean returned to the ward with her new baby girl, Gordon went back to the flat and gave the news that he was a father and both mother and baby were fine and in the ward resting. Jean's mother said 'I am so pleased and happy' and Jesse asked 'when will Mummy come home?' Gordon replied 'not yet, they will come home in a couple of days.'

'When can I see them?' asked Jesse and Gordon replied I will take you tomorrow, when I get back from work.' 'I can't wait' replied Jesse and then carried on asking 'what does she look like? Has she any hair? What colour is it?' Jean's mother said 'stop asking all these questions. You will see her tomorrow.'

The next day when Jesse had come home from school she was so excited. She had told her friends all about having a sister and that she was going to see her today after school. Her grandmother said 'I am glad you are happy. You now have to help your mother with house work as she will be very busy with your sister.'

When Gordon returned from work he took Jesse and her grandmother to see Jean and the baby in hospital where Jean was waiting.

Jean got out of bed and took Jesse to the baby ward, picked her up her baby and gave her to her mother and said to Jesse 'you cannot hold her yet, she is too small and she is asleep. We do not want to wake her.'

Jean decided to call her little girl Michelle, and Gordon agreed it was a lovely name.

When Jean went home from hospital, Gordon picked her up. Jean was packed and ready. Jean thanked the nurses and they walked out of the exit to the car. Jean held Michelle in her arms on the way home, where both Jesse and Jean's mother were waiting for them to arrive. It was a cold day and there was snow on the ground so they were happy to be home in the warmth. There were smiles on the faces of her mother and Jesse. Jesse said to Jean 'I am glad you are home Mummy, I have missed you.'

They decided to christen Michelle at the church were Jean and her mother went, St Paul's Church in Leicester Street.

It was now December and everyone was looking forward to their first Christmas together as a family. Michelle was growing and feeding well and the doctors and nurses were happy with how she was doing. She weighed 8lb 6oz at birth and now was over 10lbs. Michelle was a happy baby with smiles always on her face with her little dimple on her chin and big blue eyes like her father, she looked just like him. Gordon was a very proud father and loved both Michelle and Jesse the same way, they were his little girls whom he loved very much.

Jesse helped her mother feed Michelle with a bottle and took out the bucket with the nappies ready to be washed out to be used the next time. Jesse held her sister in her arms over the watchful eye of her mother making sure that Jesse held Michelle's head up, and that Jesse held her tight in her arms. Jesse loved holding her sister in her arms while her mother would wash Michelle's nappies or make the tea.

Christmas day came and Jesse woke up first and went into the lounge to see if Father Christmas had been. Indeed he had, she started to open her presents as she did her mother came into the lounge holding Michelle. She said 'Jesse what has Father Christmas brought you?' Jesse turned towards her mother and showed her the presents, and then said 'here are yours and Gordon's and there is one for Michelle and nanny too.'

Jean put Michelle in her pram and opened her presents with Jesse sitting by the Christmas tree, a large real one with the smell of pines. Jesse told her mother this was the best Christmas ever.

Christmas came and went, it was now January the 1st and it was the start of a new year for Jean and her family. They all were looking forward to the year and wondering what it would hold for them.

Then Michelle started to get sick. She would be crying a lot and always hungry and she had a temperature. Jean took her down to the doctor who looked at her and said she appeared to have a cold and told Jean to keep her warm and to watch her and if she got any worse to come back.

There was no medicine that Jean could give to Michelle as she was too young, she was only six weeks old. Jean took Michelle home and told both Gordon and her mother what the doctor had said. The next week Michelle got worse. Jean phoned the doctor from the public phone box and arranged for him to come out to see Michelle. Within half an hour he had arrived, when the doctor looked at her he said she needs to go to the hospital now I will take you and her in my car.

When they arrived the doctor told them to wait outside in the corridor while he took Michelle in his arms to another room. He came out and said 'I will have to take Michelle into theatre now, she needs to be operated on.' Jean, Gordon and Jesse waited about an hour. The doctor came out to see them and said 'I am so sorry but Michelle has meningitis. We have operated on her but unfortunately she is getting worse. I think it would be good to see her now and say goodbye as she will not see the night out.'

Jean asked if both herself and Gordon could go in and see Michelle but the doctor said only one could go. So Jean went into the room where Michelle was laying wired up to a machine. Jean held Michelle's little hand and stayed with her until she died. Then the machine made a sound and the doctor told Jean that Michelle had gone. With that Jean screamed out loud and said 'oh no please come back to me Michelle I need you.' she was begging the doctor to do something to bring her back, but the doctor said 'I am so sorry there is nothing I can do. She is at peace now.'

Jean ran towards where Gordon and Jesse were sitting with tears running down her face saying 'she has gone.' Gordon held Jean in his arms and he too started to cry. Jesse held on to her mother crying and the three of them holding on to each other crying in the corridor. The doctor came out and told them that with meningitis the symptoms are that it appears like a cold, it is very hard to diagnose, and again told them how very sorry he was not to be able to save Michelle.

With that they all left the hospital and went home where Jean's mother was waiting after she had heard to the news about what had happened.

CHAPTER EIGHT

Jesse's Note

To those concerned in this cruel world

You took away my childhood and in return gave me pain and anger and so much hurt.

Gone was a young, innocent child filled with love and fun and play. Willing to learn about life as she grew up, playing with her dolls and being held by grown-ups who protected her from the outside world until she was able to protect herself, with the knowledge she obtained through life itself. From the grown-ups came help, support and so much love, enough to keep her safe.

So why did you do this to me? What did I do that at the tender age of eight years old I deserved to be raped and beaten for your pleasure? Made to stand outside in the wet and cold for no reason, just your voice saying 'You are no good. You're not wanted. Die out there, go on catch a cold and die. We don't want you. We don't love you. Just go to hell, little girl.'

And then you let me in, soaking wet, you just laughed. And then you raped me. And then you made me watch you fucking your lover. And while you did that your words to me were 'You watch me fucking my lover. See how to do it. Your mother does not know how to fuck.'

And when I turned away and cried you hit me with such force, but never on my face where it would be seen. Always on my body. When my mother asked the question 'where did you get these marks from?' you would say 'She is so stupid, she fell again.' Then you just looked at me with that smile.

Why, oh why me? Now I am the denied one.

CHAPTER NINE

Silence

For two years Jean and Gordon could not talk about their feelings over their loss of Michelle and all that they had gone through. The pain never went away even though people said time will heal things and life will go back to normal. Gordon and Jean dealt with their pain by sitting alone either in their bedroom or the kitchen. Sometimes Gordon would go the local pub on a Friday after work to have his own time to think and to be on his own, just having a couple of pints of beer before going home to see his family.

Jesse was now 12 years old and happy at school and very much into music. She loved David Bowie, Jimmy Hendrix and Pink Floyd, and many other rock musicians of that era. She would play her records on the record player Gordon had bought her for her birthday.

This was her way of expressing her feelings. In her family you did not show your hurt and pain, you dealt with them on your own and got on with it, as crying in public showed your weakness, as her grandmother had once said to her. Jesse learnt to not show her feelings and turned to music instead as the songs that she would play would show how she was feeling at that time. It would ease her pain as she thought that the people singing the songs somehow were sharing her pain and knew what she was going through.

One day when Jesse was at school, an older girl came up to her and said 'your name is Jesse Benjamin,' Jesse replied 'yes. Why? Who are you?' The older girl had another girl standing by her side who just stood there looking at Jesse, saying nothing. The first girl said 'this is your sister' pointing a finger at the girl who was standing beside her. Jesse replied 'no, she is not. My sister died when she was six weeks old. I do not have any other sister, why are you lying to me?'

The girl said 'no I am not lying to you, it is the truth.' She then went on to say things about her family like the names of her mother and grandmother and where they came from. Jesse stood there in silence as she knew that the things that this girl had said to her about her mother and grandmother were the truth. The other girl then said that she was Jesse's sister but she was a year older and she was adopted when she was a baby. That she had a lovely family now and she was very happy. That she knew she was adopted and that she had a younger sister who was living with their mother.

All that day Jesse was in a state of confusion and felt hurt that her own mother had not told her that she had an older sister and that she had to find out while she was at school. This hurt Jesse and made her angry.

She felt betrayed and was hurt that her own mother could keep this secret from her. Why did her mother do this, she was so hurt inside that the rest of the day she could not concentrate on her work in any of the lessons. She just wanted to go home and face her mother with this news of having an older sister that she had never heard of in her life before and to tell her mother what the news had done to her, especially hearing it from a stranger.

When school finished, Jesse walked home feeling so very hurt inside and angry towards her own mother. She started to cry but as she approached the back door she wiped her face and took a deep breath and walked into the kitchen. Jesse looked at her mother as she was standing by the kitchen door. Her mother asked 'how was school today, Jesse?'

Jesse replied 'it was ok' then she told her what had happened. She explained how this older girl had told her the girl standing by her was her older sister. Jean stood by the sink,

136

on her face was a look of shock that now Jesse knew the truth. She knew that she would have to explain about both of Jesse's sisters and what had happened to them and why they both were not living with them anymore.

This hurt Jean as she had to relive the past which had been very painful for her to go through, but now she had to go through it all over again to make Jesse understand the reasons why this was done, how she had never forgotten her two sisters and how she still missed and loved them very much. How she had lived her life with regret that they were not living with them as a family and they now had families of their own.

After Jean explained to Jesse, she then asked her mother 'does Gordon know all of this?' Jean replied 'no he does not.' Jesse asked 'Why did you not tell Dad? He should know the truth as you are his wife and you know about his life and family. He has the right to know like I did.'

Jean replied 'I could not tell him any of this as he might leave us and he might stop loving us and not want anything to do with me anymore.' Jean broke down in tears and said 'I am so sorry. I did not want to hurt you or anyone. I just wanted the best for you and I thought that by telling you and Gordon both of you could not handle that. Both of you would be too hurt by this and knowing what had happened to Michelle. I did not want you to go through any more hurt and pain as I am going through. I just wanted to protect you both as I love you so much.'

Jesse put her arms around her mother and said that she understood and that she would never say anything to Gordon, that it would remain their painful secret and they would not talk about this subject again.

The kitchen door opened, it was Gordon, home after he had finished work at Lockheeds, a factory in Leamington Spa where he had worked as a tool setter since he left school. The three of them sat and had their meal together without saying much as Gordon was tired.

Jesse could not sleep because all she could do was to think of what had happened that day, what her mother had told her. Now she knew that two days a year when her mother told her that she had a bad day and was not in a happy mood, it was because it would have been one of her sisters' birthdays. How her mother must have felt knowing that her daughter was not with her and wondered how she was getting on with her new family and what she had for her birthday.

Jesse cried herself to sleep and then woke up very tired. She had tossed and turned all night, thinking of her mother crying in her arms. It was a bad experience for Jesse, something she had never gone through before. As soon as she saw her mother downstairs in the kitchen she walked up to her and gave her a big hug and said 'I love you, Mum, so much.'

After a few weeks, Jesse began to get back to normal. She never saw the girl and her sister again, somehow they seemed to have kept apart as the older girls were in the year above her. The school was new, with both boys and girls, another change for Jesse to deal with. They had moved from an old building to a brand new one, high on a hill. It was a lovely new building, warm in the winter whereas the old school had been dark and cold.

It was time to break-up for the school holidays. They had six weeks break from school in July. It was also Jesse's birthday, she would be 13 years old. Jean, Jesse and Gordon, who Jesse called Dad, went on holiday to Devon for two weeks. They stayed at a half board guest house where Jesse had her own bedroom in the front.

The weather was sunny and hot as it was summer time. Jesse wanted to swim in the sea so her mother and Gordon after breakfast went to the beach and laid out their towels on the sand. Jesse set off for a swim, Jean reminding her to be careful and not go too far out to sea, to stay where they could see her. Jesse was a very good swimmer, she had won races at school and against other schools.

One day Jesse saw a girl swimming as well as she did. It was not long before the two girls were swimming together and having so much fun they soon became friends. The girl's name was Gemma and she was a year older than Jesse, a tall, blond, slim girl. She lived in Devon, not far from where Jesse and her family were staying. Every day the two girls would meet up at the beach and swim together. Then they would sit down on the beach on their towels close to Jean and Gordon sitting on their deck chairs.

The girls would go to the ladies toilets to change into their swimming outfits. Then they would leave their towels on the sand and go into the sea for a swim. They would come back to their towels, read their magazines and talk about what music they liked.

On the second week of Jesse's holiday, she met up with Gemma on the beach and they went to the same ladies toilets to change. They always went together and this day was no different. After they had been sitting on the beach reading for a while Gemma said 'I am going to the toilet.' Jesse said 'I am ok. I will stay here and look after the towels and magazines.' Gemma said 'Ok, see you in a minute, Jesse.' Jesse carried on reading her magazine.

It was some time since Gemma had gone to the toilet and Jesse was starting to get concerned. She had never just left without saying anything. Jesse thought to herself 'where is she?' She went to find her mother and Gordon, and asked them if they have seen Gemma. They both replied they had not. Gordon suggested she may still be in the ladies toilets, 'I know what you girls are like for taking so long in the toilets. You are the same at home. Both you and your mother take for ever. Go to the toilets and hurry her up.'

Jesse walked back to the toilets and called out Gemma's name. A voice came from one of the cubicles, it sounded like 'argh' then went quiet again. There was no one in the first toilet. Jesse went into the next and called again to Gemma. She banged on the wall of the next cubicle, next door to her's, and again a voice which sounded like Gemma's cried out 'argh.' Jesse came out of the toilet and walked to the sink to wash her hands. A man suddenly came out of the cubicle next to where Jesse had been.

He turned to Jesse, grabbed her by the throat and said 'if you ever tell anyone that you saw me in here I will find you and do the same to you.' Then he left. Jesse ran out to her mother and Gordon and told them Gemma was not there but she had seen a man in there. Gordon laughed and said 'Oh you would go to the wrong toilets, you went to the men's. Gemma went off to get an ice cream for both of you.'

Jesse went back to where both their towels were, sat back down and waited for a few more minutes. She noticed a crowd of women come out of the toilets. Then the police arrived, so she thought that something was wrong. She ran back to her mother and Gordon and said 'look, there are police outside the ladies toilets and Gemma has not come back. I told you there was something wrong. And I did not go to the men's toilets, I went to the ladies and I saw a man in there.'

Gordon and Jean saw the police and people milling around. Gordon said 'let's pack up and go back to the guest house as it is getting late. It will be soon time for dinner.' So they gathered their things, left the beach and went back. By the time they arrived back, the news of what had happened on the beach had reached the guest house. A local girl with blonde hair, aged in her teens, had been brutally murdered in the ladies toilets earlier that day.

When Jesse heard the news, she said to her mother and Gordon 'I told you something was wrong. The girl is Gemma.'

And she began to cry. She felt she should have gone to the toilet with her and had she gone Gemma would still be alive. Now it was Jesse's fault that Gemma had died. Gordon said 'No it is not your fault. It is because there are some bad people in this world.' He gave Jesse a hug and then said to Jean 'I think it would be better if we left for home now, instead of in the morning.' Jean agreed as she did not want Jesse to go through giving evidence to the police, and going through hell, as she was only 13 years old and had gone through enough in her life already.

The next day they were at home and back to their normal lives. The news came on and it showed what had happened where they had their holiday. It told of the girl in the ladies toilets. Jesse said 'I told you I saw a man in there,' then she told them what the man has said and what she had heard in the next toilet. They knew that Jesse was the last person to see the girl alive and they looked at each other thinking it could have been Jesse that could have been killed.

Gordon turned to another programme. He said 'I am glad that you did not go with Gemma because we might have lost you too.' Jesse replied 'I know Dad, but if I had gone with Gemma she might still be alive because there would have been two of us.' Gordon replied 'you do not know what he would have done to both of you. You are not to blame for her death.'

Jean gave Jesse a big hug and said 'it will be fine. She is in heaven now, at peace. Please do not worry any more Jesse.' Jesse hugged her mother, made a drink for herself and went upstairs to her bedroom to play some music.

Later Jesse could not sleep. She kept dreaming of the man in the ladies toilets, and what he had said to her. She kept waking up and looking around her bedroom, and then she would see she was at home safe in her bedroom. Then she would go back to sleep. This went on for a few weeks. She told her mother of the dreams and her mother said the man will not come to hurt

141

her, he would soon be arrested and put into jail for what he had done.

In the months that went by, Jesse seemed to be alright and returned to her normal self. There was no more news of what had happened. The family carried on with their lives. Then it came to December. It would be the first Christmas that Gemma's parents would have without her. Jesse again thought of Gemma as they were going to keep in touch. Jesse would have sent her a Christmas card, now she could not and this hurt Jesse and made her feel full of guilt. The nightmares came back but this time she would dream of both the man who had murdered Gemma and Dominic, both of them running to try and catch Jesse to hurt her. In her dreams she would be running as fast as she could to get away from them. Then she would wake up, look around her bedroom and see she was just dreaming.

She told her mother of the dreams but not that Dominic had been in them. Her mother still did not know of what Dominic had done to her as Jesse knew that it would be too much for her mother to bear. Her mother had gone through so much with losing Michelle. Jesse had to keep that side of her life to herself to protect her mother from more pain, so she did just that.

CHAPTER TEN

Music to Mood

Jesse enjoyed her music and loved singing. She joined the Sunday school choir which made a record. Jean bought this as she was so proud of Jesse and also loved music, she had always played the radio at home and Gordon played his music which Jean also enjoyed. Their music would be Glenn Miller, Johnny Cash, Shirley Bassey and many more similar groups.

Jesse asked her mother if she could have a guitar for her thirteenth birthday and her mother agreed. Jean could only afford to buy a right handed one though Jesse was left handed. She had been taught to write with her right hand which was very difficult for her. For everything else, she used her left hand. With the guitar, she turned it upside down and then started to play.

When she was fourteen, on a Saturday she would go with her mother and Gordon to a local social club where there would be groups playing upstairs. Jean and Gordon would be downstairs in the bar, meeting up with their friends, knowing that Jesse was fine upstairs. Jesse sometimes brought her friend along with her to see the bands and they would dance and enjoy themselves. They would always be home by 10pm.

On Sunday after church, both Jesse and her mother would come home and there would be music playing in the kitchen, with Jesse playing hers in the bedroom and Gordon with his in the lounge. The house was always filled with some sort of music as the whole family enjoyed music of different sorts. Sometimes, Jesse would be allowed to watch Top of the Pops with her mother and Gordon. The show would play the top ten hits of that year, which was the seventies and show the groups and solo artists with their fashion and hair styles. They all enjoyed watching every Thursday night, and would laugh at what some of the groups would wear and sometimes they would like the outfits and hair do's and would discuss it for a short while, then Jesse would go up to her bedroom and play her music while she was getting ready for school the next day.

Every week, Jesse would buy 'Jackie' magazine, just for girls, which had all the latest gossip about the bands and solo artists and fashion and hair styles, everything a girl needed to know.

Jesse and her mother loved their music, they would often sing the songs on the radio or T.V. and Jesse would try her best to play on her guitar, though she had never had any lessons. Still, she made her own music, particularly when she felt overcome with any feelings of sadness in her life.

She would always play certain records that would fit her mood and her feelings at the time, whether they be good or bad, there always would be a record to suit her feeling. Jesse felt that the records she played understood what she was going through, be it pain or happiness, more than anyone could.

As Jesse got older, she was allowed out on her own to see the bands at the social club with her boyfriend at the time called Rob. He was known to Jesse's mother and was a good boy though he was four years older than Jesse. They were very happy together and they loved going to the club at the weekend to play bingo and to see the live bands.

Jesse loved to dance and Rob would either dance with her or watch her dance. The relationship only lasted a few months then Jesse ended it, as Rob was not keen on just going to the club every weekend, he wanted to stay at home and watch T.V.

When Jesse was sixteen, she wanted to go into hairdressing when she left school. She told her mother, Gordon and her grandmother. Her grandmother said she did not need a career, but should take a part time job, find a young man, settle down, have children, stay at home to look after them and be a housewife. Gordon agreed. Jesse replied that she did not want to get married at nineteen like her grandmother, she wanted to have a career instead.

Her grandmother was not happy with the answer and said Jesse would be no good at that and why was she bothering. Gordon also agreed, saying she wouldn't be good enough to be a hairdresser, particularly since she would need to go to college.

Jesse's mother said nothing, as she was brought up to never to answer back when her mother had said something, only when her mother wanted an answer.

Jesse was in town and came across a small hairdresser shop. She went in and asked if there was a Saturday job. The owner, called Sonja, said there was, and so Jesse started the next Saturday at 8.30am. Jesse left the shop with her heart filled with joy, she was so happy.

When Jesse told her mother, she was so happy and proud. Gordon was glad she had a job but did not show any real support, still saying that she would not be any good at college and she would fail as it was hard work. Jesse's grandmother also agreed that she would not be any good and that she should get a job in a shop and not have a career.

But Jean said that she was proud of Jesse and gave her the support that she needed in whatever decision she had made so long as she was happy. Jesse gave her mother a big hug, then went to her bedroom and thought how hurt she was that her grandmother and Gordon did not support her.

Though Jesse knew that her grandmother and Gordon loved her and they both showed it in other ways but never in giving Jesse any faith in what she did. It was not their fault, it was just the way that they both were, but Jean showed her support as she had never had her own mother say how happy and proud of her she was in anything she did.

In the house there was always a feeling of closeness with meals in the dining room and many times of laughter, it was a happy family home. But there was always an argument or two, it would always be about Jesse, what she was doing with her life, or boyfriends or the way that she would dress or her make-up she wore. Both Jesse's grandmother and Gordon would disagree with Jesse and it would be Jean who would stick up for her. Sometimes Jean even told Gordon to stop being mean to Jesse as she was not his daughter. Jean was so hurt by both her mother and her husband having a go at Jesse, it was not fair.

Lillian felt strongly that Gordon should not be spoken to in this way. Jean said she was sorry to Gordon but the look on Gordon's face was a look of hurt as his own daughter Michelle had died, and he did not grow up with his own mother only his father and his grandmother. He was very jealous of Jesse being so close to her mother and her mother so close to Jesse. He had felt at times left out, seeing them together laughing and talking about clothes and make-up. He loved them both so much, but the hurt of losing out on not having a mother would always raise its ugly head.

When Jesse was seventeen, she saw a band at the social club that were very good, they played both rock and the blues which Jesse loved. They came from Coventry and she had never seen them before but they became a regular band playing at the club so Jesse soon became a fan of theirs and became a friend of one of the group called James, he played saxophone. Jesse soon learned that James was a professional saxophone player and had played for many people, he had played in studios for artists and he had gone on tour.

James and Jesse became an item and saw each other every Saturday after Jesse had finished work. They would go off together and sometimes Jesse would go to see him play in Coventry.

The relationship went on for a year. When Jesse was eighteen she decided to move to Coventry and to live with James in his flat above a building society. Jesse knew she would be happy with James as he supported her in every way that she needed and this was what she always wanted and did not get from her family, even though she knew that they loved her it was not enough. She just could not stand the arguments any longer so she knew that her family would be better off if she was not there as they would not have anything to disagree over as it always seemed to be over Jesse.

This way they could all live happily and in peace without Jesse to fall out over.

Jesse knew that she could not tell her family she was moving out to live with James as this would not be acceptable in her Grandmother's eyes and it would cause a great deal of falling out, bigger than ever before. Jesse did not want to cause such pain for her family, so one day, when she knew that her mother and Gordon were going out with friends, she left when they had gone out, leaving a letter to say why she had gone and a present for her mother and Gordon, saying that she would be in touch soon and that she loved them very much but that they would be happier without her living at home.

This hurt Jesse very much to have to write this letter instead of sitting down with her family and talking about it like other families would have done but this was the only way to do it. It was the least hurtful way and Jesse knew that she would come and visit her family with James. That would be a tough thing to do, but at least her family could see that she was happy and loved by James and she was safe and that he would look after her.

And that she would never go through what her mother had gone through with Dominic as James was a kind, loving man who adored Jesse. James knew how Dominic had treated

Jesse's mother and cheated on her. James was not like that and disagreed with that kind of behaviour.

Two weeks later Jesse and James went to visit her family, this was arranged by letter. Jesse and James were worried about how things would be when they got to Leamington Spa and what sort of atmosphere they would be walking into. The journey seemed longer than normal. The front door of the house opened and there stood Jean with a big smile on her face. Jesse walked up to her mother and gave her a big hug.

Jesse introduced James. Her grandmother said Jesse will be back home soon where she belongs, it will not last, she belongs here in Leamington not in Coventry, she is too far away from her mother.

Jesse explained she was now eighteen and not a child anymore. She was a woman who can vote. Times had changed it was now the seventies and not the forties. Jean asked James about his work and he explained his day job was in a factory and at night time and weekends he played rock, blues and modern jazz in a band.

Gordon loved blues and jazz but was not so keen on rock or pop and the conversation went better than both James and Jesse had expected. As they were leaving, Jean said Gordon and she would go to see the band play the next time they played in Coventry. Jesse had given her mother her telephone number so she could ring anytime she wanted.

On the way back to Coventry, Jesse and James talked about how well the visit had gone and how pleased she was and how happy she was to see her mother, and was looking forward to seeing them again.

The weekend arrived and Jesse was looking forward to seeing her mother and watching James play in the band. The doorbell rang and there were her mother and Gordon standing outside. Jesse opened the front door and hugged her mother and led them both into the lounge.

The band venue was in a very big hall. Gordon and Jean sat down at a table in the front not far from the stage, then Jesse joined them and waited for James and his band to be introduced. The band began to play and Jesse was so pleased that her family were there with her, what a great night this was.

On the way home, the conversation between James and Jesse was very sad for Jesse was apologizing for what her grandmother had said. She felt so embarrassed. She said 'how could my grandmother say things like that to you? She does not know you like I do. That was so wrong of her to say that. I never ever thought that she was like that. I know that she is old fashioned in her ways but never thought that she could be so hurtful. She never says 'I love you' like mum does to me and I do to her'.

Then James said 'it is just her way. There is nothing wrong with that, she was brought up in a different country and different way and a different time where things were so different to how they are now. No one there lived with anyone before they were married and everyone was a virgin before they were married, like your grandmother and grandfather were. They more than likely were their first loves. How likely were they to find their true love? They loved and had children until the day your grandfather died. Your grandmother never remarried for she had found her true love and no one else would do. Unlike some of us. They found their true soul mate which would last until the day they died.'

'Your grandmother loves you very much. It is the way that she would so it sometimes, it could be hard words, but she loves you all the same. And so does your Dad, he too was brought up without his mother, by his father and grandmother. No contact with his mother or his sister, so it was hard for him too.'

Jesse's mother phoned a few days later to say her grandmother had moved into her old room because the house

149

where she was staying was now up for sale and the family were moving. Instead of renting a flat, she would rather be with Jean and Gordon.

Jean went on to say Lillian had made some changes, Gordon had to take his work boots off and leave them in the hallway and wear slippers in the rest of the house. And Grandmother did not like Gordon smoking, it was bad for his health.

But apart from that things were ok. Grandmother helped clean the house and prepare the meals. They had some fun with her, Gordon sometimes took the micky out of her and when she realised she said 'oh you are so silly you old fool you' and then they all laughed together.

Her mother asked if it would be alright if they came over on Sunday. Jesse was so excited when the day arrived with the thought of her mother, Gordon and her grandmother coming. She made sure everything was clean and tidy and in its place.

Jean admired the lounge, then Jesse walked them round the flat showing them the kitchen and the two bedrooms and the bathroom. Her mother said how lovely and cosy it was and asked about the neighbours. Jesse replied that one side was a dentist, no one live above and the other side was not in use.

James took them for lunch at an old fashioned local pub where the food was very good. When Jesse's family had left to go home Jesse said that the meal was lovely and thanked James for paying for everything. James replied that it might be Jesse's family but it was also his too. He wanted to look after them as if they were his own family. Jesse gave him a big hug and kissed him on the cheek.

Later in the week Jean phoned Jesse who asked what her grandmother had thought about the flat. Jean took a minute to answer the question then said she liked it very much but added 'you know what Nanny is like, she does not approve of anyone living together and still believes that you will come home to live.'

'Your grandmother and Gordon for once agree with each other. I am already the black sheep of the family, and now so are you for not doing things the way that my family have done. They all married and had children and have never been divorced like me so it is looked down on.'

'But that is just the way things are. I am proud of you and love you very much.'

Jesse put down the phone and thought of what her mother had said. She felt so hurt that both her and her mother had been made to feel ashamed of what they had done in their lives and been labelled the black sheep of the family. Jesse knew she loved her mother very much and that her mother had done her best for her whilst she grew up. It was not Jean's fault what had happened in the past, for they both had suffered in the hands of Dominic. They both had deep scars that do not show on the outside but were felt on the inside that had changed them both for life.

In the two years that Jesse had been living with James everything was good until one week when Jean had phoned Jesse. She sounded different, not herself, and the conversation was not a happy one. Jean seemed very down and Jesse picked up on that. She asked her mother if everything was alright.

Jean replied she was feeling very tired. Jesse could not stop thinking about the phone call, even though James was sure everything was fine and she need not worry. But Jesse still was worried about her mother as they were very close. She hoped her mother was just tired and nothing else was wrong and could not wait to speak to her again.

A week later it was Gordon on the phone asking for Jesse. Jesse said 'hello Dad. What are you doing phoning me, you never use the phone. What is wrong?' There was a long pause and then Gordon replied 'it is your mother, Jesse, she is not at all well. Will you come over and see her please?'

151

James and Jesse set off immediately for Leamington Spa. The journey seemed to take for ever and all Jesse could think of was her mother. She just wanted to see her and to make her better. She was thinking maybe her mother was coming down with some sort of virus and soon would be back to normal, feeling her old self again.

When they arrived Gordon opened the door and the look on his face was of fear and sadness. He said nothing to Jesse or James, just walked back to the lounge where Jean and Lillian were. Jesse walked up to her mother and said 'hello Mum, how are you?' There was no reply, just a blank stare as if she was looking straight through Jesse.

Jesse turned and looked at Gordon, saying 'Dad, what is wrong with Mum?' Jesse's grandmother then said 'it is your fault she is like this. She is like a child again. I have to bathe, dress and feed her.' Gordon said 'it is not Jesse's fault.' Grandmother retorted 'well you tell her what her mother tried to do with her life then!'

Jesse asked 'what is going on? What do you mean, Nanny? Tell me Dad.' So Gordon told how her mother had gone to the doctor and been given some tablets as she was feeling down and very low in her mood. 'Your mother took a load of the tablets and was trying to take them all when you grandmother caught her and took them off her. The doctor has been out to see your mother.'

Jesse's grandmother walked out as she could not stand to hear any more about her daughter that she had brought up and loved very much, it was all too much for her to bear. Gordon went on to say that the doctor had said Jean had had a very bad breakdown and needed to go to Henley House, a mental hospital, where she could stay until she was better. She would not be able to stay at home because she was too ill to look after herself.

Jesse was sitting by her mother hugging her so tight. She was very upset to hear this news and asked what she could do. Gordon said she could write a letter for him and sort out any paper work that needed doing because Jean managed the bills and kept the house running. Jesse agreed to help, but asked what the doctor had said about Jean going to hospital. Gordon replied 'I cannot sign this form to give permission for your mother to go to a mental hospital.' Jesse said 'then I will sign it.' Gordon said 'you cannot sign the form. It has to be the next of kin, which is me.'

Jesse said 'but I am her daughter. Does that not count Dad?' Gordon said 'no, I am afraid it does not. It is only me that can do that, and I cannot, I need her here with me.'

Jesse said 'I will go and see Mum's doctor and see what I can do. There has to be something, and I will keep trying until she is well again.

On the way home, Jesse said 'I will phone in to work tomorrow and say I am unwell. Then I will phone my mother's doctors.' He was once Jesse's doctor also.

Once at the surgery, Jesse heard her name called out. She got up and followed the doctor into his room. She asked what was wrong with her mother and told him what her stepfather had said. The doctor replied that her stepfather was right, he was the only person that could sign the forms. Then he went on to explain in more detail what had happened and why, and what the outcome would be if her mother went to Henley House. How they would give her electric shock treatment, which she needed to bring her out of this state of being locked into herself. At the present she could only show signs of being there but was unable to do anything for herself. She needed a shock to her system to bring her out of it.

Jesse sat there in horror at what the doctor had told her, and then asked what she could do. The doctor replied that her mother needed a shock. Could she give her mother a big shock that would bring her out of it? That was the only thing that she could do, otherwise it will have to be hospital for her mother to have electro-convulsive shock treatment.

On the way home she thought of what the doctor had said. She was so hurt inside as she knew that she had to do something to shock her mother. She did not want her mother to go to hospital and have this treatment for she was worried not only about her mother but what this would do to her grandmother and Gordon. She knew this would devastate the whole family, how could they all cope with this situation. Jesse knew the next step was with her; what could and should she do now?

Jesse soon was home, but did not notice what was going on around her, she too was in her own world, just like her mother. It was a dark place to be in on your own.

When James arrived home Jesse told him everything the doctor had told her. There was a silence for a minute or two and then James asked what she was going to do. Jesse replied 'I am going to have to give my own mother, whom I love so much, such a shock of her life. Hopefully she will react to it and snap out of it. Then she will go back to being her old self again. I do not know how, but I will think of something.'

The next morning, a Saturday, James took Jesse to her mother's. She still had no idea what she was going to do, all she knew was that day life would change for both her and her family.

While Jesse was driving to Leamington Spa with James to see her mother, all she could do was pray, asking for strength for whatever she was going to do. She knew that it would be the hardest thing in the world, to rock the world that her mother was now living and pick up the pieces and put them back together again.

As the car stopped, James looked at Jesse and asked if she wanted him to go in with her.

'No thank you, this is one thing that only I can do.'

As Jesse walked up the path, she felt sick inside as she knew that today would be the worst day of her life. She knocked on the front door and waited. Gordon said nothing as he let her in. Jesse followed him where she found her mother sitting in her chair. Her grandmother was in the kitchen. Jesse said 'Hello Mum. How are you today?' But there was no answer.

Jesse's grandmother said 'your mother is still the same, there is no change. And it is all your fault she is like this. How could you do this to your own mother?'

Gordon replied 'No, it is not all Jesse's fault. These things do happen.'

She replied 'Not in my family they do not.' And then there was a huge argument between them.

Jesse said 'Well, if it is all my fault then I will go and marry James and have children and you will never ever see me again.' She turned to her mother and said 'I love you so much Mum, but I am going now and I will never come back to see you or the rest of the family. I am now dead to you all.'

Jesse started to open the front door to leave. As she did so, to her surprise she could hear her mother's voice saying 'No, Jesse, don't leave me.' Jesse turned around to find her mother standing in the hallway. Jesse walked towards her, gave her a big hug and said 'I love you and if you want me to come and see you I will.'

Jesse's grandmother asked if she was still going and never coming back. Jesse replied she was not going to leave and would always come to see them. Lillian asked why she lied to her mother as she was not brought up that way, she should be ashamed of herself. Jesse told her grandmother and Gordon about the doctor saying her mother needed a shock to bring her out of herself and this was the only thing that Jesse thought of doing. Because she and her mother were so close she hoped this could be the way to bring back her mother to her old self.

She had prayed for strength to do such a thing to the one she loved so very much.

Gordon said 'I am glad that your mother has spoken. She hasn't said anything to us for a while and we just didn't know what to do. We love your mother very much and it has been so hard to see someone you love change like that, and not being able to do anything about it. I am glad that your mother responded to you and now hopefully she will get back to being her old self again, to the person we loved and missed so much.'

Jesse walked up to Gordon and gave him a big hug and said 'it will be fine now.' Then she gave her grandmother a big hug and said 'I love you grandmother.'

'I am so sorry for what I said. I did not mean to hurt you, I just wanted my Mum back.'

Jean walked back into the lounge and Gordon leaned over and said 'I love you Jean.' Then Jean's mother also came over and said 'I love you, my daughter. I am truly glad to have you back.'

No one could believe what has happened. You could not explain this to anyone without them looking at you with disbelief and yet it was all true that this did happen.

CHAPTER ELEVEN

A Normal Man

Jesse hugged her mother and said 'I will never leave you. I will always come and see you Dad and Nanna. I am sorry I said what I said, that was because I was angry. Please do not worry, it will never happen. And please concentrate on getting better, I want my old mother back again, the one that laughs and is talking all the time. That's the one I miss, so please bring her back.

Jesse's mother looked at her and said 'I will get back to the old me, now I know that I have got my family around me.'

As Jesse got into the car, James asked how everything went as she was gone a couple of hours. 'I am so very proud of you, Jesse, as I know whatever you did would not be easy, I know how much you love your mother.'

On the way home Jesse was thinking that maybe she should go back to live with her mother as she could not bear this happening again. Another breakdown could be worse. Jesse was thinking how she could break this news to James.

All good things must come to an end for the both of them, Jesse had hoped no matter how painful it would be that James would see that they had to part and Jesse had to go back to Leamington Spa to live. To make sure that her mother recovered and returned to her old self.

Jesse phoned her mother's doctor and told him what had happened over the weekend, and the results of the shock treatment and how she had reacted to it. The doctor said it was good news and a very hard thing to do as it could have gone the other way. Jesse said she had to do something and that was all she could think of. The doctor promised to visit her mother later that day.

Jesse knew that she would have to talk to James about what she was going to do and knew this conversation would be the hardest thing. She was very happy with her life with James and loved by him. She had a good job they had a good life together. Now their lives must come to an end as she could not allow what had happened to her mother to happen again. She felt it was all her fault, that she had caused the breakdown as her grandmother and Gordon had said.

The one person in life that she loved so much and could not be without was her mother, and Jesse had repaid that love by making her have a breakdown. Jesse felt more worthless than she had ever felt before and it was hurting her beyond belief. And now she would be hurting someone else she loved and wanted to spend her life with and have a family of her own with.

She had told her friend at work what had happened and how she had to break up with James. Sam could hardly take a breath with such news, she just gave Jesse a big hug and said she would help with whatever. Jesse said it was not what she wanted, she was looking forward to getting married one day and starting a family with him.

When the bus reached her stop, she took a deep breath and walked to the flat. She started to feel sick inside and had to stop and take a deep breath before she could put the key in the front door and walk up the stairs to the lounge. Her legs felt like they were stuck to the ground and did not want to move, they just felt like lead. When Jesse reached the top of the stairs she could hear James singing in the kitchen. She felt so bad knowing that she would now break his heart.

James was cooking a meal for both of them as he did every night. He asked what was wrong as she looked worried. Jesse broke down and cried, she felt like hell on earth, she was hurting so much inside she just could not say anything to James.

James gave Jesse a big hug and said 'whatever it is, we will get through it together. There is nothing in this world we cannot get through together.' All Jesse could do was cry even more as this life that they had would now come to an end. She just said 'James I have something I need to tell you.'

They both sat down looking at one another. Jesse began to tell James of her decision and what she was going to have to do; the conversation lasted for two and half hours. It was a hard and painful conversation and at the end James said 'Jesse, I love you so much, I will be here for you always, no matter what happens. But I need to go out now to think about this and take it all in.'

Jesse called Sam and began to cry. She could hardly say anything over the phone. Sam said she would be round with her in ten minutes. Jesse hung up and sat down with her head in her hands crying, her face red, tears running freely.

The pain and hurt were now pouring out of her, and every emotion she had ever felt, whether she wanted it or not. She could not stop, no matter how she tried to compose herself, the pain was all too much to keep in any longer. In a way this was a good thing as it was not good to keep building up feelings inside.

Sam arrived and Jesse ran down the stairs to let her in. She hugged Sam and began to cry some more. Jesse told Sam everything.

Sam suggested they went for a drink, Jesse agreed so they both went out and sat with a bottle of wine. Jesse began to talk of the next stage. They agreed Jesse would have to leave James and would stay with Sam until she could arrange to move back to her mother's house. It was a heart breaking decision to make, but the right one no matter how hurtful.

Jesse went back to the flat and waited for James to return. She heard footsteps on the stairs and became cold with worry. He looked at Jesse with his eyes red where he had been crying. They both talked about what would happen next and how they both felt about the whole situation. Both agreed it was for the best, they went to bed and held each other until they went to sleep.

The next morning James got up first as normal leaving Jesse asleep. When Jesse woke up she felt so alone as she knew that this was how it would be without James in her life.

Jesse set off to work, her heart filled with tears and pain, for now she was single and so unhappy, there was nothing to smile about.

When Jesse arrived at work she saw Sam on another counter in the department store, they agreed to meet at break time and talk about what had happened when James came home.

Sam told Jesse she could stay with her until she was sorted out. When Jesse arrived home she told James that she would be staying at Sam's until she worked her notice and had arranged to move back home to Leamington.

She arranged a lift back to her mother's house where she was dropped off as she wanted to go in alone to see her mother and say she was coming home for good.

The week before, Jesse and James had visited her mother, even though they were not together. They agreed it would be better if they acted as if they were. This was difficult for them both, but she had to do it. If she had explained they had broken up, Jesse was worried her mother might become ill again. If Jesse was not there it would hurt her so much. This is the real reason why she and James had to part and both had to start again living separate lives.

The last week at work was very sad for Jesse, as she loved working at Owen Owen. She worked in the camera department where they sold watches and cameras. Her friend Sam worked on another department, but this week Sam was not working as she and her boyfriend were away on holiday.

She had packed her things though there was not much, only a suitcase and her record player that had been given to her by Gordon and her mother for her thirteenth birthday. That was all she had to show for her life as a women now 20 years old.

As the car pulled up outside her mother's house Jesse got out and carrying her case and record player walked up the path to the front door. She took a deep breath, knocked and waited.

Her mother opened the door and was amazed and delighted to hear Jesse was coming home for good. Her mother gave Jesse a big hug and a kiss.

Jesse told the rest of her family she had moved home for good. That it was her decision to give up her relationship with James and to give up her job and to be with her mother. Her grandmother said 'I suppose that you will want your old room back then.' Jesse said no, she would sleep in the small bedroom.

Gordon asked what she was going to do for money as he and Jean could not afford to pay for her keep. Jesse said she would go out and find a job. She just wanted to be with her Mum.

Jean said she was very welcome, it was her home. Jean took the case and went to find bed linen and towels. Jesse followed her up the stairs.

As Jesse unpacked her suitcase and looked out of the window she felt relieved that she was back home with her mother. But at the same time she felt very sad and low about leaving James, her life had been filled with everything that she had wanted, a job and friends. Back in Leamington she did not know where any of her old friends were, they could be married and moved away, Jesse did not know and was feeling alone.

Jesse went out every day looking for work. It did not matter what job as long as she got one, so she could pay her way and not rely on her family to support and feed her.

On the Friday afternoon, she received in the post a job offer as sales assistant in a D.I.Y store in Warwick. She told her mother and that she would ring them and accept. Jean was pleased for Jesse and so, too, were Gordon and her grandmother.

As the months went by, everything in the house was calm, there was a good feeling. Jesse worked hard and her mother seemed to get more and more like her old self again. Everyone was getting on with each other, the relationship between Jesse and her mother was closer than ever. They would talk about the latest record in the charts, the new range of make-up, and the clothes that Jesse had bought that week. They seemed like not just mother and daughter but the best of friends. They would laugh and talk together about everything, just the two of them in Jesse's bedroom.

One day Jesse was walking home from work when she saw a friend she had not seen since she left home. Jesse called out to her and they stopped and talked. Janet said Jesse should visit her, she was still living at home with her dad and brother, her sister had married and moved away.

Jesse went round the same evening and met another friend of Janet's called Jackie.

Janet asked about Jesse's mother as she knew she had not been well. Jesse explained all that had gone on and how she had decided to give up everything and move back home for her mother's sake. She told them how she had felt about everything. Both Janet and Jackie were saddened by the news and said they would both be there for Jesse.

In the next weeks Jackie and Jesse became close friends. Jackie would go round to Jesse's house and they would be in Jesse's bedroom talking and playing records.

Jesse's family liked Jackie very much and Jackie's family liked Jesse very much too. The two families became close as both families lived in the same area, so for once Jesse felt happy at home in her new life and now with a close friend, she was now settled down with the idea that this from now on would be her life, even though she still was hurt by leaving her old life behind, but she knew that this time it would be better as she was with her mother and every day her mother was more like her old self.

Jackie and Jesse went out together at weekends, even though Jackie was only 16 years old. They both seemed be on the same track and liked a lot of things, like music, fashion, makeup and hair styles. They had so much in common, they were like sisters.

When it was Jackie's seventeenth birthday, Jesse bought her a record that was in the top ten charts called 'Seventeen, not yet a woman.' When she took the present round, Jackie played it on her record player in the lounge. The rest of the family came in and together they all started to sing the song to Jackie, over and over again.

It was a good birthday for Jackie, she enjoyed every minute of it, and so did Jesse. She was made to feel like part of Jackie's family and not just Jackie's best friend. When it was Jesse's 21st birthday her mother and Gordon gave her a card with a big silver key on saying happy 21st birthday with some money in the card so that Jesse could go out and spend on whatever she wanted. She and Jackie went into town the next Saturday.

It was a sunny day as it was July. They looked around the shops and Jesse bought some clothes and makeup. When they returned home to Jesse's house they went up to her bedroom and looked at what she had bought earlier.

They both decided to go out to celebrate her birthday. The night was a very good one, Jesse had so much fun with Jackie. They went to a bar where there was a dance floor so they had a drink and danced the night away, there was so much good music in the eighties. With the shoulder pads in their clothes and feathers in their hair they felt like super stars.

When Jackie came around to Jesse's she looked so beautiful and when Jesse came down stairs they both went into the lounge to say good bye. Jean said 'you both look so beautiful.' Gordon responded 'Jackie looks lovely, but you, Jesse, what are you wearing?' Jesse's grandmother added 'What do look like? Your dress is too short, you are showing your arms as well as your legs.' Gordon stated 'You look like a hooker.'

Jesse replied it was the eighties not the thirties, things had changed in the world and when people go out they wore things like they had on. It did not mean anything other than they had good taste.

Jackie stood in shock, she had never been in this situation before as her family would comment on how lovely she looked, never belittling her and making her feel bad. Jackie could see that Jesse was hurt.

Jesse just laughed it off and they went on their way to have a good night. They came back home around 2am and Jesse said to Jackie good night see you tomorrow. Then she walked to her house, opened the front door and went up the stairs so quietly not to wake up the rest of the family.

The next day Jesse woke up at 10.30am. It was Sunday morning and her mother and grandmother had gone to church, as they did every Sunday, leaving Gordon at home. He would get up in his own time and then go to his allotment. He grew all his own fruit and vegetables, and flowers. He loved the peace and quiet that he had while he was there and he loved growing everything. He would bring home all the vegetables to go with the fresh meat from the butcher. Nothing was in packets or frozen, all food was always cooked fresh, this would be the norm for Jesse and her family.

When Jean and Lillian returned, Jean asked about the night out. Jesse told her what they did and how much fun that both had and what time she got home, and her head did hurt a bit but not too much. Jean laughed and then went back downstairs to start preparing lunch.

Lillian said 'Young girls should not be going out on their own at night, it is wrong. They should stay at home with their families and look for the right man who is single and from a good family.'

Jean replied 'I know what you mean, but this is the eighties and things have changed since I was a young girl. Jesse is a good girl' Lillian said 'I do not want Jesse to end up like you, a single parent and not marrying the father. I just want her to be like your brother and sisters. They have all married and then had children. This is what I want for Jesse.'

Jean said 'I know Mum, but you have to let Jesse live her own life and hope that she makes the right decisions. She will not get pregnant as she is on the pill. The pill only came out in 1960s and wasn't about for me. And, as you know, I did not know anything about sex at her age. Not like they do now. It is different nowadays. They know more about sex than I ever did. They were taught this at school, things like sex and periods and child birth. In my day you never told us about sex or anything like that, we had to find out ourselves.'

Lillian said 'In my day you never talked about that. When I got married we were both virgins. That was the way it was then. We would never be allowed out on our own, and to talk to a boy without someone there was not heard of. Things might have changed in the world, but not for the better in my opinion.'

Both Jesse and Jackie had boyfriends, but nothing serious. Jesse had told Jackie she would never marry until she was 25years old, before that she was too young. She wanted to live life and have some fun while she could as getting married meant she could not go out, have fun with her friends, and come home late. Once married she would have children and in order to do that she had to grow up and forget being single and having no responsibility out of her own.

When Jesse reached 22, she told Jean, Gordon and Lillian that she was going to have driving lessons again. She had failed her test when 17. Lillian said she did not know why she wanted to drive as she did not have a car.

Gordon responded 'I told you last time that you would fail. I failed three times before I passed. Women should not drive. Your own mother does not, she has no need to as I do all the driving in this house.'

Jesse never told them when she took her test. She passed and was told she was a good driver.

When she told the family they were amazed. Her mother said 'well done, Jesse. I am so proud of you. I could never do that. Now you will have to save up for a car.'

Gordon said there was no chance of her driving his car.

Jesse walked round to Jackie's house to tell her the news and because she felt so uncomfortable being at home.

Jackie's house was always full of fun and laughter. They would all talk about anything and everything, there were no secrets. Unlike at home where Gordon never knew that Jean had two other daughters and that she had no choice but to give them up. Jean had never told Gordon for the fear of him being disgusted and leaving her. She could not risk losing him as she loved him very much, and she knew that he loved her too. So the family secret would remain with her and her mother and Jesse, it would be theirs to keep until the day they would die.

At Jesse's house there were times of laughter such as when the rest of the family came to see their grandmother at Christmas or birthdays. It could be a house of love and laughter. For all of them it was a happy family. You would never know this was not how things were normally, you would think this was how things were all the time, all talking about what had gone on in the family and how they were, and how the grandchildren were and what they were doing.

But once the family had gone it would return to how it always was at home. They would eat together, then Jesse would go up to her room to watch her own television or play her records. She found it easier that way. Whatever Jesse said would be wrong. Jean would be in the middle of it all to keep the peace. So she spent most of the time in her bedroom, she even had her own telephone there. Gordon had said they did not need a phone since there was one down the street.

Jackie had said to her parents that the way that Jesse lived upstairs in her bedroom was strange. She did not spend any time with her mother, Gordon and her grandmother in the lounge. Her room looked more like a bedsit and not like a bedroom. Everything in there she had paid for, even the wall paper.

It was strange the way that Jesse was living at home but that was the way it was. She could only talk to her mother and then not in front of Gordon or her grandmother. Jesse told her mother everything, whether it be about work or boyfriends.

Jesse never brought any of her boyfriend's home after what had happened to James. She used to meet them down the road from where she lived. All the family knew was that she had boyfriends.

It was the opposite for Jackie. She always took her boyfriends home to meet her family. Jesse loved the way that Jackie's family treated their daughter and herself. They treated her like she was part of their family. It made Jesse feel good inside and very much loved. Not judged in anyway, all far different to her own family.

All Jesse's aunties and uncle had got married and had children. None of them were divorced, they were all happily married, unlike her mother who had been divorced and had children out of wedlock. Not the way of doing things for Jean's family way, this was looked down upon. Now Jesse was doing what she wanted, just like her mother, she too was looked on as the black sheep. There would be no respect for her, unlike the rest of the grandchildren who were born to married parents and grew up knowing their fathers.

There were good times when the family visited, but after they had gone it would go back to normal where Jesse would help her mother do the house work along with her grandmother. There was not much laughter going on but they were happy and there were very little disagreements in the house.

They were close and showed how much they meant to each other in their own way.

One day Jesse's phone rang. It was a man called Bryan whom Jesse had met when she was living in Coventry. He worked in the bank Jesse used to pay in her wages. He knew all about Jesse's situation and before she moved back home Bryan had given her his telephone number to keep in contact.

Bryan asked if Jesse was alright and if she would like to go out for a drink. Jesse agreed so they arranged a date. Jesse then went to Jackie's house and told her the news. Jackie's family were happy and asked if he could be her next boyfriend.

They would meet up for a drink every three and then two and then every week. They became very close friends. He introduced Jesse to motor bikes and they went to Le Mans in France to see the 24 hour race and then later in the relationship they would to go the Isle of Man TT. Jesse loved it.

Bryan had yet to meet Jesse's family and had to pick her up in another road. He knew why this was but thought it a bit strange.

After a year together, Jesse moved in with Bryan. Before doing so, Jesse told her mother about Bryan and asked if he could come around to meet her family. Jean said that would be nice and arranged with Bryan to come round.

Gordon and Lillian were not too happy about this because of James. They both asked many questions and Jesse told them that Bryan was ten years older than herself, was divorced and had no children. This did not go down well with both Gordon and Lillian as they both hoped for a younger man for Jesse who had not been married before.

Jesse was now 23 years old and had been seeing Bryan for a year before they decided to live together. Jesse knew it would be hard for her leave her family home, but she knew that her mother was fully recovered from her mental breakdown, and was back to her old self again. She was worried about how Gordon and her grandmother would feel about her moving in with yet another man, this time one older than her and also divorced.

Jackie had meet Bryan many times and found him fun to be with. He was good to Jesse and that was all that Jackie was interested in.

Jesse was very worried how her family would feel about meeting Bryan for the first time. She was not looking forward to this because of what had happened before with James. Jesse prayed about this and so too did her mother that everything would be alright and they would accept Bryan and welcome him into the family.

But there was nothing to worry about. Gordon and Lillian both liked Bryan and got on very well and at last for Jesse she had a man that her family were pleased with as he worked in a bank, had his own home and car and was not into music like James. He would come home at night and not go out to clubs or studios late at night or at the weekend. He was, as Gordon said, a 'normal man' and Lillian agreed. He was a family man who helped his sister look after their father since their mother had died.

After Jesse moved in with Bryan she found an office job close to where they were living as part of a sales team. She dealt by phone with customers' orders and wholesalers and loved it. Jesse was so happy with her life.

A year later, Jesse and Bryan went to a wedding. When they were getting changed for the evening reception Bryan asked Jesse to marry him. He got down on one knee and proposed to her. Jesse was overwhelmed, and with tears in her eyes she said 'yes I will marry you Bryan.' They went back to the reception, this time as an engaged couple, but without a ring.

The next day Jesse told her mother they were engaged and went off to Coventry to buy the ring. Everyone was happy with the news.

The wedding was at Warwick Registry Office with Jean, Gordon and Lillian, some others from Jesse's family, Jackie and her mother, Bryan's father, his sister and husband and some of Bryan's friends. It was a fine, sunny day and after the reception they went to Spain for their honeymoon. Two weeks later they both returned back to work as normal but this time Jesse was married.

A year passed, Bryan had now been promoted to a bank manager in Nuneaton, a market town in north Warwickshire, some nine miles from Coventry. They decided to put their house in Warwick on the market to save the daily travel.

In the middle of all this, Jesse found out she was pregnant. It was such a surprise to her as there was so much going on she just thought that because she had missed a period and it was down to stress. She found out by going to the doctors. She phoned Bryan immediately, he too was surprised but very happy.

They both went to Jesse's mother and told her the news, Jean was so very happy that she was going to be a grandmother and so was Gordon. Lillian was delighted because she would become a great grandmother. She was also happy because Jesse was married to the father of her unborn child.

When Jesse was three months pregnant, she had a bleed and the doctors told her to have bedrest for ten days. She had to give up work because she was very poorly but then after ten days she was fine and continued being well. While Bryan was away for work she told him she had sold the house for the full asking price, he was very pleased and said as soon as he was back home they would go to Nuneaton and look at houses.

They found a new three bedroom detached house in Nuneaton. Bryan had done well for himself in the bank and they could afford to live in this house without worrying too much about the mortgage.

The baby was due on the 2nd of December, Gordon's birthday was on the 3rd so both Jean and Gordon were wondering whether the baby would come on time or would it arrive on Gordon's birthday.

Then Jesse began to have her nightmares back again. She would wake up and look around the bedroom and then go back to sleep. Once she had looked around the bedroom and found that she was safe, she realised it was only a nightmare and could go back to sleep again. She hoped and prayed the baby would be a boy as Jesse thought at least being a boy he would not go through what she had done as a child.

Jesse had a difficult pregnancy. She was told that she was a small build and her hips were small too, she could therefore have trouble giving birth due to her frame. The day came when they moved out of Warwick to their new house in Nuneaton to start their new lives. All was very exciting.

When Jesse registered at the new doctors they asked if she was expecting twins, because of her size. The doctor booked her in for a scan as he thought she might be carrying twins. This confirmed that she was only having one baby though she was carrying either a lot of water or a big baby. Jesse went from being seven and half stone to eleven stone and six pounds. They never told her the sex of the baby nor gave her an ultrasound picture of the baby as in those days it was not available. So Jesse and Bryan just had to wait to see the baby when it was born.

But Jesse still had nightmares that a man was chasing her and grabbed hold of her. Then she would wake up. She never ever told Bryan of her past and what had happened to her as a child as she was ashamed of it. So too was her mother. Neither of them told anyone, apart from Jesse's grandmother who knew somethings but not of Jesse's past with Dominic, that was never spoken about.

On the 1st December 1985, Jesse decided to put up the decorations ready for Christmas. Her baby was due the next day. She decided to get everything ready before her baby was due. Bryan's father was staying with them and Jesse's mother and grandmother and Gordon were coming over for Christmas so at least if the baby had come early everything would be ready for all of them.

On the 4th December at 2.30am Jesse woke up with pains in her back and went to the bathroom where she was sick. At 7.30am her waters broke and Bryan and his father took her to hospital in Nuneaton.

After seventeen and a half hours of labour, Jesse and her baby were getting tired and the baby was suffering from foetal distress. Jesse was too weak to deliver and was rushed to the theatre for an emergency caesarean. Bryan had been with her all this time but was sent out to wait. Then he had to sign a form to save the life of either his wife or his baby. He chose his wife and signed the form.

The baby was delivered safely, a boy, at 6.59pm on the 4th of December. But for Jesse it was a different matter. Her heart had stopped and she had a dream of what was happening. She explained this later to the surgeon, telling him she had seen him and others running, one of them pushing down on her chest. She was telling them to stop but they made her jump by then putting leads onto her body to start her heart again. She told him that she could see and hear everything but they could not hear her.

With that, the surgeon looked at Jesse with disbelief. What she had told him was what had happened. The surgeon told her she had had a baby boy. Then he took a deep breath and told the truth that she had died in theatre. He had never come across someone who had an experience like hers, it was called an out of the body experience. Jesse thanked him sincerely for bringing her back to life.

Jesse laid back and went to sleep until the next morning when a nurse came to see how she was. She gave Jesse a colour picture of her little boy who was in the baby ward. She said he was 7lb 2oz and doing just fine.

Jesse did not see her baby until the third day, when she was well enough to go with Bryan in a wheelchair. Bryan had already seen his son. When Jesse saw him for the first time in his cot she could not lift him due to the operation. But she was thrilled to see her son as he slept peacefully.

Jesse said that she liked the name Liam, so that was what he was named. But Jesse was feeling so low in herself she did not share it with anyone. She stayed in the hospital for eight days before coming home with Liam. That was a lovely feeling, being able to sleep in her own bed and not to be woken up by other babies crying in the night.

The first night home she had dreams of what happened to her in hospital. Everything was so clear she awoke suddenly and looked around the bedroom. Once she knew where she was she went back to sleep again until morning.

Jesse became very clingy to Liam and did not like anyone touching or holding him. She wanted to protect him from everyone except Bryan, her mother and Jackie. She worried if Liam would live, unlike her baby sister Michelle who died at the age of 6 weeks. This played heavily on her mind, and on her mother's, though neither of them said anything to each other about their feelings.

Jean stayed with Jesse and Bryan for two weeks to help out. It was lovely for Jesse and her mother to spend time together with Liam, alone in the day time. Jean was so happy to help out with Liam and she did everything for Jesse to get as much rest as she could to build her strength back up again.

After Jean returned home to Leamington, Jesse was now home alone with Liam. Bryan worked hard at helping with the feeds and changing Liam, as well as working at the Bank during the day. But Jesse still had her bump and felt so low, as well as tired. She sometimes would cry and play her records for comfort as to her it felt like no one could see or feel how she was feeling inside, only her music could do that.

She never told anyone how she felt, as the people she knew that had babies were all fine and did not have to go through what Jesse was going through. They had all had natural births and their weight dropped off and returned to normal within weeks. Unlike Jesse. Even her health visitor said nothing helpful to Jesse, just that Liam was doing very well and she was pleased with his progress. That she would not need to come back.

Over the next few weeks, Jesse felt even worse. She felt like she was screaming out loud inside but no one could hear her voice crying out for help. She just carried on like normal. She tried some light-weight exercise following the Green Goddess. She worked at this every day to try and get back into shape, though it was hard and very tiring. Within eight weeks she had lost all the excess weight and returned back to seven and a half stone. This gave her a good feeling but now she just wanted her feelings to change and not feel so very low inside.

CHAPTER TWELVE

Sinking in the Quicksand

Liam was now 6 months old. Jesse had got back to her normal weight and was happy to get back into her old clothes again. She was still not feeling any better inside so she went to her doctor. He said that she would get better as she was suffering from the baby blues.

But Jesse was not getting any better, she still had nightmares. She was pleased she had a boy, not a girl, but feelings of her past kept coming back. She felt so alone, with pain inside her. She became withdrawn whilst everyone around her, including Bryan, were happy with their lives. Not Jesse, she felt alone with her baby Liam, who needed her.

Jesse felt so depressed at having such a low mood. She could not let Bryan and her family down by telling them that she was not coping and needed help with how she was feeling. She just carried on, pretending she was also happy with life. Yet she was screaming inside with the feeling she was not good enough, that she had failed, she could not even give birth like everyone else she knew. She had failed and this played on her mind. Once again, like her grandmother and Gordon used to say, she was not good enough. That if she wanted to do anything, she would fail, so do not bother.

All of Jesse's past came back to her. Being a new mother and having to deal with that was very hard. She did whatever she could to make everyone happy and for herself she found that her music was the only thing that helped her deal with everything in life.

Even though her mother and family, and her best friend Jackie and her family came to see her in her home in Nuneaton,

175

it did not make any difference. She just felt alone inside. She had never told Bryan of her past life, what she and her mother had gone through. Bryan's family life was so very different to hers. He had grown up with his parents and younger sister in a loving family.

To put this to him would be very hard for him to deal with. He would not understand how people could do this to someone they were supposed to love. So she chose to keep this secret to herself and pretend to have a normal upbringing, like everyone else she knew.

But the closeness that Jesse and Bryan had before had gone. Maybe it was because they were now parents. Was it all about Liam? She could see others who had children were closer than before. It seemed to complete the family package. But not for Jesse and Bryan, they were drifting apart and going back to being just close friends.

Jesse had told Bryan that things were not right, and he said he would buy her a car so she could see her mother whenever she wanted. Jesse agreed maybe that was the answer. For a short while she started to feel better, knowing she could go out of Nuneaton.

Her mother was the only one that Jesse could not hide her feelings from. One day she asked her if she was happy with her life. After a long pause, Jesse said 'I am, but at the same time I do not know why, Mum.' With that she broke down and cried. For the first time in 18 months, Jesse told her mother everything about how she was feeling, from the day Liam was born, about her dying on the operating table, what she had seen and what the surgeon had told her. She told her everything. Then there was silence for a couple of minutes whilst her mother came to terms with this.

Jean held Jesse tightly in her arms and said she would always be there for her and Liam, no matter what happened. And how lucky Liam was to have her as his mother.

This was hard for Jean as she had lost Michelle at only 6 weeks old, when Jesse was ten. The memory of that came back to Jean and she too cried, so together they cried in each other's arms, while Liam was asleep, unaware of what was going.

Liam was safe and happy in his own world and sleeping soundly. He looked so lovely in his carry cot, not aware of the outside world and the pain that his mother was in. No, it was a different world for babies, all they cared about was being fed and changed and being given a cuddle.

Then Jesse said she must being going, before Liam woke up. She picked him up and told her mother that she would come back later in the week. She also said she would be fine and not to worry.

'Thanks for listening, Mum. I do love you.'

Jesse played her favourite music as she drove home, thinking about the conversation with her mother. Then they were back home in Nuneaton and Jesse was pulling up on the drive, she looked back at Liam and smiled.

Bryan returned from work and Jesse told him she had been to see her mother. She never told him about the conversation she had with her mother and how she was really feeling because she did not want him to worry him. Bryan had a very hard job to do and sometimes he would bring some work home, so she knew she had to keep her feelings to herself and hope that they would change and the bad dreams would come to an end.

There was no reason for her to feel like this, she was in a good marriage and there were no money worries as Bryan took care of all the bills. Jesse's job was to look after Liam, the house and Bryan. The rest Bryan looked after. Everything was good in their lives and everyone was happy, except for Jesse. She was in hell, living with her nightmares and her feelings of being so low and worthless. But somehow she had to keep it from everyone else and carry on like everything in her world was perfect.

Jesse kept this up for eighteen months. Liam had been christened, and had three Godparents, one of which was her best friend Jackie. But deep inside Jesse had reached the point of no return. She could no longer pretend she was happy with her life with Bryan, so much so that she knew she had to do something.

Jesse spoke to her mother about how things were with Bryan, that they had drifted apart and she was not feeling like his wife but his friend. She wanted more than a friend, she wanted her husband back again. Jesse asked if she and Liam could come back to live at her mother's again, until she could sort out a place of her own. Her mother agreed but felt it was sad that their marriage should end. And that Jesse felt a complete failure, she had let down Bryan who was a good man and a good father to Liam. She had failed them all.

This made Jesse feel even worse inside. She would often cry when on her own, but never in sight of anyone, not even Bryan. She just tried her hardest to deal with the feelings that she had inside, and to make sure that Bryan and Liam were happy. The only one that she did not hide from was her mother. Jean knew just how low and unhappy Jesse was and how withdrawn she had become.

Jean knew that Jesse should try and talk to Bryan and see if anything could change. Bryan could not see how she could feel how she did. He said he thought buying a car would make things alright. Jesse explained they were drifting apart and she needed her husband back. That they were back to being like friends, but she needed more than that. Then she said that she and Liam were going to live at her mother's, and that he could see Liam every weekend.

The conversation went on for a while and everything that Jesse had been feeling came out. Bryan looked shocked at what

Jesse was saying. He had thought she was happy and even said so to her. But Jesse then said 'I tried so hard to make these feelings go away. I did not want to fail you and the rest of the family. But I could not make them go away. And there was no help from doctors or anyone else. It was left up to me to deal with this and carry on with life. If I stay with you any longer I would have to change my feelings for you, Bryan, and then we would start to argue in front of Liam. That is not what I want. I want to remain good friends with you. But to lead separate lives.' Bryan could then find his true love.

It was very sad, but they both agreed it was for the best. Bryan would keep the house and have Liam at weekends and holidays.

Jesse moved back to her mother's and found it very hard. She knew her grandmother and Gordon would not be happy and would tell her how they were feeling.

Lillian said 'In my day, there was no such thing as being married and then leaving the marriage. You just stuck together no matter what. Once you were married you were married for life. Until one of you died, like your grandfather. You do not split up the family. You are so very weak. Like your mother, she is weak. But at least you got married first and then had a child. Your son knows his father and will always see him.'

Gordon however said the opposite. He said that Liam should have stayed with his father like he did when his parents went their separate ways. Bryan was a good father and had a good job, so Liam would be better off with him and not Jesse. She had nothing to give Liam but love.

Jean was on Jesse's side and said that she would rather Jesse and Liam live with them and not in some bedsit like she had done when she had met Gordon.

With that the room went quiet, no one said a thing.

Jesse and her mother went into the kitchen. 'Don't worry about what they say,' said Jean, 'I am pleased that you both are here and I will help you all that I can.' Then she gave Jesse a big hug.

Jesse had put up Liam's cot in her old room that her grandmother used to use when she was living at her mother's house and Jesse used the other bedroom so all three bedrooms were now in use.

The day came when Jesse had to get Liam's things ready to take to his father for the weekend. It was hard for both Jesse and Bryan. Gordon, Jean and Lillian welcomed Bryan as they always did, there was no hard feeling towards him, just sadness that things had not worked out.

Gordon was not happy that Liam was now living with Jesse. He had only lived with his mother from birth to six months, then she returned him to live with his father and grandmother. His mother left his life forever.

So now Gordon was feeling very jealous that Liam was with his mother and would see his father, whilst both his parents would live their own lives, not together but they would always be in Liam's life. This hurt Gordon very much, seeing how much Jesse loved Liam and watched her playing with him and giving him all the love that any mother should do to their child. It made Gordon feel like it was his fault, for he was a boy and his mother had not wanted a boy.

Gordon told Jean his feelings and she in turn told Jesse. He could not play with Liam or even hold him, it hurt him so much, though he would never show it to anyone.

Jean and Jesse were in the bedroom changing Liam. Jesse asked 'Does Gordon love me or does he just tolerate me because of you?' Jean replied 'He does love you very much, and so does your grandmother. They just do not show it like we do. They will not say 'I love you' and give big hugs like I do.' Jean then went on to explain that when she was a child, Lillian did not give her hugs or tell her that she loved her. That was just her way and she did not mean any harm.

Jesse returned to the lounge and gave her grandmother a big hug and said 'I love you, Nanny' and then walked up to Gordon and gave him a big hug and said 'I love you, Dad.'

Then Jesse went to find Jean in the kitchen with Liam and told her what she had just done. Jean looked at her and said 'You are such a lovely young lady. One day I hope you will find true love again, and this time it will last forever. Like I have now found with my Gordon, though it took some time and a lot heart ache along the way. But I have found my true love at last.'

'And we will be together until one of us dies. In Gordon I have found a true, good, loyal and loving man. We have never felt this way about anyone else. He is my soul mate and I am his.'

Liam began to change. He became fractious and shy and wanted to cling to Jesse. The health visitor came to see Jesse and Liam because of her change of address and noticed Liam's distress. She told Jesse she would have to talk things over with Bryan. She asked how he had taken the change of circumstances. This left Jesse again feeling she had failed both Bryan and now Liam. She felt totally useless as a mother and a wife, she was no good to anyone. Jesse shared everything about the health visitor meeting with her mother.

Jean put her arms round Jesse to console her, telling her that whatever she decided, she would be there to support her. She also told her it would be hard for her, but whatever she did needed to be for Liam's sake, not hers or anybody else.

This reminded Jean of what she had gone through with Jesse's two sisters, the pain and hurt. How she still thought of them on their birthdays and Christmas. Every day that had gone by, Jean had never forgotten them and never would until the day she died. She would always remember her two little girls that she had to give up and would never see again.

And now Jesse was about to do the same thing. But this time her son would not leave the family, he would live with his father and Jesse would see him at weekends and holidays. Jean knew how hard it would be for Jesse, but at least Liam would grow up knowing his parents and the rest of the family.

Even though this was the nineteen eighties, Jean knew some people would not be nice to Jesse for doing this, that she may come across some abuse, but at least she could say she did this for her son and his father. She would not let anyone take Liam from her and put him to live with another family he did not know and never see his own parents and family.

Jesse met up with Bryan and told him what had happened, and what was suggested. They both agreed that Liam would stay with Bryan for a week to see what was upsetting Liam. Whether it was leaving the place he knew and having to go to his Nanny's.

For a week Jesse went over each night to give Liam his bath and put him to bed. Liam returned to being his happy self, not being shy and clinging to Jesse when anyone came. He did not get upset when only his father was there.

The following week both Bryan and Jesse agreed that it was for the best for Liam to go back and live with Bryan and his father. Jesse packed up all Liam's belongings and left for Bryan's house. It appeared that Liam was unhappy moving away from the home he knew and living in Leamington.

When Jesse returned back to Leamington, she went upstairs to Liam's room and noticed she had left Liam's soft toy that he had slept with every night since he was born. She knew he could not sleep without it, so she grabbed the toy and drove as fast as she could back to Bryan's house, as it was nearly Liam's bath and bed time.

Jesse pulled up on the drive and knocked on the front door. Bryan opened it and Jesse told him why she had come. He thanked her and said she could put Liam to bed. Jesse went upstairs to where Liam was playing and showed him his soft toy. Liam looked up and smiled with his arms open wide. She picked him up and said she would put him to bed. With that Liam was fine and happy. She kissed him on his head and said 'Goodnight. I love you, Liam.' Then she put out the bedroom light and went downstairs.

As Jesse was driving back to Leamington Spa she drove faster than ever, with the tears running down her face. The music she chose was a Pink Floyd track called Comfortably Numb and this was just how she felt inside. She could not feel anything, she was drained. She could not stop the tears even if she had wanted to, they just kept coming. All she knew was that she failed her son and her family, in fact everyone. She was a failure.

She did not notice anything on the road, just her sense of failure. Nothing else mattered, whether she lived or died. She did not care anymore, she was filled with numbness inside, just like the song.

Another record was by David Bowie, called Quicksand. The words were also how she felt, lack of faith in herself and feeling down and low.

When Jesse arrived back, Gordon asked if she was going to get a job now she did not have Liam to look after. Jesse replied she was. Jean gave Jesse a hug and said that everything would be alright, she should not worry as she has done the right thing for Liam. She was proud of her for doing such a hard thing.

Gordon said he was glad Liam was living with his father. He had been brought up by his father and he turned out well. He did not miss his mother one tiny bit. Then Jesse's grandmother said she was not proud of Jesse, and in fact she was ashamed of her. 'You are not my granddaughter, how could you do this to your own child? In my day, this would never happen. The child stays with its mother, not its father. That this is so very wrong.' And she never forgave her.

This hurt Jesse. But she never showed it in front of her grandmother as crying in public was a sign of weakness. She had learned this from her grandmother at a very early age. She did not cry, even though she wanted to let out the pain and anger that was building up inside her.

Jean stood up 'That is very wrong of both of you to say such things. Can't you see how Jesse is right now? She has just lost her child and I know just how she feels.' Jean and Jesse walked into the kitchen and broke down, crying in each other's arms. The pain they felt about losing Liam, even though Jesse would see her son. And Jean's pain, she had lost three girls and would never see them again.

Jesse found a job to apply for, she knew she needed one to help provide for Liam. She was asked to go for an interview.

The next day a letter came for Jesse from the health visitor saying she had now amended the details and it was on record that Liam was no longer living with Jesse, that he was now living with his father where Liam was born. She wished Jesse all the best for the future.

This letter was a relief for Jesse, knowing that Liam was fine and there would be no more involvement from the health visitor. They now could all get on with their lives.

The next day was the interview. She got up early, made herself very smart in a suit, with hair carefully done and make-up on, she looked the part. In the interview she told them what she had done in her working life and why she was now living in Leamington. She also told them about Liam and that she could not work on the weekends.

The lady that interviewed Jesse was also a mother, she was very understanding about the situation. On Friday morning there was a letter for Jesse from the agency. Her mother took it to Jesse's bedroom. She opened it and read it out loud. It said Jesse had been successful and they wanted to her to start the following Monday morning.

They both jumped around in Jesse's bedroom, hugging each other, with big smiles on their faces. What a great day for both of them.

Later, the whole family was eating dinner. Gordon said 'Your mother told me you have a job. I am very pleased for you. Now you can start to pay for board and lodge. And you can buy your own things as well as those for Liam.'

After dinner, Jesse went to see Jackie to tell her about the news. The two of them were happy and arranged to go out that night to celebrate.

They had a good night out and were both looking forward to the weekend when Liam would stay with Jesse. Jackie would spend time with them as Liam's Godmother. She loved him very much and was so glad he was still in the family and had not been taken away.

Things were different at Jesse's home. She would have tea with Jean and Gordon, then spend her time in her bedroom. She had paid for it to be painted, bought her own TV and installed her own phone.

Jackie found this very strange. In her family, they all sat and ate together then only went to their bedrooms to sleep. But Jesse was a loner. Her family would only be together at the weekend when Liam came.

After three months, Jesse's contract finished. Then she accepted a temporary position with Flavel, a long established maker of cookers and catering equipment, who were also in Leamington. The job was full time as personal assistant to the factory manager, who was responsible for the running of the factory and all the personnel employed there. She loved the position.

On a Friday, she would finish the same time as Gordon. He also worked in a factory but at Lockheed, another big employer in Leamington who made brake systems for the automotive industry. He worked as a tool setter and had been on the same machine since he was 16 years old.

He would pick Jesse up around midday and they would go to his local pub to have a drink and wait for Jean. She helped make lunch for the pensioners at the local church, St Paul's, where Jesse and her mother went every Sunday. Jean loved doing this. She arrived at the pub at 2.30pm after she had cleared the kitchen.

This was the only time that Jesse spent on her own with Gordon. He introduced her as his daughter. When Jean came in everyone knew that she was his wife and they all sat down and had a drink together as a family.

Then on Saturday it would be again family time with Liam and Jackie. They were such good times for all of them, even though in the week it was so different.

Four months later, Jesse decided to seek a divorce, to let Bryan and herself live their separate lives. Then, if either of them found the love they wanted, they could get married and start a new life.

The divorce took four months from start to finish, including both having parental rights over Liam, and each having a say over his schooling, They both agreed on all the issues with no arguments, including the house. They remained friends.

Jesse did not attend court for her divorce, she just could not bear the fact that she had failed Bryan and Liam. On that day, after work she went home and told her mother that she was now a single mother. She told her how she felt inside about the whole situation, then she decided she wanted to be on her own and stayed in her bedroom playing records that showed her anger and pain. It was ACDC and Black Sabbath, Iron Maiden, Phil Collins, Pink Floyd, David Bowie, all of which shared how Jesse was feeling inside. This allowed her to get out the feelings and she just cried her eyes out. She sat there alone drinking a bottle of wine.

While Jesse was in her bedroom, she was just filled with the memories of her past. All of it came back to her like it was yesterday. The things that happened to her when she was a child from the age of eight upwards to the present day. She felt so low and hurt, she just wanted to die, and wished she had died when Liam was born, and had not come back from the dead. She felt Liam and Bryan would be better off if she was dead as they would not have had to go through what they had gone through.

Bryan would have met someone else and Liam would have a mummy that was better than his birth mummy. Jesse just felt that she had failed everyone in her family and the fact that her grandmother, who she loved so much, and had so many good times with, spending with her at the weekends when she was younger, had told her that she was no longer a granddaughter of hers, for letting Liam go and live with his father and not stay with her. Jesse knew that her grandmother was different in her ways and that the child never ever stayed with his father, that was not the way.

And Gordon was glad that Liam was now living with his father. Just like Gordon had done as a baby, he had lived with his father. He told Jesse that, as he said that she would not be able to give the life Liam needed, like his own father. That she was not good enough for Liam like his father was.

The only person who was on her side, apart from Jackie, was her mother, who loved and supported her, and stuck up for her every time. She felt so alone and prayed to God, asking why she had not died and was still alive. She thought it was better for all if she was dead. Everyone would get over it and have a better life without her.

The next day, Jesse woke up still feeling the same. She knew she had to carry on with life and she had to not show how she was feeling. She did not want her mother to be upset. Though she had told her how she felt deep down inside. Jesse put on a smile and hid her feelings deep inside so no one could see how see really was feeling. She pretended she was fine and acted like it.

When she came back from work, Jesse told her mother she felt like she had failed everyone. That she was not a good mother. Jean said 'You are a good person. Look how you are with me. Every Mother's Day you always give me flowers. You help out with the cleaning and shopping. You do everything that you can. Please do not say things like that.'

Jean went on to say 'You made sure that Liam will grow up knowing his parents and knowing his family. You didn't let him grow up not knowing his parents and family. I know that it is hard for you now but at least you and the rest of us will see Liam. You have done the most unselfish thing anyone could ever do in their life. I am so very proud of you and love you so much, more than words can say.'

Jean gave Jesse a big hug. Jesse said 'I love you so much too. I do not know what I would do without you, Mum. You are always there on my side, no matter what I do.' She thanked her then went upstairs to her bedroom. She felt a lot better for the talk to her mother, knowing that at least her mother was on her side, even if the rest of the world was not. Then she started to play Michael Jackson, and sat down to listen to the words. Then she put on Simply Red and listened to that. Then her mother came upstairs and knocked on the bedroom door and said to that tea was ready.

So Jesse turned off the music and went downstairs, where Gordon was already sitting at the table. He never said a word to Jesse. She sat down and her mother came in with their dinner.

Jean asked how Jesse's day had been. She replied she had been very busy day but she loved it. The staff on the factory floor were now starting to treat her like they treated one of their own and not like a white collar management person, but like one of them. This does not happen normally as there are two types of workers- the management, who are the white collar and the factory workers (the blue collars) and neither of them mix. Yet this time they were with Jesse, but not with her manager.

Gordon said 'You are lucky. As you know, I am only a factory worker. We do not mix with the white collar people. They look down at us. You are very lucky that the factory workers accept you as one of them and not white collar management who would look down at them. How is it that they are like that with you then?' Jesse replied that she said hello in the morning and asked if there is anything that they need help with. 'I treat them the same way that I wanted to be treated and that is all that I do.'

Gordon explained that in his factory things were different. There was no one like Jesse, so the factory workers kept themselves to themselves and so did the management.

Gordon was quite surprised at how Jesse was received at her place of work, and wished that it was like that where he was and how nice it would be if everyone was like that.

The days went on and turned into weeks and then months and everything in the house was fine and Jesse still stayed up in her bedroom and her mother and Gordon still stayed in the lounge and everyone was happy with this arrangement and Jackie who when she came to see Jesse always went straight upstairs to Jesse's bedroom and not downstairs to say hello to Gordon, but this was the way that it was at Jesse's house.

CHAPTER THIRTEEN

Wish you were here

It was now 1989 and Jesse had met someone called Alan, whom she thought was a good man. They had known each other for a year before they got a mortgage for a one bedroom house in a nice area of Kenilworth, a small town between Leamington and Coventry, well known for its castle.

Jesse was now working full time at a solicitors practice, as personal assistant to one of the partners. Alan was a self-employed driving instructor. They were happy in their lives and decided to get married. Gordon did not like Alan and refused to go the wedding but Jean went and was happy for Jesse because she was very joyful.

When Jesse went to see her mother, Alan did not go, he did his own thing at the weekends when Jesse stayed at her Mother's to have Liam, before going back to Alan on Sunday when Liam had gone home with his father. Jesse was only away on Saturday night.

The marriage only lasted six months as Jesse found out that not only had Alan cheated on her, but he had a bad temper on him. This ended up with Jesse being hit and raped by him. Jesse told her mother and she then moved back home. She made arrangements to collect her belongings, but when she arrived with a friend, she found a 'for sale' sign in the front garden. She rang the estate agent to get in the house and he arrived with the keys. She told him she did not know anything about this, and he told her the house was being repossessed by the building society. She went in to find a black bin liner in the middle of the lounge, when she looked in it she found what was left of her clothes which were all burnt, the rest of the house was empty.

She was very upset by this. How could he have done this to her, after all that he had done to her while were together. To find this was like a kick in the teeth. How evil he really was, and how glad she was that she went back home and did not stay with a man who would hit a woman and cheat on her.

Jesse returned home and told her mother and Gordon what she had found at the house. Her mother was so angry about his behaviour to her. Gordon said he had never liked him, there was something strange about him, which was why he did not go to the wedding or have anything to do with him.

'You should have listened to me when I said do not marry him, he was no good. There was something odd, I don't know what, but I did not trust him. But you had to have it your way as usual, so serves you right for not listening to me.'

'Now I suppose you want to move back to live here again.'

Jean said 'Of course she will move back here to live and get her life back.'

Jesse arranged to see her boss, one of the partners in the practice. She was very nervous for this time it was her personal matters. He was very caring towards her and said he would arrange for her to see one of the other solicitors in another office, this would be better for her.

This was the worst year ever for Jesse. Now she was going through a divorce and had lost her home as well. It was back to the start again. This was the second time she had to go through a divorce, but this time it was not like before. The first time it was dealt with quickly and in a friendly way. There was no one else involved in the split up of the marriage. And she was never beaten up by Bryan like she had been with Alan.

Her mood was now very low. Jesse tried very hard not to show it, she gave the impression she was on top of everything and nothing was getting her down. She was fine and that was the part she played for everyone, even to her best friend Jackie and her family. But her mother did not buy this. She knew Jesse was not in a good place, no matter how hard she tried to convince her otherwise.

Jean told Jesse what she was thinking about and how concerned she was for her. Jesse said 'Mum, please do not worry about me. I am fine and I am dealing with everything. Soon things will go back to normal, and then I can start a new life again. I am like you and Nanna, so strong, so please do not worry.' She gave her mother a big hug and kissed her on her cheek and then went upstairs to her bedroom.

Her music was the only thing that she could relate to, as she felt that the music could always understand how she was feeling.

Things went from bad to worse. Gordon was not happy with what was going on in his house, with Jesse back home and going through yet another divorce, and her mother caring for her every need, sometimes spending more time upstairs with Jesse than with him. This took its toll, he felt left out. He already had to deal with his jealousy of the relationship between Jesse and Jean, which was very close. He could not understand why they were so very close, he had not known such a relationship, as he did not have any such relationship with his mother.

This caused him a great deal of being uncomfortable in their presence. It was hard to deal with him in turn as it caused him to get so jealous of Jesse. He then began to get to a point that he did not feel at home in his own house. For Jean it was also hard to deal with, trying to show her love for Gordon and her daughter at the same time. Trying to keep the peace between them both, when they would argue over something so simple and not even worth mentioning. But they both did. And then Jean's mother would show her disappointment over the whole thing, with Jesse now going through her second divorce. And saying that this never happened in her time, that Jesse was like her mother, the black sheep of the family. The rest of the family had all married and had children and were happy. How proud of them she was.

And how much shame both Jesse and her mother had brought on the family and how very upset she was about the whole situation that Jesse was now in, having a child that was not living with her but with his father. That was not acceptable.

Jesse stood up and said to her grandmother 'it was a hard thing for me to do. It was either Liam living with his father or with another family. Then we may not have been able to see him grow up. So I made my choice. No one knows but Mum and me how this has affected me deep inside. The only person here that has given me any support or even held me in their arms is Mum. Not you or Gordon.'

'You told me that I am no longer your granddaughter. How do you think I feel about that? Being called a black sheep. And my mother is. Well it hurts, as I love you. I am the oldest grandchild, the first born. How close we were once. Now you have put Richard as your favourite grandchild. Telling Mum and me how proud of him you are, when you come back from London. How proud you are of all of your grandchildren, except me.' Then Jesse turned to her mother and said 'sometimes I wish I had died when Liam was born. That way, you would all be much happier, without me around to remind you of what a great disappointment that I am to you all.'

Jean got up and said 'How could both of you be so cruel to her? She has done nothing wrong. She just had the wrong partners. Now she is paying for this. She is my daughter at the end of the day. I am so proud of her, and will support her in every way I can. Even if you both do not.' Jean walked out of lounge and went upstairs to find Jesse playing Pink Floyd 'What do you want from me.'

Jean saw how upset Jesse was, sitting on her bed, her head in her hands, with tears running down her face. Jean sat down and gave her a big hug, saying 'I love you and I am always here for you Jesse.' Jesse hugged her mother so tight as if her life depended on it. Together they sat there saying nothing, just hugging each other. Then Jean began to cry in Jesse's arms.

Jesse asked 'Why have I caused so much pain for you all, and so much disappointment? I meant what I said about dying. I am right that Nanny and Gordon would not have to be embarrassed by me. And neither would the rest of the family. You all would be better off if I was dead. And I wish that I was.'

With that, Jean cried even more and said 'No Jesse, what about me? I could not live without you in my life. I have lost so much. Out of four daughters, I have only you left in my life. How could you think that I would be better off? No. I would not. I would be worse off, you were the one that shocked me out of the deep depression. It was you, not your grandmother or Gordon. It was you that I needed most of all to pull me through those bad times in my life. So I need you more than you will ever know.'

Jesse replied 'I am so sorry that I hurt you by saying that. I love you so much, more than words can say. Please forgive me, Mum. I love you so much. It feels like it is us against the world.' Jean then said 'Yes, it does, and I guess it will always be like that for us. We are the black sheep of the family and everyone else is so perfect, unlike us.'

Jesse responded 'Who wants to be perfect? I do not. I am glad that I am different and the black sheep, like you. We are different, and I am so proud to be like you. And I am proud of being the black sheep. At least there is no one else like us around, and we are not boring or ever will be.' With that, they both laughed and Jean said she was going downstairs to be with the normal boring people.

It was Sunday lunch time when they always had their meal together. But this time it was different because of what had been said earlier. The meal was eaten in silence. The looks on their faces said everything.

Next morning things seemed no different, and Jesse went off to work as usual.

There was a deep feeling of despair and pain within Jesse, but she did not show this at all at work. The workplace seemed to be a comfort zone for her. It kept her from thinking about her life and what was going on within it. The way things had changed in the house and the feeling that soon something would have to change. She did not know what that was. She could not afford to move out and get a place of her own as she did not have any money to put down as a deposit. She did worry that one day Gordon would get so fed up with her he might tell her to leave.

Things did not get any better for Jesse. Christmas season arrived with her still spending most of the time in her bedroom. She only saw Gordon when they all ate together, then she would quickly be back alone in her bedroom. Except when Jackie came.

Then they would be getting ready to go out or just listening to music, and chatting, but never about what Jesse was going through. She did not want her best friend to worry like her mother.

The arguments were getting more frequent, and the feeling of jealousy between Gordon and Jesse was getting worse. At lunch time on Christmas Eve 1990, they were sitting around the dinner table with Gordon at the head, Jesse's grandmother next to Gordon and Jean opposite Jesse. There was a bottle of Lanson champagne which Jesse had bought and a bottle of cheaper champagne bought by Gordon. Gordon and Lillian only had a small glass, they preferred their own drinks, a ginger beer for Lillian and a brandy for Gordon. Jean then would drink the rest of the champagne herself. Things were going well for a change.

Until they finished their pudding.

Then the conversation changed. Jean asked 'what is that drink like Jesse? Can I have a sip please?' Lillian queried how much it cost and Jesse said it was £15.00 a bottle. With that Gordon then said 'Oh, so the champagne we bought is not good enough for you then!' Jesse responded 'Of course it is. Why did you just say that? I bought it because I had already tried it before, that is all.'

Gordon already felt he was not good enough for Jesse or Jean. Now, with the champagne, that was all it took for a full blown row between them. Lillian tried to calm things down by saying 'it is Christmas Eve, and you should not be like this. It should be a happy time.' With that, Gordon stated 'This is my house and I will do whatever I want to do in it. No one is going to tell me what I can do in my own house. I pay all the bills.'

Jean responded 'There is no need to speak to my mother like that. And, there is no need to speak to my daughter like that either. What has gotten into you, Gordon?'

Gordon took another drink of his brandy and said 'I am just sick and tired of all of this. It is getting too much for me. I do not feel I belong here anymore.' Then he said to Jesse 'I want you out of my house now. I am sick of the sight of you in my house. You cause so much trouble. I cannot stand it anymore. Just get out of my house. Leave now, go upstairs, pack your bags and go.'

'No Jesse, you stay where you are' said Jean. Lillian intervened 'Gordon, you cannot throw out my granddaughter onto the streets on Christmas Eve. You are an evil man. Where will she go?' Gordon retorted 'She can sleep on the streets for all I care, so long as she is not in my sight.'

With that, Jesse got up from the table and went to her bedroom, leaving the rest of the family still arguing amongst themselves. She phoned a friend, told her what had happened and asked her if she could stay with her until she could sort herself out. Her friend said yes of course. Jesse immediately packed a bag, then her mother came into the bedroom and asked what she was doing. Jesse replied that she was getting out of Gordon's house because, since she had been back, things had not been right for a while.

There was a knock on the door. Jesse said 'That is my friend, she will being putting me up.' She took her bag and went down the stairs. Jean followed, Jesse turned to her and said 'I am so sorry for everything I have done. I did not mean to cause so much trouble for you, Mum. I love so very much.' Then she kissed her on the cheek and left.

Jean went back into the dining room, very angry with Gordon and what had just happened. She said 'I hope you are happy, now that you have just kicked out Jesse, your stepdaughter. She has gone to stay at her friend's house for Christmas, instead of being with her family.' There was no answer from Gordon, he just got up, walked into the lounge, sat down on his chair and began to watch the television, leaving Jean and her mother alone. Lillian said 'I do not believe what has just happened. One minute we are all fine and happy and then the next Gordon just changed into a monster. Why is he like that? I know it has been hard for him but it has been hard for all of us, especially for Jesse. She is the one who is going through it the worst of all.'

Jean replied 'I know she is, and I will never forgive Gordon for this. He has gone too far this time. It is Christmas, and not having Jesse here is not right. It is very painful for me as she is my only child. Not to have her here will feel like it is not Christmas, just another ordinary day at home. It will not be filled with happiness and joy opening presents together on Christmas Day.'

Christmas Day came and Jesse phoned her mother to say Happy Christmas and to tell her she loved her and hoped she liked the present she had bought for her, and to thank her for her Christmas present. Jesse explained her friend was not there and she was on her own watching television, and there was plenty of food and drink. They both said they missed and loved each other very much and then hung up.

Jean and Gordon went off to the local pub as they always did, but this time without Jesse. Normally they would then go back home and all sit down to have their Christmas lunch together, having fun pulling Christmas crackers, reading out the jokes, putting on the paper hats and having a good laugh. Then they would all go into the lounge and at 3.00pm Jean would stand up to salute the Queen whilst she was making her speech. Gordon would always say 'Oh woman, sit down.' And her mother would say 'Sit down, you are making a fool of yourself.'

Christmas was always a good time. In the afternoon, Jean would go with Jesse to Jackie's house where there was more fun. They would play games in the front room with the whole family while back at Jesse's home her grandmother and Gordon would be asleep in the lounge.

But this year there would be none of that. Jesse would be on her own and Jean would be without her daughter, having to stay at home with both Gordon and her mother just sitting in the lounge watching the television. Jean did not stand up at 3.00pm for the Queen's speech, she did not feel like it at all. She just sat in silence just like Gordon and her mother.

No one was happy. It was just like an ordinary day, not how Christmas should be. There was no laughter or smiles, just silence. And when the day was coming to an end it was the worst Christmas Jean had ever had, and it would have been for her mother too.

It was the worst time for Gordon to throw Jesse out and it ruined Christmas for the whole family. Gordon was the only one who seemed to enjoy his Christmas, as his wife, for the first time, at home with him and not off with Jesse to Jackie's house. This made him very happy indeed, and he said to both Jean and her mother he had the best Christmas ever.

This upset Jean and her mother very much, but they did not say anything to Gordon. They just sat in silence. Lillian went to bed leaving Jean and Gordon alone, sitting in silence, still watching the television.

Jean then went to bed, leaving Gordon downstairs on his own. When she started to put on her nightdress, she just broke down and cried, all she could think of was Jesse. And how Gordon had thought it was the best Christmas ever, without Jesse being there, she thought how cruel it was of him to say that.

Jean was so very hurt inside but she still cried alone as she had done so many times before never showing her weakness, as her mother would call it.

Meanwhile, Jesse too was feeling the same, and she too just cried on her own in her friend's house. It was the worst Christmas ever for her. She had never missed Christmas with her mother and her family. It hurt like hell for Jesse. Even though she had spoken to her mother, it was not the same as being there with her and her family.

Not only having to deal with this, she was also out of work as her contract had ended just before Christmas. She was not only homeless but unemployed at the same time.

Jesse wondered what 1991 would bring her, as the last year was the hardest and most painful one ever. She was looking forward to a brighter year to come.

Jean helped cook lunch for the over sixty's at St Paul's Church, Leamington and was aware they ran a women's refuge. They agreed to take Jesse and had a room available.

The age of the women was normally from 16 to 30 and Jesse was now 31.

Jesse took the offer up on New Year's Day, moving into her new life in a small room and shared kitchen and bathroom. She did not care, she was now free to start again.

Jesse was so happy, even though she was the oldest one there. Soon she had become the mother of the house and loved every minute of it. They all seemed to like Jesse and they would each in turn spend time with her in her room, talking about why they were living there. Each had a tale to tell, some very sad and painful. They all shared the same thing, they were all rejected by their families, for whatever reason. They all felt that for once they were not alone and felt safe. They could now start a new life on their own.

Jesse was there for six months and had her 32nd birthday there. Everyone made sure she had a good day, they got her a birthday cake. Even though no alcoholic drink was allowed, they still managed to bring some in to celebrate Jesse's birthday. They all brought Jesse presents. For her it was such a good birthday. Jesse had also seen her mother that day and received a present from her.

In September, the refuge arranged for the council and a housing association to visit and to see if they could help with getting some of the women rehoused. Jesse was put forward for a flat because she had Liam and he could not spend much time there with her. She was looking for somewhere to live, where she could have more time with Liam.

She was offered a one bedroom flat, only about ten minutes away from her mother. She took it as soon as she saw it, signed the paperwork and now had a long term tenancy meaning that providing the rent was paid she could stay there as long as she wanted.

Because she was not working she thought what do about the rent. She then had, for the first time in her life, to sign on to get benefit for herself. Then, to get the things needed for the flat, she filled out a form to get help with everything because could not do it on her own.

Since Jesse left home, things were much better with her mother and Gordon, and Jesse got on better with Gordon and her grandmother. In August 1991, the worst news that anyone could have was that Gordon was told he had lung cancer, and a secondary small brain tumour. The cancer had gone too far for them to treat. He was offered a place at the local hospice with full time care, but Gordon decided that as he was going to die, he would die at home with his family around him.

Jesse went to see him and her mother every day. The time Gordon and Jesse spent together was full of fun with a lot of talking, something they had never done before, about their feelings and what they meant to each other. Gordon gave his car to Jesse and insured it for her. He also told her that he was so jealous of the relationship that she had with her mother as he never knew that love, and said he was sorry for not being a good father to her.

Jesse replied 'No Dad, you are the best Dad in the world and I love you so much.' She then lent forward to him and both of them hugged each other and said to each other 'I love you.' It was so nice for Jean to see the two people that she loved so much now holding hands and talking together about their feelings, which they had never done before. This at last was a family getting on and acting like a real family. Jean was so happy, even though it took Gordon to become ill and on his death bed to show his true feeling for Jesse and to make up to each other.

So in September Gordon knew about the flat and also knew about Jesse's divorce which came through the day after she had signed for the flat. Everything was coming together for Jesse, and Gordon was there to see it happen. He was so happy for Jesse and told her so.

On Friday morning 10th of September at 9.30am the phone rang at the refuge where Jesse was still living. She was going to move the next Friday. She could hear her mother's voice in tears on the other end of the phone 'Your father is dying and he might not last the weekend.'

Jesse ran as fast as she could to be there for her mother and Gordon. When she arrived, the door was opened by the next door neighbour, Connie, who had known her family since they first moved in, about 35 years ago.

Jesse went into the lounge where her stepfather was on his bed, lying there with his eyes closed. She thought she was too late, but her mother said 'No, he is not gone yet.' The Macmillan nurses came every day to make sure Gordon was comfortable and give morphine injections to ease the pain. He could not tell anyone how he was as the morphine kept him in a coma.

Gordon could not open his eyes when anyone walked in the room or even when they held his hand. He could only communicate by holding hands tightly. He would hold them tight and let go if you wanted to go out of the room. On your return, he would hold your hand tight again.

Jesse, her mother, and Connie spent the weekend by Gordon's side, talking to him. On the Sunday, there was a knock on the door. It was Gordon's sister, who he had not seen since she was about 5years old. She was younger than he was. Somehow, Jean had managed to track her down and she came straight away to see her brother.

Jesse looked at her and could see how much they both looked alike. Jesse introduced her to Jean who gave her a big hug and said 'please sit beside your brother.' She sat down and held his hand saying 'I have missed you so much and I have often wondered what happened to you, and how you were. Our mother never ever talked about you or our father.'

She whispered 'Gordon I love you, and I am now here holding your hand. Can you hear me?' There was a tear running down Gordon's cheek and she said to Jean 'he is holding my hand so tight he can hear me.' Then she too started to cry.

Jesse and her mother sat by his bed holding his hands, going in turn to the kitchen to make drinks for all. They talked to Gordon, telling him the news and what was going on.

After tea time, Jesse had a headache, and took some painkillers. Connie returned and suggested she and Jean had a break. Jessie went for a lie down whilst Jean made a drink in the kitchen. Whilst they were both out of the lounge, Gordon passed away. Connie called out to Jean who rushed into the lounge. Then she ran upstairs and told Jesse and together they held each other.

They came downstairs to where Gordon was lying peacefully. They both sat down beside him, held his hands for the last time and cried. Connie phoned the doctor, then Jean phoned her sister in Coventry who came straight over.

The doctor signed the death certificate. Jean's sister, Mary, and her husband then arrived. Everyone was filled with sadness and many tears were shed. The last to arrive were the funeral directors to take Gordon to the place of rest.

Jesse was concerned for her mother, who had stayed in the lounge with Gordon. She opened the kitchen door to find her stepfather's body in a black plastic bag being carried out with her mother behind, crying her eyes out, saying 'I love you Gordon.' Then Jean closed the front door and walked back to the kitchen were her family were waiting for her.

They all gathered around Jean, held each other tight and cried together for the loss of Gordon. Afterwards, Jesse stayed with her mother overnight and in the morning they started to sort things out. From then onwards, Jesse was beside her mother, helping her as much as she could, sorting out Gordon's clothes, including what to wear when he was buried. It was very hard for both of them, even though Gordon and Jesse had not got on in the past. She had loved him very much, and at the end they both managed to clear the air and tell each other how they really felt about each other, how much they had loved each other but showed it in many different ways.

And Gordon went to his grave knowing how Jesse loved him.

The day for Gordon's funeral came. It was so hard for Jesse and her mother. This was the first time Jesse had been to a funeral. She could not even cry as she walked behind Gordon with her mother. She was holding a wreath from herself and a small wreath from Liam, both of red roses. She put them on top of the coffin and then sat down by her mother's side holding her hand.

In the next few days after Gordon's funeral, Jesse kept herself to herself, only seeing her mother, then going back home to her flat. She kept playing a special record, 'Wish You Were Here' by Pink Floyd. She missed Gordon so much, and the hurt of losing him was so great inside she could not face anyone.

For her, music was the only thing that seemed to understand how she really felt. She had always done this whether it be happy music or sad or angry music, it was the only way that she could express herself throughout her life.

The weeks turned into months after Gordon had died and things were getting back to normal. Jesse was now in full time work and could pay for things to help her mother out and to try and make her happy.

For Mother's Day, Jesse decided the kitchen was old so she arranged for a complete new one. Then she decorated it for her. And she bought flowers, and took her out for lunch, just to see her mother's face with a big smile.

Jesse was now the protector of her mother and if anything needed doing which she could not do, she sorted it out. Jesse would not let anyone in her mother's house without her being there, she would protect her at any cost. If her mother went out at night, Jesse made sure that she had a lift there and back with her friend or she would take her mother and bring her back again.

If her mother went on holiday to see her family in London, she would take her to catch the train and then pick her up again. She would tell her mother to ring her as soon as she got there to make sure that her mother was safe, so that Jesse could then relax. She could not wait for her mother to return home again.

Jesse's mother had settled down and life was returning to normal for both Jean and Jesse, even though they both missed Gordon very much. Jesse would take her mother to the graves of Gordon and Michelle and they would place flowers there and talk about how they both felt. One time, her mother said, after putting the flowers on Gordon's grave, 'if anything happened to me like it did with Gordon, please do not let me suffer like he did. Let me go in peace.' Jesse replied 'Oh Mum, please don't talk like that. I may go before you anyway.' But Jean insisted 'promise me, Jesse, you will not let me suffer.' 'OK, I promise I will not let anything happen to you, Mum, and you must promise me the same if anything happens to me. Please do the same thing.' Jean replied 'I promise I will.'

Once they had placed the flowers on the graves, Jesse drove her mother home and nothing else was said. It was as if they both needed to know that they would never suffer like Gordon had done. They both then had spent the time watching someone they loved suffer, and not being able to stop the suffering that Gordon had gone through. They both had watched him cough up phlegm and fight for breath, then go into a coma. The only thing they could do was hold his hand tight, right up to the day he died.

CHAPTER FOURTEEN

Stranger in This Town

Work was good for Jesse, and she had decorated her flat. Jackie came and stayed over when they went out. Things were also slowly getting better for Jean, her family and her mother came round frequently, but Jesse was always there for her.

Jesse had broken up from her boyfriend just after she lost Gordon. She met someone new the following May at a local pub where she was working. She had been taught how to pull pints, serve drinks and deal with the till. On one of her shifts, she met a lovely looking young man, who was with his work mates. They were American, all working for one of the American companies based in Leamington Spa.

They were not like the local men that Jesse had come across. They seemed much more polite. They treated women with more respect than some of the men that she had come across in her life.

At the end of the evening, he asked her if she would like to have an Indian meal with him. He was not drunk, in fact very much sober, he had only drunk two pints. Jesse knew by talking to him that she would be alright, and the Indian restaurant was just over the road from where she was working. She knew the owners as she had been there with Jackie many times before, so she knew that she would be safe.

Jesse and the young man, who was called Anthony, went for their meal. It was a lovely time for both of them, they got on like a house on fire. They laughed and talked and at the end Anthony said 'would you like me to take you home?' Jesse paused and then said 'Yes. That would be nice.' Anthony said he did not want anything else, just to make sure she got home alright. Jesse thought how nice this was, not what she was used to.

Anthony walked Jesse home and said goodnight. He asked if he could have her phone number and maybe they could go out again for a coffee. Jesse agreed, they said good night but there were no kisses, just words. For Jesse, this showed total respect for her, which she had never experienced before. She had always had a good night kiss from other men but they were all English and not American, maybe this was how they were.

Two days later, Anthony phoned and they arranged to see each other. Jesse was not expecting to hear from him, she thought he had changed his mind as he did not live in England.

The day came and she was so excited, looking forward to seeing him again. He seemed to listen more to what Jesse was saying, and took a deep interest in her. This was someone she knew she needed right now in her life, someone who took every word seriously and listened to her, not just heard what she had to say. This made her feel so good inside and she felt happy. She hoped they would be good for one another for as long as Anthony was in England. She knew at the end of it all he would go back home with some good memories which she would also treasure.

Jesse did not think for one minute they would ever become serious about each other. They just had fun being together. She was happy with that, and did not expect anything else. She needed it in her life as she was still going through nightmares that had again returned to haunt her and left her feeling alone, in pain and with heart ache. With Anthony she felt safe and in a good place.

They went out for a year and a half and got closer and closer. Then one day she met him in a car park, he sat in her car and kissed her cheek. He could see that Jesse was not alright, she was quiet and not herself.

Jesse still had very bad nightmares, they would come and go, but always remained with her. They would always be about her childhood, what had happened to her with Dominic, and how he had treated her. No one ever knew about this, not even her own mother. She kept it to herself. She felt she could not, as it was too painful to explain. She kept the hurt inside, the only sign of it would be she would go very quiet and sometimes she would sit in silence with her pain.

But Anthony knew that she was not herself. He knew that something was wrong and asked if she was not feeling too good. Jesse replied she was just in deep thought and he did not need to worry. She would be back to normal the next day.

Anthony said if there was anything upsetting her, she could trust him and tell him anything. It was not good to bottle things up, far better to share and get it off your chest. He went to his car and Jesse sat in hers watching him. She thought that was close, she must try harder to keep her feelings from showing, as she must not be weak. She did not know what could happen if she showed any weakness, he might harm her.

They drove to an Italian restaurant. Sitting at the table chatting, Jesse seemed to relax and Anthony also was relaxed after a long day working as a draughtsman. It was a good job and he loved it very much. He did this at home in Michigan, U.S.A. where he had a house.

Jesse was thinking how good Anthony was at listening to her. He then asked again if she was alright as she seemed to be more relaxed. She sat there again in silence and as much as she tried to hide her feelings deep inside, this was not working for her. Anthony seemed to see straight through her, not convinced that there was nothing wrong. In the end he asked 'Have you ever been abused in any way?'

He asked because he had had a breakdown in his own life. He could see she was hiding something which was hurting. He told her he too had demons that he had to deal with, and told her what had happened to him. Though he was not abused as a child, he had gone through hell and back. Through therapy, he had dealt with his demons and he was now in a better place. He could now get on with his own life and not be troubled with the demons of the past.

Jesse sat there with a blank expression on her face as she could not believe anyone else had suffered like herself. He too had gone through hell and back. She went through something different to him and she did not know if she could tell him, as she had never even told her own mother. She knew it would hurt her, and she did not want to put Anthony out of her life by being damaged goods.

Anthony then asked 'have you?' And before he could carry on, Jesse said very quickly 'Yes. Alright I have, at eight years old.' She went on and told him what had happened to her and by whom. Then she said nothing else, just sat there, her head down, she looked like she was holding her head in shame.

Anthony took a deep breath. He held Jesse's hand and told her he would never hurt her, he would look after her. He said she was so very strong to deal with this on her own, carrying all the pain inside. And protecting her mother, whatever the cost. He then said 'what a loving woman you really are. You always think of others. You should never feel that you are worthless, because that is one thing you are not.'

After this very deep conversation, they realised they had more in common than anyone they had gone out with before, which made them closer. They felt comfortable with knowing what each other had gone through in life. Though it was tough to deal with, they had done it all the same and shared everything. For once, Jesse felt not alone with her demons, she could be heard and not judged. She was comforted by someone who knew what had hurt her, and never judged her or tried to change the subject, as some people would have done, when it was too painful to deal with.

At last they both felt at ease with each other. The relationship grew stronger. There was deep meaning and understanding between them.

It was not long before Anthony had to return to the U.S.A, his contract was only for two years and they had been together for 18 months. Before he left, Anthony said to Jesse that he would like her to come over and to see him and to meet his family, as he had met her mother and Liam. She said she would love to, as soon as she could, but in the mean time they could talk on the phone.

When Jesse was alone in her flat she would often play Stranger in This Town by Richie Sambora as this was how she felt. She had bought the CD in 1991 after her stepfather had died. It was so fitting for her feelings then, alone with her demons. They came out to haunt her with nightmares almost every night. They would appear to her in one form or another, they just did not want to stop.

Now the one person who knew about her demons had returned home to the States. At least she had now shared her demons with someone who did not judge her, but was hurt by it, gave her the understanding that she needed and allowed her to be herself. Instead of having to put on the clown's mask, showing only the smile on her face and telling everyone that she was fine, when she was far from it.

The only way she could be herself was on her own. Then she could take off the mask and show her real self, with the tears of a clown running down her face, and playing music like One Light Burning and Mr. Bluesman by Richie Sambora. The music seemed to share Jesse's feelings. The artist seemed to understand her so much, it was like they were there together in the room and she was no longer alone.

In March 1993 Jesse had a phone call from Anthony saying that he had posted a letter to her. It contained a surprise for Valentine's Day but he had not been able to send it for the right day. When she returned later, there was the letter. She opened it and to her surprise it was not only a letter but also tickets for a trip to the U.S.A. It explained they would meet up in Orlando and stay there for a week, then fly to Detroit and drive to Michigan, where Anthony and his family lived.

The tickets were booked for three weeks time, so Jesse jumped up and down with joy at the thought of seeing Anthony again. It had been a while since he had left. They had never lived together, as he had his own flat whilst he was in Leamington. They spent every night together and at weekends, seeing her at her mother's house and spending time with her son Liam. Even though he had never married or had children, he adored Liam and Jesse's mother. They all got on so well as a family. They talked about maybe one day they too would get married and start a family of their own.

The day before Jesse was due to fly, she was so excited she hardly slept a wink. In the morning, she woke at 4.30am and checked five times that she had everything ready. Then it was time to go.

The journey was long, but once she arrived at Orlando airport she knew that Anthony would be waiting for her. Then she saw him, looking at her and smiling. She ran up to him, leaving her case behind, and hugged him very tight. Then he got her case and they walked to the car he had hired for the week, before driving to the hotel where they would be staying.

The next day, after breakfast, they drove around and saw lots of sights and shops, and had a good fun day together. In the evening, they had a meal in the hotel and then an early night. Jesse was very tired after her journey and a long day; she just wanted to relax together with him.

The whole week was good. They both enjoyed being with each. It felt they had been together for twenty years but in reality it was only two.

Then it was time to fly to Detroit and the two hour drive to where Anthony and his family lived. When they landed, Anthony said 'I have another surprise for you.' When they walked out of the airport, there was a white limousine with a driver in his suit waiting for them.

The driver opened the car door and both got in. The driver put their suitcases in the boot then drove them to Anthony's house in Michigan.

It was a large house with three bedrooms, a garden in front, a garage and room to park four cars. It was lovely inside with two bathrooms. Jesse felt so at home there, with Anthony she did not feel uncomfortable in anyway.

Anthony introduced Jesse to his family and friends. They all welcomed Jesse into their homes and their lives, they were all happy to meet the woman who had changed Anthony and made him very happy and no longer feeling alone, just working hard.

In the middle of the week they went out to an expensive Italian restaurant. On his mother's side they were Italians, though she was born in the U.S.A. His father's family were all Americans. The restaurant was big and very Italian. To Jesse it was very romantic.

They sat at a table set for two, with a candle already lit. The lighting was low and they talked over the meal about everything, including their feelings towards each other, instead of over the phone as they had done so many times before.

Then Anthony got up from the table and went down on one knee. He said to Jesse 'you know how much I love you and your family, and how much you mean to me. How alone I feel when you are not beside me. It would give me the greatest pleasure if you would marry me. Will you be my wife and spend the rest of your life with me? Will you let us start our own family?' Then he kissed her hand and looked up at her.

Jesse's face was full of a beaming smile, her eyes were filled with tears of joy. She said 'Yes. I will marry you.'

Anthony got up and leant over Jesse, then gave her a big hug. They just looked at each other and together they both said 'I love you so much.'

The next day, Anthony phoned his mother and arranged to visit that evening for dinner. Both Jesse and Anthony were so excited to give the news to his family. It was received with joy and lots of hugs and kisses. The whole family was so delighted. They all celebrated together as one big happy family.

Suddenly the holiday was coming to an end. Jesse was going home the next morning. She was now wearing the ring she and Anthony had chosen. They talked all day. Then it was time to go back to Anthony's house. They both felt so down and were filled with sadness. Jesse had said many times that she always felt at home with him and everything felt so natural, nothing was hard work at all.

The last evening was filled with the two of them talking and crying together at the thought of Jesse leaving. It felt so wrong to do this. It was not a natural thing to do. They both felt like she was leaving for good. They both felt hurt by her leaving, but knew she had to go back. She was not leaving him, but it just felt like that.

Saturday morning arrived with Jesse and Anthony getting up early, for Jesse had to catch a flight from Detroit to Orlando and then to Heathrow. He drove her to the airport, there was no conversation, just silence. They were both hurting deep down inside at the thought of them being apart once again.

After Jesse had checked in, they hugged each other so tight, as if their lives depended on it. They watched other passengers go through to get on the plane, then it was just Jesse left. 'I am sorry, but you are the last passenger we are waiting for' said the check-in lady. Anthony said 'you have to go now,' and Jesse replied 'I do not want to leave you.' Then they both looked at each other and said their goodbyes. Jesse walked off to the plane looking back at Anthony until she lost sight of him.

At Orlando, Jesse went onto the flight that would take her back to England. Her mood was low and filled with sadness at leaving Anthony. She spent the next nine hours thinking about the good times she had spent with him and his family and how happy they both were.

She arrived home very tired, and felt so alone inside, as though she had lost Anthony and would never see him again. She thought 'no, of course I will see him again. I am engaged to him and soon will be his wife. I will live over there in Michigan.' Then she thought about Liam and her mother, and how that would all work. Liam was still living with his father and she could not then see him every weekend. And what about her mother? She could not leave them behind.

This worried Jesse a great deal. The next day, she went to see her mother who was very happy for her and Anthony. Jean asked if Anthony would return to England.

'I am sure that will be the way. We could go and see his family when we have the money to travel. Liam is only nine years old and I would never ever leave him, or you. I need you both and you both need me. This will never happen, so please do not worry, Mum.'

Over the next few months Anthony tried everything he could to find work in England. But there was no way he could. He would also need to apply for a work permit again and this would not be easy as he had only recently returned to the USA. His employer had no other work in England. He was not a resident of the UK so he would have to leave after six months. He did not have a permanent job in England which would allow him to get married and then apply for residency.

After six months of trying hard to make things work, the only thing left was for Jesse to move to the States and get married there. This would mean seeing Liam once or twice a year. Her mother could go to live with Jesse. This was not an option for Jesse, and Anthony knew that.

So when Anthony phoned, she talked about what she was feeling and how hard it was for her to say things would not work out. They talked about her mother and Liam. She said she was sorry but thought it would be best if he found someone in the States who could give him what she was unable to do. 'For you are the best man I ever could have wished for in my life. You have given me something that I had always wanted but never had, and that was your emotions in both words and showing them. You are the only one who knows me deep down inside. I can be myself with that. I thank you and love you. It hurts me very much that I have to let you go and search for another woman to take my place. To be loved by you and not me anymore. This will hurt me forever. I know you will be the only one that will ever know me fully. Know and understand what I have been through and how it has affected me.'

Then they said their goodbyes and hung up.

It took some time for Jesse to get over her feelings for Anthony. She knew that she would never meet anyone else like him, someone who was so in tune with his emotions and feelings. Unlike English men.

Anthony never phoned Jesse again after they had parted. They both went their separate ways in life. Jesse just kept working and looking after her mother and doing whatever was needed.

Then in 1997 Jesse's grandmother died aged 95. This was a hard time for both Jean and Jesse. Once again, they were losing someone they loved so much. For Jean, it was her own mother. She had lost her father when she was only eight years old, fifty-four years ago. She had seen how that had affected her mother, and now she too felt the same pain, losing someone so close. This hurt Jean very much indeed. And for Jesse, this too hurt, as they were once very close.

On the day of the funeral, Jesse was sad. She did her best to comfort her mother. All the family came, from London and other areas. The family carried in the coffin. Afterwards they all met up and had something to eat and drink, then they went their separate ways, leaving Jean and Jesse to go back to Jean's house.

Jesse had moved from her flat to a two bedroomed house, still in Leamington, not far from her mother. The house had a small back garden for her rescue dog called Maxwell, who had been mistreated. He was half Alsatian and half Labrador and so loving towards Jesse, and very protective towards her.

Jesse felt it was a shame that her grandmother didn't see her new house or meet Maxwell as she would have loved both, and been pleased that now she had somewhere for Liam to come and stay.

Liam was now thirteen. He was very happy that his mother had her own house, and so was his father who would pick him up from Jesse's house. Jean would have lunch with her and Liam, it was so good at last.

1997 was a difficult time for Jean and Jesse. When it came to Christmas, Jesse suggested having Christmas at her house and Jean agreed. They spent the first Christmas in Jesse's new house together. Liam came on the day before Christmas Eve and opened his presents, everyone was happy. On Christmas Day, Jesse phoned Liam who was with his father at his father's sister's house, as that was what they used to do since they had gone their separate ways.

In 1998, she met a man who used the same bar where she worked. It was about six months before they got together as they knew the same people. They soon became close and one day Bob asked her to marry him. Jesse said yes as he was a nice man with a good job, and they got on well. They had both been married before. Jesse was told by Bob that she would be his second wife. He knew he would be Jesse's third husband

and that she had a son called Liam. He also had a son, older than Liam, called Mark.

In December 1998, they got married at Warwick Registry Office, where Jesse had been married twice before, and, like before, she hoped this time it would be for good.

But that was not the case. It only took six months to find out he was not all he had seemed. When Jesse met the rest of his family, she found he had a daughter and an older son who did not have much to do with their father. One night, when they were out with his family, a woman came up to Jesse with Bob's daughter who said 'this is my mother who is my father's second wife.' Jesse stood there with disbelief on her face, and said 'he told me I was his second wife' and the woman said 'no, you are his third wife. And now you have found out he is a liar. Like I did. So please be careful.'

Bob could see Jesse was talking to his second wife and came over to her, saying 'Now you have met my other wife.' Jesse straight away replied 'yes, I have. And why did you tell me that I was your second wife?' Bob responded 'I thought that I had. Never mind, you have met her now. I think it is time we went, as we have both got work in the morning.'

On the way home, Jesse was so angry she could not speak to Bob at all. She just sat in silence.

After that Bob changed and became more loving towards Jesse, as he was not about to lose her 'over one small thing' as he put it. Jesse told him 'no more lies. I will not stand for anymore. If you lie again, that will be it for us.' Bob agreed that he would never lie again to her.

After a while things looked good for them. Both had jobs and their children got on, though they did not see much of the older ones. One day they went to Honiley Dogs Trust and Jesse fell in love with a nine month old puppy called Toby, a cross between a Rottweiler and a beagle. Jesse had a chance to take

217

him out for a walk with Maxwell around the grounds and they both got on well.

The next week Jesse and Bob with Maxwell picked up Toby and went back home. Everyone got on well, the two dogs were so close as if they had been together from birth. Jean looked after Maxwell and Toby when they were both at work, she loved the idea and took them out for walks.

One day Jesse came home from her work in Coventry on contract as a personal assistant for the Law Society. She loved it very much. Bob worked in an office Leamington. When Jesse came home, Bob said to her 'I need to tell you something. Let's go out for a drink.' He told her he had lost his job by being made redundant because they were making cut backs. As he was the last one to be employed he was the first person to be let go.

This was a shock to Jesse, she told him they would manage. He said he would start looking for another job, no matter what it was, even if it was through an agency, he would do it.

Jesse started to notice a change in Bob. He would have a drink every day, and his behaviour towards Jesse was becoming bad.

Bob would throw things and shout at her. He even threw a crystal vase at the garden wall knowing that it would smash into small pieces. It had been given to her by a girlfriend for her birthday.

Jesse was worried for herself and the dogs. She took the dogs and put them in the car. Bob came out screaming at her. When she started to drive off, he kicked the passenger door. She drove with the dogs to where she knew they would safe. She did not care what he did in the house, she could replace things there, but she could not replace her two dogs.

Jesse drove to a pub where she knew some friends would be. She told them what had happened. One of them had a look at her car and said she must go to the police station and report him. Jesse did that and they went to the house and arrested Bob. Jesse could then go home. He stayed at the police station for the night. The next day, she took the two dogs to her mother's and left for work. She was hurt and upset at what she was going through. She did not know what he would be like when she got home, so she decided to leave Maxwell and Toby at her mother's while she went home.

Bob was not there when Jess arrived. He returned much later. He was drunk and not in a good mood after what Jesse had done to him the night before. He thought she would never do that to him and told her as much. Then he started to break things in the kitchen. He hit her and she ran out of the house and drove to her mother's. She told her what had happened and then said she would not have that situation, being afraid to go home. She thought he could end up killing her.

Jesse stayed at her mother's house and the next day she took a day off work, saying she was ill. She changed the locks on all the doors to her house, then went to a solicitor where she used to work to start divorce proceedings. When Bob came home he could not get into the house. Jesse told him what she had done and he should leave her alone or she would get the police out again.

Bob left and Jesse relaxed, knowing he would not be living there. She was invited the next day to a birthday party at the local social club. It was a family Bob knew, but it had been arranged for several months that he would not go because he was looking after his son that day.

Her friends knew the situation between her and Bob so they were not expecting him to show up, so everyone could enjoy themselves at the birthday party.

Around 9.30pm, a woman came in saying a man had driven into the parked cars. A few of the party guests went out and saw what was going on. Some tried to stop him from doing any more damage. The driver was in fact Bob. He was drunk, and had driven his car from seeing his son. He just drove his car at the others in the car park. He broke up the happy times that people were having. He had seen Jesse dancing and having fun and that got him annoyed. He had a bottle of drink in the car and drank it, getting madder and madder until he decided to drive into the parked cars to spoil everyone's night.

Then he drove off, leaving complete devastation in his wake. People were looking at their wrecked cars. Once they knew who had done this, they started on Jesse, saying how were they going to get home? Look at what your husband has done. And what sort of man is he.

The police were called and Jesse had to say who the driver was. Bob was arrested again, taken to the police station and charged with drink driving and damage to other cars while they were parked.

Again Jesse had to go through hell with this man, who seemed to have a drink problem. Even though she knew he liked a drink, she never saw anything to tell her he might have a problem, otherwise she would not have married him in the first place.

Soon after that, Bob returned to Jesse's house at night. This time, Jesse was out with some friends. Her dogs were at her mother's house.

A phone call came for her on the pub's land line. It was the paramedics saying her husband had taken come pills and he looked very poorly indeed. He wanted her to come home. He would not go in the ambulance. Jesse had told them this was what he had done to her before, then he had not taken anything. It was to get her attention. She told them they were not together anymore and he did not live there.

The paramedics were then aware of the situation. Bob then told them he had phoned someone else and Jesse did not need to come home, it was just to let her know. Jesse hung up knowing that Bob was just trying again to ruin her night out. She carried on and told her friends what the situation was.

The next day Jesse heard from her solicitor that the divorce was going ahead, and as Jesse had not put Bob's name on the tenancy he had no right over the property, or anything in it. He told her Bob had asked for half of the dinner plates and cutlery, and Toby. He said that he had paid for him and not Jesse, so Toby was his. With this, Jesse supplied the receipt for Toby that she had paid by cheque.

Bob ended up in a mental hospital, he had problems with drink and anger management. There he could get the help he needed. After there, he found somewhere to live and started a new life on his own. And so could Jesse. In 2000 she was divorced from Bob.

Jesse found out that while she was with Bob he had been sacked from his job through turning up drunk at work. She thought about the bottles of drink that she had found after he had moved out of the house, and why he did not put the bottles in the bin.

One day Jesse mentioned this to a friend who told her he was a secret alcoholic. She had heard he had done this before and treated his other wives the same way. They too were fooled by his lies. She was not the only one to go through this and she was better off without him in her life. Jesse agreed and was glad she got out quietly, unlike the other wives who had it much worse.

It was now 2003 and things had returned to normal. She was on her own and still working hard. She only went out with her friends. At weekends, she would have her mother and Liam, and Jackie would come down on Sundays to have lunch. Things were looking good again, after all that she had been through, she was happy being on her own.

One day she saw a man called Ryan in the local pub. She had said hello to him many times and he knew what had happened to her. Jesse was standing at the bar waiting to be served, Ryan came to order a drink and they both started talking and having a laugh.

Ryan was also divorced, and had three children, one son and two daughters. His son aged thirteen was still at school, and one of his daughters lived with their mother. Things between Ryan and his ex-wife were fine, and he worked full time. He was not a drinker or a wife beater, like Jesse's ex-husband.

He seemed to be a good man. He played pool and was in a local team. He invited Jesse to see him play. She went to watch him play a few times and they got on very well. Then they went out as a couple for a while and she met his friends and his son called Matthew. He was a nice boy and well behaved. Jesse then introduced Ryan and Matthew to Liam and they all got on very well. Ryan also met Jesse's mother and Jackie.

Ryan had his own rented flat but he spent most of his time at Jesse's. Then his landlord told him that he was going to sell the flat, so Jesse said he could move in with her. Ryan was the same age as Jesse which was 43years old.

On a night out together, Jesse saw a friend called Andy and introduced him to Ryan, Jesse had known him from the age of eighteen when he had not long lost his mother. He and his family were close to Jesse, and Andy used to call Jesse 'Mum' as she looked after him when he was low. He was so much younger than Jesse she could have been his mum.

Now he had grown up and Jesse had not seen him for a long time. Andy told her he was now married to an older woman who had been married before. She was ten years older than him, and they were very happy together.

They all met and got on very well. It was good for Jesse and Andy, they had much to catch up on. They shared with their partners what it was like before when they first knew each other and the good and bad times they had both gone through. Now they were back together again as one family, but this time they had partners, Jesse had Ryan as a boyfriend and Andy his wife, Lucy.

They spent times in the week together. At weekends, Ryan went to see his family and Jesse hers. They all got on well and Andy's wife was taught to play pool by Ryan.

One day, Ryan lost his job due to cut backs. Andy said there was a job going in the warehouse where he worked. Ryan was given the job and was happy working again, as he had always worked and supported his family.

A few months later, Jesse missed a period, and went to the doctor. She thought she had an infection. Neither of them had talked about having a family as they already had children of their own. She did not for one minute think she could be pregnant, but a test confirmed she was. She thought that at her age she would never get pregnant again, even though she was on the pill. She had been suffering with an infection which caused diarrhoea, and this was why she caught while she was on the pill.

Jesse was pleased at the news, and had time for it to sink in before Ryan came home. She shared it with her mother who was surprised but glad for her. She wished her well, as she had suffered whilst she was carrying Liam, and told Jesse to rest as much as she could and not to stress about anything.

When Ryan came home, Jesse told him the news. Like Jesse, he was surprised but very pleased at the same time. When she told Andy, he and his wife were happy that his second mum was going to have another child. Jesse had been on her own for two years before she had a relationship with Ryan.

She had to go to Stratford Hospital to have her first scan when she was five and half months pregnant, her baby was due in November. She went with Ryan. When the nurse did the scan, Jesse could see the baby was a boy. He had his thumb in his mouth and looked like Liam did when he was asleep.

Then the nurse said to Jesse that she could not see the heartbeat of the baby so she would do another scan, but this time it would be internal, which would be a more accurate reading. She did this scan, then the nurse turned to Jesse 'I am so sorry, but your baby has died.'

With this news, Jesse just burst into tears, and could not stop crying. Ryan leant over and comforted her, saying 'It is ok. You have another son, so it does not matter. And I have a son also.' Then he leaned back in his chair, there were tears running down his face. He never spoke about this again, nor did he hug Jesse in her hour of need. He just sat on his chair and waited for the nurse to come back in the room. When she did, the nurse said to Jesse 'I have made arrangements for you to go to Warwick hospital from here as you do not live in Stratford area.'

Jesse got dressed and they walked to the car park. Ryan did not hold her hand while they walked out of the hospital, nor did he speak to Jesse. He lit up a cigarette as they went to the car.

The journey back to Warwick was in total silence. Jesse was in disbelief with the news that her baby had died. She was carrying a dead baby inside her, and now she was going to Warwick Hospital to have the baby taken away. This was just too much for her to deal with, so she just shut down inside.

When they arrived at the hospital she was told to sit in the hallway as they did not have a bed for her, even though they knew she was coming. Jesse and Ryan sat down next to the mother and baby unit, seeing mothers with their new babies. Jesse had to watch them going home to start a new family life. After half an hour, she went to the Reception and said 'you have put me in the hallway where the mothers and their new babies are coming out. I have a baby that has died inside me. I cannot sit there any longer. This is hurting me more. Can you please find me a bed as soon as possible?'

They found her a bed and she lay down on it. Then she was taken to the theatre. She was told she could not give birth as she was only five and a half months gone.

Afterwards, Ryan took her home where she went straight up to bed, and stayed there for four hours. Then she came down and sat with Maxwell and Toby beside her, as they both knew that something was wrong. They never left her side, just kept licking the tears which ran down her face.

Ryan said that while Jesse was in bed he had taken the dogs out. If she did not mind, he would go out for a while, he would not be long. Jesse knew that even though he had not talked about what had happened, he was hurt like herself, she did not mind.

Two weeks later, in the morning, Jesse was in the kitchen when she felt such pain in her tummy. She just wanted to push for some reason, then she went upstairs to the bathroom and sat on the toilet. She just pushed, then there was a big splash. The pain of it all felt like she was in labour again, just like she had gone through with Liam. When she looked down at the toilet she saw big pieces of what looked like liver coming out of the toilet water. She went downstairs to the kitchen, phoned her doctor and told him what had just happened. He said to get to the surgery as soon as possible.

Jesse phoned Ryan at work and asked him to take her to the doctor. Ryan replied he was too busy and she would have to drive herself and then hung up.

Jesse could not believe that Ryan could act like that, it was his baby too. Then another big pain came again. When she looked down she found another piece of liver so Jesse put it in silver foil and took with her. She got into car, still with a lot of pain, and drove to the doctor.

She went into the doctor's surgery and showed him what she had. He looked at it and said it should never ever have happened. It was no wonder she was in so much pain. He also commented that she looked very pale and grey. She said she had been feeling hot and sweating a lot, and felt very tired.

The doctor gave her some medication and told her she was suffering from blood poisoning, and this was dangerous as she could have died. He dictated a letter to the head of the hospital department complaining about what had happened to his patient. He told her to have complete rest for a few days and then come back and see him again.

She made something to eat as it was now getting on towards lunch time. She then lay down on the sofa and waited for Ryan to come home. She left the French doors open for the two dogs and fell asleep. When Ryan returned she told him everything that had happened.

In the following weeks Ryan changed towards Jesse. He started to row with her over nothing at all. When they went out with Andy and his wife, Ryan would change and be very nice to Jesse. He would always play pool with Andy's wife and have fun with her and Andy, but not with Jesse.

One day Andy phoned Jesse to ask where Ryan was as he should be at work. Jesse replied that Ryan had left at the usual time.

When Ryan came home, Jesse said she had a phone call from Andy asking where he was. Ryan stood there in the lounge with a look on his face as if he had just been caught out. Once he had thought about it, he said he had a phone call about a family matter and he had to go and to sort it out. He told Jesse he would go into work the next day and would phone Andy to explain what had happened.

The next morning Ryan went to work and came home at the same time as usual and did not take any more time off work again.

It was time for Jesse to go back to the doctor for a check-up. She saw the doctor she had seen before. He said how sorry he was about losing her baby and not being able to give birth. Jesse said the baby's name was Nathan and how hard it was not having the chance to hold him and say goodbye. All she had was a scan photo. She told the doctor how she was feeling inside and how she felt that she was deprived of not having a grave for him that she could go and visit.

The doctor asked if Ryan was alright and did they talk about Nathan and what had happened. Jesse replied that they did not talk about Nathan at all. He just got on with things like work and going out to play pool, he did not sit down with her at all. He acted as though he did not want to be with her. When they were out with friends, he acted differently, enjoying their company, but not hers.

The doctor said that maybe Ryan was dealing with his pain differently to Jesse and that time is a great healer.

Jesse went home to find Maxwell was not acting the same as usual. He was a very active 12 years old dog and had never been ill in his life. Jesse took him to the vets. He looked at Maxwell and said he would take some blood samples to find out what was wrong. He gave a steroid injection which helped him return to his old self.

The next day Maxwell was fine but three days later he was getting worse again. She took him back to the vets where they had received his blood test results. Ryan had to carry Maxwell in his arms because he could not stand and was very limp. The vet said the blood test showed Maxwell had leukemia and at his age there was nothing they could do. More injections would have no effect and he would suffer.

Jesse agreed to have Maxwell put to sleep, even though she did not want to lose him. She knew that she had to let him go and she held him while the vet put him to sleep. After a few minutes, Jesse took off Maxwell's collar and asked the vet if

Maxwell could be cremated. She kissed Maxwell goodbye and left to go home with Ryan.

When Jesse and Ryan arrived home, she hugged Toby and told him that Maxwell was not coming home. She just broke down and cried her heart out, while Ryan was in the kitchen making coffee. He never cried for the loss of Maxwell. He told Jesse the following week Maxwell was only a dog not a human being so he could not understand how Jesse could get that upset over losing a dog.

This caused arguments between Ryan and Jesse and she felt that he was behaving like he did not care about her or her dogs, only himself and his friends. A few weeks later, Jesse met up with a friend to have a drink. Her friend asked about Ryan and whether they had split up, as she had seen him with another woman.

Jesse said she must be mistaken. Ryan was not with her at the weekends as he saw his family then, and sometimes in the week he went out alone to play pool. As he was part of a team, he had asked Jesse not to go with him as he needed to concentrate on his game.

Her friend then described the woman in full detail. Jesse took a deep breath and said that sounded like Andy's wife. Her friend said she did not know the woman but she did know Ryan and he was with her.

Jesse phoned Andy and gave him the news. He was devastated. They thought about when they were not with Ryan and Lucy and it turned out they had been away at the same time and dates. So it was true.

Andy told Jesse he would sort this out when Lucy got back home, and Jesse said she would also. Jesse went back to her seat and told her friend all about the conversation she had with Andy. 'You were right. They are both having an affair behind our backs. And, on top of everything else I am going through, I do not need another liar and cheat in my life. So Ryan is now gone. And when I get back, I will pack his bags for good, and I will live on my own, just Toby and me.'

Her friend gave Jesse a hug and said 'I will be there for you any time. I hope that now you can get on with your life without him being in it. At least you never married him. It will be hard, but easier in the end to move on without solicitors involved.'

Jesse learnt that Ryan had been seeing Lucy for a while. And he was glad that Nathan had died because otherwise he would have had to pay child support to Jesse for Nathan. Lucy also was pleased he did not have another child, as she would be uncomfortable with the relationship with Ryan, seeing Jesse as well as his son Nathan. So they were both pleased, as they could now start a new life.

When Jesse was told this, she was so upset at the thought of them being together while she was pregnant with Nathan. It made her feel like she was not good enough for Ryan. She thought of all the times they all went out as a foursome. How Ryan and Lucy were always playing pool together, and how they looked at each other when they were all together.

And now knowing that they were seeing each other, with neither Jesse nor Andy aware about it. They both acted so well. How could they do that, knowing that Ryan was about to be a father again. To Jesse this was the unthinkable thing to do. 'You must be so shallow to do this to someone who you are supposed to be in love with' she thought.

Jesse's mother was very angry at what had happened, having to deal with losing Nathan and Maxwell, then finding out that Ryan was having an affair with the wife of one of Jesse's closest friends. Then to hear they both were glad that Nathan had died. Jean was so hurt by all of this, finding she could have lost her only daughter as well. This hurt her and made Jean so mad with grief. She hoped never to see or hear from Ryan again.

In the weeks that went by, Jesse tried to carry on as normal, but she was getting low in her mood and started to feel that maybe it was all her fault that all her three marriages had ended. That the relationships since then, including with Ryan, were all her fault. She must have done something wrong to them all to make them all not want to love her anymore and leave her in the end.

Jesse started to have her nightmares back again. She would remember, when she was growing up, her family saying 'do not try this, you are not good enough, you will fail.' Jesse remembered that her grandmother loved her but she never had any faith in her, and neither did Gordon, nor her mother. But her mother used to always say to Jesse, when they were on their own, that she would support Jesse in anything she did. She was so proud of Jesse and loved her very much. Jesse could always talk to her mother about anything in her life. But she could not with her grandmother or Gordon.

Jesse's low mood was getting worse as the weeks turned into months. She was still working as hard as she could, as this stopped her from thinking about herself. But all she was doing was working hard, then going home and listening to her music on her own.

Her music was the only thing that reflected how Jesse was really feeling inside. Sometimes she would play Metallic or Iron Maiden or Black Sabbath, these were all heavy metal music and just how she felt inside. The one thing she could not do was to truly tell her mother and her son and her best friend how she was. She was trying to protect them from her feelings as much as she could. She knew she was a very strong woman, who had already been through so much in her life. She thought she could go through hell and come out the other side ready to start again, as she had done so many times before.

Liam was away in the R.A.F. Jesse waited to see him in person to tell him the full story. He knew his mother had lost

Nathan but he did not know the rest. She told him everything on one of his visits. Like his grandmother, he was very hurt. Not only he had lost his brother, but he could have lost his mother as well. And to find out that Ryan and Lucy where glad that his brother was dead made him mad with anger.

Jesse had to keep her feelings to herself to protect her family and her friends. She thought more about others than her own self. She was finding it harder and harder to put on a brave face. When she was on her own she could take off the mask and reveal the real Jesse, the one who was so very hurt and low in mood and feeling completely worthless inside, no good for anyone.

She was finding it hard to sleep and did not want to see her friends. She just withdrew from everyone except her mother. This went on for a few weeks until one day she had a phone call inviting her out for a drink in the pub on a friend's birthday. She agreed as she had not been out for some time.

She got dressed, still feeling she did not want to go anywhere. She walked to the local pub and saw her friend there, they talked and her friend commented she had lost some weight, but she looked good. They all had a good time.

Later, another friend said they were all going back to a house to continue the party, would she like to come. Jane said it would be such a shame to leave now as she had not been out having fun for some time. With what Jesse had been through, she needed to relax. It would help her to sleep well, after a few drinks.

Jesse agreed to go back with them. The house was five minutes walk from the pub. Everyone was happy, there was food laid on and the music was playing, music that Jesse liked such as Pink Floyd. It was great, Jesse thought, she was starting to relax for once, something that she had not done in a while.

Around 1.30am, Jesse noticed people were going into the dining room and wanted to know what was there. She opened the door to find three people taking lines of cocaine. Jesse had never taken any drugs in her life, so she quickly shut the door and went back to the lounge. She saw her friend Jane and told her what was going on. Jane said 'It's ok, you do not have to take anything you don't want to, Jesse. It just relaxes you, and you feel very chilled out after taking it.'

Jesse had not been drinking much, she only had four small glasses of wine, and had been eating. She was still feeling at times a bit low inside, but she did not show it on the outside, she still had on her happy face mask, but the pain inside still remained.

She looked around the room and all she could see were her friends and others all having a good time. They were all relaxed, even the ones who were saying their goodbyes. Everyone was leaving relaxed and happy. But Jesse was not, she had put on her happy mask yet she was not. She was worried about going to sleep that night, as her sleep pattern was not good. She was having bad nightmares about her past and this always made her wake up.

As she stood in the lounge, she noticed Jane walking towards the dining room so Jesse followed her. She told Jane she could not sleep and Jane suggested having a line of cocaine, since it helped her to sleep.

So at the age of forty three, Jesse had a few lines of cocaine and afterwards began to feel relaxed, more than she had ever felt before taking the drug. After a while, she went home.

She was now feeling tired and went to bed. Toby was with her mother overnight. The next morning, when she woke up, she felt so good and not one bit tired, as she normally would do. She had not been woken up by any bad dreams, she just slept right through until 10.00am, which she had never done before. She always woke up early.

She got dressed and went to pick up Toby from her mothers. She thought about how she was feeling, so much more awake and not one bit tired. She had more energy than she would normally as every day was an effort to do anything. Everything was such hard work, but she still carried on doing the best she could.

She took Toby for a long walk by the canal. It was her time to think, just Toby and herself walking along, seeing the moored boats and the countryside that she enjoyed, with Toby running along beside her.

She thought what a difference a couple of lines of cocaine had done for her. There were no side effects at all. So on this thought Jesse decided to phone Jane and invite her for a meal to thank her for the previous night and to tell her how she was now feeling, that she had had a good night's sleep, something she had not had for a long time. To sleep more than 5 hours was very good indeed.

Jane said it was the cocaine that had given her the long awaited sleep that she needed.

Over the next six months Jesse would go out with her friends and take cocaine. She would feel so much better, as she now had a good feel about herself. She had the confidence to handle anything that came her way when she was on cocaine. But neither her mother, Liam nor Jackie knew about what she was doing, they all thought she was starting to get her life back and how well she was doing, so much better than they expected.

Then one day after work when she had arranged to go the local pub to meet up with friends and have a meal and drinks, she was waiting to be served when another friend, Gary, came over to say hello. They had not seen each other for a long time. Gary looked at her and said 'Are you ok Jesse?' Straight way Jesse replied 'Of course I am, why are you asking?' Gary said 'Come over here a minute, where it is quieter.' He took her hands and said 'you are acting very strangely, it is not the normal you. Are you drunk?'

Jesse replied 'No, I am not. I have only just got here. I have not even ordered a drink. You asked me over here to talk. Why do I look different?'

'You act like you are full of energy. Like you are bouncing of the wall. You are to talking very quickly, not like you normally would. You normally are much calmer and less energetic. You would normally stand still when people talk to you, but you are waving your arms around. This is not you, it seems to me. But you are so happy, more than normal. I have seen you happy before, but you were different then to now.'

Then Gary looked in Jesse's eyes and said 'Your eyes are wider than normal, which gives me an idea. You are on something. Please tell me what it is, and please do not say that you are not taking anything. I can tell from your eyes.' With that, Jesse admitted she had been taking cocaine and it had helped her to sleep and relax.

Gary took a deep breath and then said 'Oh no Jesse. You have never taken drugs in your life. Now at the age of forty-three you are taking them. Why Jesse? Why have you done this to yourself? This is not the way to go about things. You have to stop this as it can get addictive. Then you will be in trouble. You will lose your job and everything that you have worked so hard for. And, does your mother and son know? What about Jackie, does she know?'

Jesse replied, with her head in her hands with shame, that all she wanted was to get some sleep and relax. Now she would have to stop, and this was not what she wanted to hear from anyone.

And certainly not from Gary, who was a good friend. Gary continued 'If you carry on, I will tell your mother, Liam and Jackie. I do not think for one minute that they know about you taking drugs as none of them would stand for it. So I am telling you now that I will not hesitate to tell them. I might sound harsh, but I am telling you for your own good.'

'Please stay with me and have a drink. If you see your so called friends then tell them what I have said and do not take any more cocaine.'

Jesse was trying not to cry so she said to Gary that she was going to the toilets where she broke down in tears at what she had now become, a low life woman, one who took drugs. How could she do this to her family and how would they feel if they found out by someone else. This made Jesse so mad with herself for letting her family down yet again. She felt she was a failure and no good for anyone. At least Liam was in the R.A.F thinking that his mother, like his father, was doing well in her life. Little did he know that his mother was living in hell and so low in her mood she could not sleep and felt so alone with all of her pain.

Jesse, feeling full of shame with what she was doing, knew she had to make another change in her life. This time it would be for the better. She also knew that she would have to tell her mother, Liam and Jackie. How shocked and disappointed they would all be.

When Jesse came back, Gary had bought her a drink. He gave her a big hug and said he was sorry to have upset her, but it was for her own good. Jesse replied she realised that and was glad he had said what he had. She knew she should never have taken anything like cocaine, but could not see what it had done to her. Gary had seen the difference it had on her.

'Thank you so much. If you were not such a good friend, you would never have talked to me like this. It has made me see sense, and what could have happened if I had carried on taking drugs. How I could lose everything that I have worked for, as well as my family, and what it would have done to them.'

Jesse arrived home and thought she had to phone Jane. She hoped Jane would not fall out with her as she would no longer be taking drugs. She did not like to upset anyone as she always had other people's feeling at heart, sometimes more than her own.

Then her phone rang and it was Jane asking where she was. She was worried about her. Jesse explained she was not going to take any more cocaine and thought it would not be a good idea if she went out with Jane and her friends again, as it would be too much of a temptation.

Jane said that was fine, they said their goodbyes and Jesse hung up. She sat back down on the sofa and thought to herself that it was for the best, and how Gary was so right in what he had said to her. And how pleased she was to see him again as she had not seen him for some time.

She knew she would have to talk with her mother about cocaine and this would not be easy. Her mother believed that Jesse had never taken drugs in her life, but now, at the age of forty-three she had been tempted.

The next morning, lying in the bath, she thought about her life and what she had done. How very disappointed her mother, Liam and the rest of the family would be when they found out. And Jackie, who had never smoked or taken drugs. They would all be disappointed in her. But Jackie would understand more than her family, and be more supportive.

When she pulled up outside her mother's house she was filled with dread inside, and her heart was going ten to the dozen with the thought of what she had to say. How her mother would react to the news of what has been going on over the last six months. Jesse had not told anyone about it. Now she had thought of what it could do to her, and how it could affect her in the long run. Now she had stopped and would no longer be taking cocaine.

She never would take cocaine again.

She was very sorry for letting her mother down. She would tell Liam when she saw him next, but he was away on tour in another country. And she would tell Jackie.

CHAPTER FIFTEEN

Is there any Music

Jesse's mother was extremely upset that her own daughter had gone through such problems with drugs. On her own. Jesse explained she had tried to get on with things and did not want her mother to worry, she was only trying to protect her. She was no longer taking any drugs and would not take them again. She was very sorry and now was trying to sort things out in her life, to start again on her own, just with Toby.

Her mother said she was pleased, though she was still worried about her. She would always be her mother and that is what mothers do. She gave Jesse a big hug and then Jesse took Toby and drove home.

She phoned Jackie and told her what had been going on. Like her mother, Jackie never knew all the things that had been happening in Jesse's life and especially not about the cocaine. Jesse knew that Jackie would be worried and ask why she did not tell her how she was feeling as she was her best friend. She always told her everything that was going on in her life and now she was hiding things.

Jesse was right about how Jackie would react. Jesse had to explain why she did not tell her, how she did not want her to worry and how she was just trying to protect her.

Jesse arranged to meet with Jackie the next weekend and the two of them sat down and talked face to face. They were together again, as they had not been for a while.

Jesse never heard from Jane again, for which she was glad as she did not want to go back on cocaine. She was dealing with the pain of all that was going on in her life.

Jesse helped her mother in her house. One Mother's Day, she arranged for a brand new kitchen to be installed as well as flowers. Jesse would always take her mother out for lunch on Mother's Day. Jesse was always there with her mother to make sure everything was alright.

Jesse loved her mother so much she would do anything she wanted and saw her every week. She had done this since Gordon had died.

Jesse and Jean became even closer than before, they needed each other so much and loved spending time together. They acted like it was them against the world. Every week Jesse took her mother to the graves of Gordon, her sister Michelle, and Jesse's grandmother who died the year that Jesse had moved into her house, to place flowers there. They would talk about them while they were there.

On one of these visits, Jean said 'Please promise me one thing, Jesse. If I have an incurable disease and would be in pain and suffering and could not lead a normal life again then please withdraw any treatment to keep me alive. Let me go in peace. It was so hard to see Gordon suffering the way that he did at home. I do not want that to happen to me.'

Jesse just looked up from putting flowers on Gordon's grave and said 'Mum, please don't talk like that.' Her mother replied 'We have to talk about things like dying and make arrangements while we can, it is an important thing to do, Jesse.'

Jesse promised she would carry out her wishes and Jean also promised that she too would carry out Jesse's wishes if it came to it. After leaving the cemetery and driving home there was silence as they both thought about what they had promised each other. Jesse knew her mother had made a will and she would need to make one herself.

Jesse only had her mother and Liam. They were all very close. Jesse missed her grandmother and Gordon very much and so did Jean.

The following weekend Liam came to stay with his friend from the R.A.F. Jesse thought she had the opportunity to tell him the whole truth about his little brother Nathan, and about taking cocaine for six months, but now was no longer taking any drugs. Why she did it in the first place, what she had been going through on her own, why she thought she had to protect them all from this as she did not want it to affect them in any way. She was trying to deal with everything herself as well as work and there was no support from anyone.

There had been no professional help with dealing with anything, it was up to her to deal with everything by herself and she did not deal with it very well.

Liam arrived, he was only eighteen years old. Jesse and Jean were so proud of him. Jesse opened the front door to find him standing there, he was six feet two inches tall whilst Jesse was only five foot five inches. Jesse said to him 'Come in, how are you?' Then she said hello to Liam's friend, Jason, who she had seen before. After they put their things in the bedroom, Jesse suggested they went out for a meal.

Things were going so well, they all were happy and laughing, things were good. But deep down inside, Jesse knew that she had to talk to Liam about things she wished she did not have to, but she and Liam had a very close relationship where they could talk about anything going on in their lives. She knew she had to tell him everything about what was going on while he was away on tour and why she had to see him to tell him face to face as none of this she could tell him over the phone.

Jesse brought over drinks for both Liam and Jason, and a large vodka and tonic for herself. It was one of the hardest things she had to do and she needed a stiff drink to do it. When

239

they all were seated, Jesse took a big mouthful of her drink and then said to Liam 'There is something that I need to tell.' Liam asked 'Is it Nanny? Is she alright?' Jesse replied 'No Nanny is fine and well. It is to do with me.'

Then Jess explained in great detail what has been happening in her life, about the drugs and Nathan his brother. Everything, nothing left out. It was so hard for Jesse to tell her son and to see the expression on his face, the look of anger and disbelief of what his mother had gone through on her own and how she was now.

When Jesse finished there was silence while Liam and Jason were trying to get their heads around what they had been told. Then Liam said 'I am sorry Mum, but if I ever see Ryan in the streets I will be doing time afterwards, because he will end up dead.'

Jesse said 'No son, you will not do such a thing. You cannot do that, I know that you are angry right now, but there is no need to talk like that.' Liam said why he felt this way, 'I have lost my brother and I could have lost my own mother at the same time. And Ryan could not care less about either of you. You said he already had a son so it did not matter. Well it does matter to me and I am so angry that he had an affair. And then both of them were glad that I had lost my brother. I could have lost you too, Mum.' Liam hugged his mother and Jesse broke down in his arms and cried for the loss of Nathan. It hurt her to see Liam who was so hurt and upset and angry all at the same time. This hurt Jesse so much that she too became so angry with the world and what it had dished out to her.

The next Sunday, Jesse, Liam and Jason went to have lunch with Jean. They were in a quiet mood, and not laughing like they would normally be. Liam came downstairs and hugged his mother saying 'I love you and I am the man of the house. No one is ever going hurt you like Ryan did ever again. I will not let anyone do that.'

'I know son. You will always be the head of the house. Please do not worry as I am fine now that you are here. I am so sorry that I had to put you through this. It is not easy for me to do as the last thing I ever wanted to put you through is the pain that I had to go through, as I love you very much. I was only trying to protect you like I did with Nanny.'

Jesse had explained to Liam that she had told her mother and Jackie everything that had gone on. They were also very angry and hurt.

Nothing was said while they were at Jean's house. They all had a good time and there was plenty of laughter and plenty of news of what Liam had been doing on and off tour. It turned out to be such a good day for all of them. At the end of the day when Jesse, Liam and Jason had to leave, they all gave each other big hugs and kisses, said their goodbyes and left to drive back.

Liam and Jason left Jesse and she was on her own with Toby. She felt such relief that she had told Liam everything that had gone on with her life and now was sorting things out. She was working hard and dealing with her pain like she used to always do, through her music, as it was the only thing that she knew could help her through. She would never feel alone with her pain as the records shared her pain with her like no one else could.

It was now 2008 and Liam was 22 years old and he had a daughter. The two bedroom house where Jesse was living was getting too small when Liam visited with his partner, their daughter and his partner's two girls. Jesse's mother would stay at Christmas and sometimes for birthdays. It was now getting to the stage of being uncomfortable in the house so Jesse was looking to move to somewhere with three bedrooms where there would be more room for everyone. A friend told Jesse one of his neighbours wanted a smaller house. He would ask if she would be interested in a swap as they both were living in houses owned by the same housing association.

Everything was set to exchange houses, Jesse from a two bedroom house to a three bedroom house, and things were now starting to look like they were going well for a change. Jesse and her mother were very happy at this.

Jesse moved into her new house on 6th April 2008 and was so pleased. It took all day to get the house filled with boxes of things and to put up Jesse's bed and her wardrobe and then Jesse stayed at her new house overnight on her own. She was so excited that she did not sleep well that night as she was not used to sleeping alone without Toby by her side.

The next day Jesse woke up still excited about her new home. She got changed and went straight to her mother's to get Toby, then took him back to his new home. Together they would start a new life on their own, just the two of them. This time there would be plenty of room for all to stay and be happy whatever the occasion. They would all have enough room to enjoy themselves and be happy together.

The thought of a Christmas in a new home for Jesse and her mother was so exciting, something to look forward to, and leave the bad past behind. This was a very good feeling. Her mother had given her some money to help get the house the way she wanted. She was very grateful, she had always helped her mother in the past and this time her mother was going to help her.

With the money she could buy things for the house and decorate it to the way she wanted. She was a very house-proud person and everything had to be in its place. The colours had to match in every room, that was how Jesse was.

It took six months of hard work and the house was now the way Jesse wanted. She was so proud of it. Jean would come and spend the weekend with her and together they were so happy. Then it was Christmas and the house was filled with everything to do with it. Jesse loved this special season. There were festive lights and a Christmas tree standing six foot tall by the window. They had their first Christmas together in the new house, just the two of them as Liam was away with his daughter.

Jesse took her mother home on New Year's Eve and Jean looked after Toby. There were always fireworks that night and Toby hated the noise, he would always be with Jesse's mother were she would give Toby a cuddle and make sure that he was alright.

Jesse always went out for New Year's Eve with Jackie. They would be together for the New Year, having fun as they always had over more than thirty years they had known each other. Jesse, Jean and Jackie looked forward to 2009 and wondered what it would bring.

Everything started out well. Jesse was still settling down in her new home and sorting and changing things as she always did, but that was her way.

In September, Jean had a fall but had not broken anything. She was very bruised on her nose and Jesse took her to the hospital, but all was well. Jesse said she must go the doctor and tell him of what had happened. Jesse wanted to take Jean home with her, but her mother would not go, she just wanted to stay in her own house. Jesse did not like the thought of her mother on her own so she stayed the night.

The next morning they went to the doctor. He took her blood pressure and temperature and everything was fine. Jesse treated her mother to lunch.

Mid October Jesse received a phone call from one of her mother's friends to say that Jean had collapsed in church. They had called the ambulance and she was in hospital in Warwick. She drove straight to the hospital, found her in bed and gave her a big hug. Then she went to find someone to ask what would happen next.

The doctor said they had given her an MRI scan to see what had happened and why she had collapsed. They had found a large shadow on her brain indicating vascular dementia. Unfortunately, this was untreatable. The only thing that she could take was aspirin to thin the blood. They could not operate as this was a disease of the brain.

Jesse was devastated and so hurt that her mother would die of this. She would lose her mind and no longer be her mother. She would change and maybe not be able to recognize her or the rest of the family.

Jesse learnt that her mother would have be moved to St Michael's, a hospital for people with mental health issues, where they would look after Jean until they could see what care she would need, after more tests.

A few days later Jesse had come to see her mother and have a meeting with the doctors. Jesse had seen the changes with her mother and how she was quiet and withdrawn, did not laugh at anything Jesse said to try to make her smile again. It was like her mother had lost her sense of humour.

A nurse came in and said to Jean 'The doctor would like to talk to Jesse. I will stay with you,' and she sat down beside Jean. Jesse walked to the reception to say she had an appointment to see the doctors. She was taken into a room with five people already seated, waiting for her.

As she walked in, one of the doctors invited her to take a seat. The doctor who was treating Jean explained the situation with her mother and said she would now need special care. Jesse said she would give up work and move into mother's house to look after her.

'I will do everything for her. After my step-father died, I did everything for her. It will not make any difference this time, as we are a very close family. So when I can take my mother home?' She did not expect the answer they gave her. This was the worst thing Jesse had ever heard in her life.

But the answer was unfortunately there was no way this could happen. The doctor explained Jean would get worse and need 24 hour nursing. 'I know you and your mother are very close, but you cannot be awake 24 hours a day. You are not a nurse and do not have any special training this situation requires. That is what your mother now needs, unfortunately you alone cannot give her that. But you can do what is right for her and that is to let her live in a nursing home where they have 24 hour care with fully qualified staff. Your mother will need that from now on.' Jesse asked how long she would have left to live as people with dementia can live a long time. The doctor told Jesse that her mother would only have five years left as the disease was a more progressive one.

The doctor went on to explain more about her mother's situation. Her form of vascular dementia was quick acting and would kill more quickly than other types. She should treat every time she saw her as possibly the last time and make every minute count. Her mother could collapse again due to having mini strokes which could turn into a big stroke. 'We do not know when this could happen, it could be months, weeks or years. We just do not know any more than what we have told you. I am so very sorry for giving this troubling news but at least you are now well informed about the situation.'

Jesse thanked everyone for helping her understand. Then she walked out, knowing she was about see her mother, wondering what she was going to say about what has been told. And how her mother would react.

This played on Jesse's mind. She had to tell her mother she would never be able to live in her own house again. Jesse walked very slowly down the hallway back to where her mother was. She opened the door and saw the nurse. 'Can you please stay a few minutes?' Jesse sat down and explained as much as she could in a way that her mother would understand.

That it would be the best for her in the long run. Jean agreed, and then Jesse went back and told the doctor.

Jesse did not tell her mother how she would be, that she would have good days or weeks or months but then would start to go downhill little by little. She would go down and get worse. She would have more falls and mini strokes until one big stroke that could be the end but no one knew what or when or how.

Jesse knew she had to treat every day as if it could be the last time. It was so hard for her to deal with, but she had to all the same. She had to tell the rest of the family so they too were in the picture could make arrangements to come and visit Jean.

Jesse had to sort out the nursing home where her mother would live. This was hard for her as the only thing she wanted was for her mother to come home to her house where she had lived for 43 years, and for Jesse to look after her until she died. But this was not going to happen, which made Jesse feel like she had failed her mother and family once again.

Jesse met with the social worker to help find a suitable nursing home. Jesse knew her mother did not like staying in hospital, she could walk around and was not ill enough to be in bed, so would settle down more if she had her own room with her own things around her.

It took a month before her mother could be moved. On the day, Jesse packed her things like photos of the family and the ambulance came to take her.

Jesse said she would follow behind in her car and be there to help her settle in. Her mother was fine and relaxed about everything and excited about leaving the hospital for good.

Jean moved to the nursing home on the 5th November 2009, and a firework display had been arranged for the residents that same evening. Afterwards there was a buffet for everyone including the families of the residents.

Jesse knew about this beforehand and that this would make her mother happy.

She pulled up in the car park outside the nursing home which was called The Westhouse. It was a lovely old building and so big. As Jesse walked up to the front door, there were the owners. They welcomed both Jean and Jesse to their home and one of the nurses helped Jean to her room. Jesse followed and sorted out her mother's things. Then they went round the home to see where everything was. The staff were introduced to them. The owners said Jesse would be welcome anytime for lunch and also for Christmas dinner which made Jean very happy.

After the fireworks and buffet, the nurses came to Jean and said it was time for her medication. Jesse asked what it was and was told it was aspirin and anti-depressant tablets to help calm Jean's nerves so she would have a good night's sleep in her new room.

In the weeks that followed, Jean began to get back to her old self. She joined in with the activities and was happy there. She had visitors from the church and the luncheon club where she used to cook for the OAPs.

Christmas came and Jesse spent lunch time with her mother. She took her presents and her mother had a present brought for Jesse by one of the nurses. They opened them together, like they always had done. This would be the first one that would not be at one of their homes. From now on it would be at the nursing home instead, but at least they would be together as Jesse had never been without her mother at Christmas.

2010 was the start of a very hard year for Jesse. She had a meeting with her mother's doctors and her social worker. All explained what she needed to do as the next of kin, she was the only one who could make decisions on behalf of her mother.

Together, the social worker and Jesse had to explain to Jean what would have to happen. At this time Jean was like her old self and could comprehend what was going on. Jesse had to tell her mother that she would have to sell the family home after 43 years of being in her possession. The money was needed to pay for her accommodation. Jesse could not afford to pay.

This came as a shock to Jean as she thought that the Government would help pay for her rent and she could live off her pension and not have to sell the family home. She wanted to give it to Jesse and from Jesse to Liam. But this now would not happen, which made Jean upset. Jesse had to again explain the reason why it had to happen and she too was very upset at this situation.

Jesse had to obtain power of attorney for her mother so that she could act on her behalf. She did not care how much it cost as long as it was done for her mother.

Once Jesse had filled out the paper work for the Court and they in turn had vetted her to see what sort of person she was, to see if she had a criminal record and whether she had been in trouble with the Police, they granted her legal guardianship for her mother.

The hardest thing for Jesse to do was to clear her family home after 43 years of both growing up there and bringing her son there as a baby. So many memories were in that house and now she had no choice but to clear out everything. Only leaving behind the memories the walls of the house could tell. They would be good and bad, happy and sad, every tear that was shed and laughter that was heard in the house.

It had three good sized bedrooms and one small box room so in fact it was a four bedroomed house. It was filled with so many things that her mother and stepfather, Gordon, had collected over the years. As well as her mother's clothes, there was her important paperwork. Jesse had given her a briefcase to put this in.

In the meantime the rent for Jean was paid by the local authority, they knew they would get the money back after the sale of the house.

But there was so much to do with the house and it felt so wrong. Knowing that her mother was ill was bad enough, but this was worse.

It took months for all the paper work to come through in order for Jesse to deal with her mother's affairs and be able to sell the family home. This was on top of seeing her mother every day. Jean was settling in and taking her medication to calm her down. Jesse noted all the changes her mother went through, remembering the doctor had explained she would go up and down, be on a high, then normal for a while. Then she would go down slowly. These changes could go on for a long time.

In fact Jean was on a high for all the important things that had to be done. She even gave her own views on things. Jean told Jesse what she wanted to keep and the rest went to charity.

Jesse explained that once everything was sorted, the money would be put into Jean's bank account to pay for her accommodation and anything else she wanted. The rent that has already been paid by the council would have to be paid back. Anything bought out of her money would be recorded and Jesse would keep all the receipts for the accounts, which would be shown to the courts.

Jean agreed and understood everything that Jesse had told her. She wanted to give Liam some money. Jesse said she would give him a cheque. Then Jean said she wanted to give Jesse some money but Jesse refused. Jean persisted, reminding Jesse she had a bad crash and her car was written off. Jesse was travelling by taxi and not able to take Jean to the cemetery. Jesse reluctantly agreed that Jean could pay for another car for her.

The next week Jesse turned up in her new car. She had told her mother about it and knew she would be excited. She could see her looking out of the dining room window with a happy smile on her face. As Jesse walked up to the front door her mother was already waiting in the hallway. Jesse said 'Come out and see the car, Mum.' Her mother replied 'Oh I like the colour.' Jesse explained 'The roof goes back. It is called a soft top,' with that her mother laughed.

Jesse told a nurse she would take Jean to the cemetery. She took her mother's hand and walked to her the car. They both drove off, her mother asking 'Is there any music in here?' Jesse put on the CD she was playing and Jean said 'I like this car and I like the music. Can you put the top down to show me?' Jesse said she would when they arrived.

But for now they just listened to the music and sang along to it, her mother was so happy. Jesse could see the joy on her mother's face. It was good see her mother as she used to be.

When they returned they had their lunch together and afterwards Jesse sat with her mother in her room. Then Jean gave her some letters she had written to post for her.

Jean stood by the dining room window and watched and waved Jesse goodbye.

Once home, Jesse sat in the lounge thinking what a lovely day they had together. How her mother was like her old self again. This made her happy inside.

In 2012 Jean began to go downhill. She had two falls but did not break any bones. She had bruises on her face and arms and this worried Jesse. She had been told that if she had any mini strokes this would happen and there was nothing anyone could do.

The changes had begun to be noticed by everyone. Jean had gone from talking and joining in with anything that was going on in the home to just sitting in her chair in the lounge and not talking to anyone. Her weight had begun to change as well, she was once a size 14 and had gone down to size 12, the same as Jesse.

This carried on. Jean was changing so much, she became inward and just wanted to hold Jesse's hand. To only to stay in the home. She became unable to dress herself and had to wear pads.

Jesse used to sit and look at her and she would look back at Jesse. It was as though her mother was looking straight through her with a blank look on her face. This hurt Jesse so much, she knew that this woman looked like her mother but her mother had gone. This was only a shell of what her mother once used to be. She would no longer talk to Jesse and not even tell her she loved her and give her a big hug.

In 2014 Jesse had a phone call from the home. They told her that her mother had again had a fall but this time she had broken her hip and was in hospital in Warwick. She grabbed her handbag and mobile phone and rushed to the hospital to find out what had happened and how her mother was.

When Jesse arrived she was told a doctor would see her. She went to her mother's bed and found her asleep. She had her legs under a cage to make it more comfortable for her. She took her mother's hand and kissed it, then Jean awoke to see Jesse looking at her. Jean said 'Hello.' This was good as she did not speak much, she would be asleep most of the time when Jesse visited her in the home.

Jesse sat with her until the doctor came round to see Jean and talk about what had happened and what the treatment was that her mother was on.

Two weeks later it was May and the sun was out. Jesse was again visiting her mother. A nurse told her the doctor had requested to see her when she arrived.

There were two doctors in the room, one Jesse knew because he was looking after her mother. The other she did not know and was introduced to him. They asked Jesse questions about whether her mother had ever said anything to her about if she was very ill. Jesse said when her stepfather had died of cancer and was at home for six months, that he had died at home. Both her mother and herself, with the help of McMillan nurses and the doctor, had nursed him at home. It had been tough for both of them, to see him suffer and not be able to do anything for him but just watch him slowly die.

And one day while they were at Gordon's grave, her mother had said 'Please promise me that if there was anything wrong with me then let me go in peace. Do not let me suffer like Gordon,' and Jesse promised her mother that if anything like that happened she would agree to let her go in peace and not let her suffer.

Then Jesse queried why they were asking this. The doctor she knew said her mother had broken her hip again and had had a second hip operation. She had had an MRSA infection which she got over but now had double pneumonia. She was not getting over it and was getting worse. She could not have another hip operation and would have to live with a broken hip for the rest of her life. She would be in a wheel chair and in constant pain.

'This is why we had to ask if you knew what your mother would want now this has happened to her. Would she want to be in a wheel chair and in pain for the rest of her life?' By now Jesse was trying to get her head around this information and not saying anything at all to the doctors. She was being asked to make a decision to stop the treatment as it was not working for her mother. To let her go in peace.

She also knew her mother's sister had arrived with her husband. Jesse had said to them 'I will be back in a minute as the doctors need to speak to me about Mum.'

Jesse was thinking of this as she sat there. How she would tell the rest of the family of what she has done. How would they feel about the decision that she had just made.

Jesse came out of the room and walked to her mother's side. She looked at her Auntie and shook her head as if to say 'No, she is now dying so say your goodbyes.' Then she sat down and after her Auntie and Uncle had left she phoned Liam and told him. Later Liam came to the hospital and said his goodbyes to his grandmother and so did his father the next day. Then on Monday the 19th of May Jean passed away in her sleep and Jesse was all alone.

In July it was Jesse's birthday, but this time without her mother to share the celebration. Jesse was not herself as she felt so alone. She had always had her mother with her, no matter what. Now she was on her own and she could not cope, no matter how hard she tried. She told her doctor how she was feeling and he arranged for her to go for therapy. She had been suffering from post traumatic stress disorder which came out after her mother had died. She was suffering from deep depression, and had kept it to herself, not showing it to the world. But this time she could not hide it any longer and she knew it.

Her friends and neighbours did the best they could for her birthday. Then it came to Christmas and this again was so hard for Jesse. She had never missed out having Christmas with her mother. Like her birthday, this would be the first of many without her mother.

June 2015 Jesse had gone to work and she collapsed in the toilet. She was found by one of her colleagues and sent home. They phoned the agency and told them what had happened. Jesse went home in a taxi as she still did not feel good. She made an appointment to see her doctor and told her what had happened. And that she was having really bad headaches, more than she had ever had before. She also told her what had happened to her mother.

The doctor made an appointment for Jesse to see a specialist to try to find out what was going on. Jesse went home and tried to relax but could not for worrying that she could have what her mother had.

After a few months of tests, Jesse got the news of what was going on with her health. She had Cadasil, a rare genetic disorder affecting the small blood vessels in the brain. Her mother had the gene which caused this, so Jesse was told to have the test to see if she too had the gene. Fortunately she did not, so Liam was now safe.

This news was too much for Jesse to bear. The therapists who were treating her were fully aware of the situation going on in Jesse's life and knew how to deal with her emotions. She shared these with them but only them, this had helped, along with her music. She always played her music to comfort her in her hours of need. Like her mother, she knew there was nothing to be done and eventually she too would suffer from falls and bad headaches. But she knew that this was now her life and that she would have to make the best of it, and that is what she has done.

The music plays on. Jesse listens and remembers.

#0032 - 221117 - C0 - 210/148/14 - PB - DID2036933